Armageddo

Volume Four

'The Longest Night'

ANDY FARMAN

Copyright © 2014 Andy Farman

All rights reserved.

ISBN: 1499619367
ISBN-13: 978-1499619362

DEDICATION

To my wife and son, Jessica and Edward Eric, with all my love.

Templar Platoon, Z Company, IJLB, Oswestry.
Guards Company, IJLB, Oswestry.
The Guards Depot, Pirbright.
2nd Battalion Coldstream Guards.
C (Royal Berkshires) Company, 2nd Battalion Wessex Regiment.
253 Provost Company, Royal Military Police.
'B' Relief, South Norwood Police Station.
Z District Crime Squad, Croydon.
Thornton Heath Robbery Squad (Temp)
4 Unit, Special Patrol Group.
4 Area Specialist Counter-Terrorist IED Search Team.
'D' Relief, Norbury.
A Team (North) Walworth.
The East Street Market 'Dip' Squad.
Peter O'Rourke, Steve Littel, John & Wendy Allen, the best CAD Operators in the business.

To everyone out there who gets up in the morning, and does good things for others!

"The Depot'

I visited the Guards Depot the other day,
only it's the 'The Depot' no longer, all the Guards gone away.

A place once alive with martial noise,
for the creation of men from that of mere boys;
the British Army's best, and no idle boast,
now 'The Depot' is silent but for the wind and the ghosts.

'Cat Company', which sat beside the square,
had borne a board of memorable dates there,
remembering battles fought on foot, horse and tank
by those who had skirmished, and of men stood in rank
It honoured their courage on many a foreign field
but the board is now empty and the paintwork has peeled.

No Guardsmen, no Troopers, no Corporals-of-Horse,
no men from the battalions returned for some course.
The ranges are silent, Sand Hill overgrown
The Queen Mary is mildewed, forlorn and alone.

I visited The Depot the other day
but the Guardsmen have gone, up Catterick way.

(Andy Farman. Pirbright, 1996.)

CONTENTS

ANDY FARMAN

ACKNOWLEDGMENTS

Where to start? There have been so many who have helped and encouraged with the writing of this series. Time and advice given freely, but here we go, and in no particular order, and with added thanks to the several hundred of you out there who comment and contribute to the blog and online page regularly.

My Mother and Father, Audrey and Ted Farman, who taught me to enjoy books more than the goggle box (I hasten to add that it did not include any affection for text books, however.)

My Uncle Richard and Cousin David, (From the Farman's colony in the Americas) for technical advice on matters maritime, nautical and the Chinook.

Jessica of course for putting up with it all, and an apology to little Edward for only playing with him before his bedtime because I was writing all day.

Bill Rowlinson and Ray Tester for inspiring two of the characters, and Bill's bountiful knowledge of firearms and police tactics.

Friend, actor and author Craig Henderson has qualities recognizable in young Nikoli, the Russian paratrooper. It is inevitable that people we meet will rub off on characters who appear in our stories.

Jason Ferguson of the US Army and National Guard PSI for his sound advice on all things US Military, translating my Brit mortar fire controller orders into the US variety, and test reading.

The lovely and witty Irina Voronina for her advice on low byte sources for graphic tools (one of several of her current post-Playboy careers.) Another former glamour model, now turned TV Producer (when not partying) Tracey Elvik, for adding some wisdom to Janet Probert's character, I almost made Janet a Mancunian too.

Nick Gill and Andy Croy for their invaluable help with the editing and waking me up to how bad my writing had become since leaving school. Adrian Robinson for invaluable help with the file size reduction problem for map insertions.

Paul Beaumont knowledge of radio communications and military 'Sigs'.

Paul Teare for test reading, Brendan McWilliams for helpful suggestions which were predictably along the lines of 'more paras.'

Chris Cullen, Paolo Ruoppolo, Tobi Shear Smith and Steve Enever, test readers extraordinaire.

Lyynard for HTML indexing the book.

Prelude

Arkansas Valley, Nebraska, USA.
Saturday 20th October, 0001hrs.

"Mister President, the Missile Defence Agency confirms a nuclear detonation in the ten megaton range, one minute ago above Sydney, Australia."

The President was still looking at the speaker, hoping that this was some communications error and that Commander Willis would continue.

"My God, what do I do now? How do I respond to that?" The earlier heady feeling that all was going well following the report of the sinking of the Chinese ballistic missile submarine *Xia*, had evaporated.

"Henry?"

The President looked for the Chief of the General Staff but saw faces staring back at him, shocked and unbelieving despite the awful toll already racked up in the war, or they still stared at the wall speaker.

The incoming-call lights were still flashing on the telephones, and each of those calls was from an agency either with information for the people in the room, or they required information and instructions.

Terry Jones replaced the receiver he had been holding and clapped his hands, breaking the spell for some and having to raise his voice sharply to snap the others out of the unbelieving state they were in, back to the job at hand.

This was a job General Henry Shaw had fulfilled without effort. By professional inclination, Terry Jones, CIA Director and former field agent, was not naturally attuned to stepping onto podiums to take charge. He had not survived his first twenty years in the CIA by being high profile. Terry was most comfortable at the back of the crowd, and preferably stood behind someone taller. Henry, however, had walked out the moment he heard the sound of his daughter's and his eldest son's ships vaporizing in Sydney Harbour.

"Listen in people." He addressed the room. "Game heads on, now!" Clapping his hands again for emphasis, he pointed to the telephones.

"You have jobs to do, so do them."

"Where did General Shaw go, Terry?" the President asked him.

"I do not know sir, but I do not think that anything anyone says to him right now can be of any real use." Terry said with concern.

"However, I think you will agree that we do need General Carmine in here to represent the military because now is not the moment for a timeout."

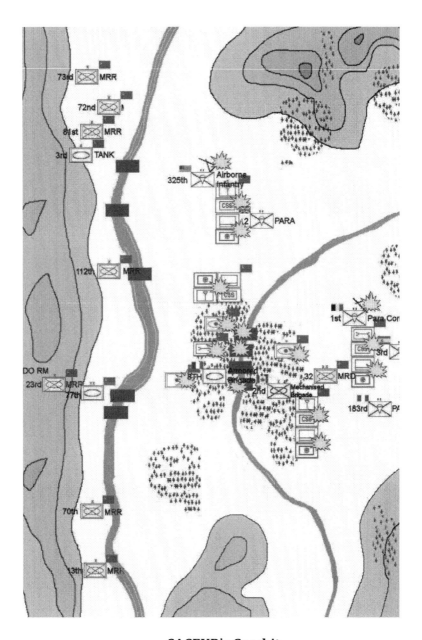

SACEUR's Gambit

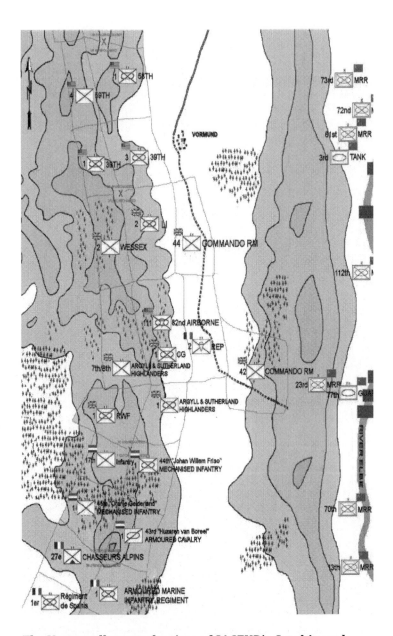

**The Vormundberg at the time of SACEUR's Gambit, and
The first appearance of the enemy in 'Fight Through'.**

"And gentlemen in England, now abed, shall think themselves accursed they were not here; and hold their manhood's cheap whiles any speaks that fought with us upon Saint Crispin's Day."

William Shakespeare

'The Longest night'

CHAPTER 1

The Vormundberg

If not for the burning vehicles in the valley it would be as dark as a grave on the hillside, but silent it was not.

"AMMO!"

The cry came from the gun controller of a GPMG in the sustained fire role and its gun crew from 'C' (Royal Berkshire) Company, 2 Wessex, who were firing on a DF he would not even be able to see in daylight.

The GPMG was almost at its maximum elevation as it fired bursts of twenty, with every fifth round being a tracer to aid correction. The rounds arced away into the night but not to a pre-registered Defensive Fire, a DF, in front of their own position, they were disappearing over a protrusion of higher ground to their right to plunge down at a target 1700 metres away.

The gun pit was not situated for direct defence but instead to provide enfilade fire support for other companies or units on the flanks. The GPMG was particularly well suited for this as the 'beaten zone', the pattern in which the rounds from a burst of fire landed, was cigar shaped and therefore more effective when employed against advancing infantry.

Likewise the companies and units on either flank would fire on their neighbours DFs.

Its sight was the C2, the same as that used on the L16 81mm mortar, and similarly used in conjunction with an aiming post to register targets they may, again, not have direct line of sight to, and to be able to lay onto those targets again at any time, come day or night. A Trilux lamp was clamped to the top of the aiming post for night shoots.

When 'registering' the target, once the fall of shot was landing where it was required the bearing and elevation were recorded. In this fashion a good crew could unlock the guns swivel mount, swing it onto the desired bearing where after a little fine adjustment they could put rounds on the ground in exactly the same place, in very short order. If it was necessary to engage targets to their front, the gun was dismounted from the tripod and used in the light role over open sights as the tripod was below ground level.

Some twenty three DFs were registered carefully in waterproof chinagraph pen along with three FPFs, Final Protective Fires, that would be called in in the event of units coming into close quarters with enemy infantry.

Thus far they had fired on those FPFs some eleven times this day, and the day wasn't over yet.

In a trench to their rear a young soldier slung his rifle across his back and squatted to grip the metal handles of two ammunition boxes. The boxes were from a stash left by the CQMS and the yellow stenciling identified the contents as 7.62 mixed link. The boxes were heavy, the handles slippery with mud and he used the remaining boxes as steps to exit.

"NO...crawl!" shouted the gun controller before flinching at the sound of a high velocity round, its sharp crack hurting his ears as it passed by at a velocity exceeded the speed of sound.

"Ah, *bollocks!*" Lance Corporal 'Dopey' Hemp snarled with feeling, tearing his eyes away before turning to the gun's No. 2, yelling into his ear.

"Back in a jiffy Spider, but get ready to throw smoke when I shout?"

"I've only got the one."

Dopey checked his pouches, but he had only L2 fragmentation grenades, the Brit version of the US M26.

"Bugger it..." Roger was busy doing his gunner bit so Dopey checked his pouches for him, and he was out of smoke too. He would have to use a wet and muddy route back to the trench behind them and save the smoke for the return journey.

"Where'd the shot come from?" Spider asked.

Dopey nodded downslope where Soviet AFVs and tanks sat disabled or burnt-out in mud that grew deeper with each new attack's churning sets of tracks.

"The smart money says he...or they, will be five hundred odd metres away in amongst that lot down there."

Downslope beyond their own units positions was known as the Thin Green Line, the ground held by the Royal Marines of 44 Commando who had allowed a group of enemy tanks and AFVs to roll over their forward trenches before engaging them where their armour was thinnest and knocking them out with infantry anti-tank weapons.

The NATO forces best tank killers were still the guns of their own MBTs, but attrition was at work there too on this seemingly endless day and night.

Clearly not all the enemy who had reached the defenders on the Vormundberg were dead as two members of D Company, 2LI, at whose rear the gun pit sat, had also fallen victim in the past hour.

Private 'Spider' Webber did not stick his head up to look; he had learned that lesson early on.

"I wonder what the Argyll and Sutherland guys will call us when we are the forward line of troops?"

"Same as always, I expect..." replied Dopey, stripping off his bulky fighting order and adding with his best attempt at a Glasgow accent *"...yon fockin' wee Eng-lish bast-ads."*

Spider checked the wind direction and decided he would have to toss the smoke to the right front of the gun pit, and not too far either as damp air made the smoke 'hang' in the rain rather than drift with the breeze.

Unburdened by the webbing Dopey slipped over the lip of the gun pit, keeping as low as possible he snaked through the mud into a depression carved out by this constant rain. He couldn't remember when he had last been dry and neither could he recall when last he had last felt safe. He followed the depression on his belly for twenty metres up the slope.

Bracing himself, swallowing down the fear and forcing it away he left the depression with a dive and roll, and the lance corporal kept on rolling until he reach the other trench, dropping over the edge and back into cover.

He landed on a pair of legs, but the owner did not object, he lay where he had toppled backwards over the trench's lip.

Dead eyes which had been alive but a few minutes before now stared back. The soldier's face was in shadow until illuminated briefly by a Soviet parachute flares sulfurous light and Dopey saw it held a look of surprise. He checked for a pulse anyway and it confirmed what he had learned to judge by sight, the difference from the living and the dead, so he wrested the ammunition boxes away from the body. Crouching below the edge of the trench he braced himself before heaving each one up and over, lofting not only those boxes but the six remaining boxes of link cached there.

There were also two boxes of 7.62 ball ammunition which could be belted together with the growing pile of expended links below their GPMG. One at a time he tossed these over the lip of the trench toward his own gun's position. His arm and back ached with the effort.

The small arms fire from the both his 2LI hosts and 44 Commando rose to a crescendo seemingly at the very second he opened his mouth to call to Spider, and he froze.

Streams of tracer, almost akin to lasers, ripped through the air high overhead as the marine's called in defensive fires.

Gradually the angles of the outgoing tracer altered, engaging DFs closer to the marine's positions before again dropping plunging fire onto a FPF as the Hungarians closed almost to grenade range.

Mortar fire missions arrived on target and overhead the outgoing artillery rounds droned mournfully eastwards, the sound punctuated by those of Challenger and Chieftain's main guns deliberate fire.

Dopey's heart pounded and it would have been so very easy to just stay where he was, put his shaking hands over his ears and resign to fear, but the firing slackened from that of a deafening roar to one of a few desultory shots in the dark.

At times like this the good soldier does not grit his teeth and fight on for Queen and country, he does not risk his skin out of regimental pride either, what he does do though is to think of his mates and it is that spurs him out of safety and back into harm's way.

"SPIDER!" he waited for an answering shout.

"SMOKE!" Dopey yelled.

There was a pause until Spider judged that line of sight between the trench and the suspected firing point was sufficient.

"GO!"

Perhaps the sniper was now dead? But if not he was unlikely to have moved on as his last victim had emerged from this trench carrying ammunition boxes, so it was a potentially good source of targets.

Dopey did not leave the trench the way he came in, he left the far end and rolled again, pausing only to check that the smoke was where it should be before slithering quickly downhill to where the boxes had landed.

The smoke was thinning out by the time he had tossed the last one the remainder of the way to the gun pit and rejoined the rest of the crew.

They were none of them regular soldiers, although Dopey Hemp had served a tour attached to The Queens Regiment in Iraq. They were all three of them part timers from Britain's Territorial Army, a diverse mix in terms of background, education and employment in their day jobs, far more so than amongst the ranks of the regular army. 'Dopey's' given name was Mark and he was a barman by trade, pulling pints in a pub in Dedworth on the outskirts of Windsor. He didn't know what Spider Webber's Christian name was, but Spider was a machinist somewhere on Slough Trading Estate. The gunner was Roger Goldsmith, a real estate agent from Eton Wick and young man lying dead in the trench behind them had been a college student in Maidenhead.

Dopey and the others from 2 Wessex who were on loan to the Light Infantry were filling dead men's shoes, and in their case manning one of the 2LI Machine Gun Platoon 'gimpies', the L7A2 General Purpose Machine Guns.

The carefully recorded bearing and elevation sight settings were not written in Dopey's hand and they did not ask what had happened to the light infantrymen who had been the original crew, the sandbags lining the gun pit were torn and ripped in places from an air bursting artillery round's shrapnel, but the rain had washed away the blood.

Now back in the gun pit the barrel of the GPMG glowed red, the rain hissed and sizzled on the metal but the fire mission in support of 1CG's left flank company was complete.

It is possible for the barrel of a GPMG to become white hot with constant use, and with that the barrel will warp and become unusable, but before that occurs then rounds will cook-off in the breach due to the heat. Three spare heavy barrels are part of an SF kit and carried in a thick woven bag of '37 Pattern webbing, and it is but the work of a moment to replace a barrel that is glowing red orange with that of a spare.

According to the SASC, the Small Arms School Corps, the hot barrel should be placed to one side and allowed to cool naturally in order to prevent the metal eventually becoming brittle. But at one side of the gun pit stood a 16" high aluminium storage tin that had once held twelve shermouli para illum tubes, it was now brimming with rainwater and had two heavy barrels for the 'gimpy' sticking out of it. Had it not been raining and the locale arid, then the tin would have been filled with the crew's urine and the pungent odour of a public urinal on a hot summer's day would have hung in the air.

A wonderful tool is a soldier's urine; it has softened boot leather for centuries and cooled barrels since the invention of gunpowder.

In a cramped shelter bay dug into the side of the gun pit Roger was working on the third barrel with a wire brush from the weapons cleaning kit, also a webbing bag. Carbon builds up rapidly in the SF role and if unchecked it will adversely effect accuracy as it fills the rifling grooves. The barrels gas regulator also collects carbon residue each time a round is fire and this eventually leads to stoppages.

Having once cleaned the inside of the barrel Roger removed the gas regulator and carefully placed this, along with its two small semi-circular lugs into an old compo ration tin. He dropped them into two inches of clear fluid that was already in the tin where they fizzed. If the SASC frowned up the method of cooling the barrels that the Berkshire men employed, then they would be seriously upset with the regulator being immersed in rust remover. Nothing, however, removed carbon quite as quickly and thoroughly as an acid solution. The gunner was far more concerned with husbanding his limited supply of Jenolite than he was of the SASC's wrath.

The position had a field telephone with a direct line to a man-portable telephone exchange at company headquarters and he reported the death of their ammunition carrier to the D Company 2LI CSM.

"What was his full name?" the CSM asked.

"I dunno sir, his surname was Crowne." Dopey replied, pausing to look at the other two, almost indiscernible in the dark.

"Fucknows." Spider offered unhelpfully, and Rogers shrug went unseen in the darkness at the back of the shelter bay.

A few months ago they would all have been greatly embarrassed at not knowing the name of one of their unit who had been killed, but that was then and this was now.

"He was a new guy...and we are down to six boxes of mixed link."

"And smoke!" Spider reminded him.

The CSM could be heard calling out to the Q Bloke at the other end but the company's quarter master sergeant's reply was a mere nod. He was a busy man this day.

Dopey hung up the old fashioned handset and sat beside Spider on empty ammunition boxes in the entrance to the shelter bay, their boots squelching in the mud with each movement as the boxes of 7.62 ball ammunition were opened.

They were all deathly tired, and not just from lack of sleep. Fear produces adrenaline and adrenaline has a toll on the body but they squatted, silently creating fresh belts using spent links. There would be no tracer rounds in these belts so they would be carefully stored in the boxes the rounds had come from and placed with similar belts as their final ammunition reserve.

"Anyone got any scoff?" Roger asked "Me stomach thinks me throats been cut."

Dopey fished out a small tin from a cardboard ten man ration pack beside him, tossing it across.

Roger worked his compo tin opener industriously in the dark interior of the shelter bay before giving the contents an exploratory sniff.

"Bacon Grill? What kind of grub is that for a good Jewish boy?" he grumbled "Hasn't this man's army heard of religious diversity?"

There was the usual banter that went on between soldiers who lived in each pockets day in and day out. Complete irreverence towards each other's religions, football teams, school and home towns. Only family was sacrosanct.

At the end of the day nothing outside of their small circle was going to save them from harm, they had only each other and the absolute trust that came with that. Professional motivators are fond of stating "There is no 'i' in Team" but if they had consulted each member of the team they would realise their error.

"I trust them, and I won't betray their trust in me."

Roger tried to feign offence at a remark, but he failed and joined the other two soldiers giggling like demented schoolboys at the bad, and very old joke, before bending the newly removed lid of the tin slightly and using it to scoop the contents into his mouth, taking care not let his tongue touch its jagged edge.

When Roger finished his cold, al fresco repast he stamped the empty tin and lid flat.

"Stick a brew on Spider"

"Bollocks...what did your last slave die of?"

"Disobedience" Roger replied "and make mine three sugars, mate."

As handy as the pocket sized army issue solid fuel cookers were, the hexamine fuel gave off poisonous fumes in confined spaces so Spider pulled his camping gas stove from a bergan side pouch and set it up. Each man contributed their water bottles to the filling of the 'kettle', a circular L2 Frag grenade storage container. The lid and fastener kept soil and dirt out, and the heat in for quicker boiling.

Roger fished the gas parts from out of the compo tin and grunted in pain as the rust remover attacked the tiny cuts on his fingertips that seem to appear as if by magic on infantrymen's hands as soon as they get into the field. Roger's discomfort was a minor thing, akin to getting lemon juice on a cut and the reassembly and reattachment of the gas regulator to the barrel went in silence.

The newly field cleaned barrel replaced the old one, and a brief hiss sounded from the shermouli container that one was doused too.

The white noise issuing from the radio headphones cut out abruptly.

"Hello Four Six Delta this is Nine Four Bravo, over?"

The trio paused in what they were doing.

"Four Six Bravo, send, over." replied Dopey.

"Nine Four Bravo...shoot Delta Echo Three Six Echo, over!"

"Here we go again." muttered Roger.

Bloodhound Zero Three, Germany: West of Bremen. 2049hrs.

Of the fleet of converted Boeing 707-300 airframes currently in service with the USAF, the one presently carrying the callsign Bloodhound Zero Three was the oldest of the JSTARS.

Forty years before, it had taken to the air in the livery of Pan Am on the long-haul transatlantic routes, but it now wore pale grey as it traced its north/south race track route.

Retired from commercial service some time before the sad demise of Pan Am she entered military service via a make-over at the, then, Grumman Aerospace facility. Since the end of the first Gulf War, or 'Desert Sword' to some, this old lady had sat in the dry desert heat in Nevada, just another retired airframe left out for spy satellites to count until this, the Third World War, necessitated a hurried refurbishment and installation of a surveillance suite several generations superior to the one previously carried.

Tonight, high above a solid cover of rain heavy cloud Bloodhound Zero Three was watching events unfolded to the east.

The Russian 77th Guards Tank Division had completed its awkward reverse course and the opposition had worn out two other divisions in keeping up the pressure so NATO could not exploit the situation. It had not all been for nothing, not all a complete waste as a minor breakthrough had occurred between two defending units, always a weak spot. Romanian tanks and AFVs from the 91st Tank Regiment were through that small breach before hard fighting by 3 Para, plus A and B Companies of 1 Wessex, had choked it off, battering the follow-on infantry.

The Hungarians had smashed into the US and German sections on the Vormundberg, making some gains, only to lose them again in vicious hand to hand fighting as the Americans took back their fighting positions trench by trench, with grenades, bayonets and sheer guts. Once the last trench was retaken they poured fire into the former German positions, assisting their allies as they too fixed bayonets and counter attacked.

Only in the sector held by the composite battalion of 82nd paratroopers and Coldstream Guardsmen did the enemy have a foothold and the Czechs of the 23rd Motor Rifle Regiment used that position to pry at the neighbouring 44 Commando, Royal Marines.

Bloodhound Zero Three saw it all and reported each turn of events despite twice having to run from Red Air Force fighters.

The NATO Air Forces were joined by carrier air groups and their brief was to get 4 Corps to the front, so only helicopter assets were on station where the ground fighting was taking place.

It was SACEUR's call, his decision. Did he allow the enemy to pound 4 Corps with their fighter bombers, or did he load up his own fighter bombers with air to air ordnance and use them as well as his remaining fighters in fully supporting the newly arrived US and Canadians in their drive to the front?

If 4 Corps failed to arrive then the war in Europe was lost, and it had to get there before the blockage he had caused in the enemy supply line had been cleared.

So as far as fixed wing air support went the front was on its own for the time being.

General Allain could see that one of the two main dangers on the ground was the armour that had broken through and disappeared into the forested foothills south of the Vormundberg, was it now heading for the junction of Autobahn's 2 and 39 to the east of Brunswick?

He was not a man who held much reliance on computer aided digital maps and although there were a battery of plasma screens displaying all pertinent information, it was a paper map of Germany with a plastic overlay that he was studying and according to the grease pencil symbols, C Company, 2/198th Armored Regiment, a Mississippi National Guard unit, was defending it. Two tank platoons, an ITV, Improved Tow Vehicle, and a pair of M125 81mm mortar carriers were dug in covering the approaches. There was also an engineer section ready to drop the flyover if Vormundberg fell. Additionally there was a section of military policemen doing what MPs do, waving their arms at the traffic.

The reality of the matter, however, was that one of those tank platoons was made up of elderly M1 Abrams MBTs from a prepositioned equipment depot, as their own rides had only arrived at Zeebrugge with 4 Corps.

The M1 had much thinner armour than the M1A1 and was technologically its inferior on most other levels too, in addition being armed with a 105mm main gun, not the heavier 120mm.

The second tank platoon was in the infantry role and as such under-strength in comparison to that of an infantry platoon.

General Allain was about out of options and bereft an armoured reserve when he really needed one.

In regard to the other matter, the divisional commander at Vormundberg had already informed SACEUR that he had wanted to pull out 44 Commando from their current location once they had thoroughly mined and booby trapped each position. They would then carry out a reorganisation on the hurry-up before going into the dead ground behind the forward companies of 2 Wessex, in readiness for a counterattack. General Allain had been doubtful as to the wisdom of the proposed action, the guardsmen and paratroopers had been in the line since the beginning, and they were about used up. The marines of 44 Commando were fresher, so why not carry out a relief-in-place? They had some artillery to spare that could provide a limited covering barrage whilst the maneouvre was carried out?

"Grudge match...and I want that artillery for the Czechs when they are out in the open, not to keep their heads down." was the divisional commander's reply.

Both the guardsmen and the marine commandos had a score to settle with the Czechs of the 23rd MRR.

"Those Geordies and Yorkshiremen want payback for what those Czechs did to the prisoners and wounded at Wesernitz, and Forty Four were watching when those guys did the same to 42 Commando."

Major General Dave Hesher had been Brigadier General Hesher and commanding the US 4th Armored Brigade twenty four hours before, now he was commanding a division thrown together with such haste no one had found time to even give it a name or number.

Despite his recent command of an armoured unit Dave Hesher had spent most of his service in the Rangers and Green Berets; he knew the value of unit pride when the odds were stacked against you. Attachments over the years to British units such as the Gloucester Regiment and Royal Welsh Fusiliers had brought home the value of joining your regional regiment for life rather than being posted to different ones every few years. Only the Airborne had anything like a similar setup in the US Army.

The Canadian had been silent for a long moment as he considered the words.

"The Czechs outnumber them, Dave."

"Sir, the 23rd were a full strength motor rifle regiment at the Wesernitz..."

"A motor rifle regiment is equivalent to one of our infantry brigades, as you well know." interrupted General Allain. "Together, the Coldstreamers and Commandos make a superannuated battalion...hell Dave, I combined what was left of two Brit mech' *brigades* and together there's still barely more than three grand's worth of them on their bit of that hill."

"There are Jim Popham's boys too sir, 1CG and his guys are joined at the hip." It was a desperate shot as even with those three units combined they were still outgunned, but Dave Hesher was betting that the Czechs were about to try and build on their earlier success and he wanted to kick them in the balls and regain the lost ground at the same time. He believed the amity, the brotherhood that had built up between American paratroopers and British guardsmen, if combined with the enmity the guardsmen and marines had for the Czech 23rd, would compensate for lack of numbers.

Pierre Allain had been the one who had originally ordered the remnants of the battalion of the 82nd that had fought its way out of Leipzig Airport, and the half strength Guards battalion to combine. It had been geography and circumstance that had made the *temporary* arrangement a logical one at the time, it had been expeditious and Pierre had not envisaged the odd union lasting beyond the time it took to re-establish NATOs defensive line.

The last he had heard was that troops in both units had exchanged items of uniform and kit so that now, not unlike two soccer teams at the final whistle, the paratrooper from Washington, Illinois was indistinguishable from the guardsman from Washington, Tyne and Wear, unless they spoke of course. The odd union had lasted months.

Pierre Allain was not one to change a winning team before the cup final.

"The 23rd have been quiet for an hour now." Major General Hesher had said. "I'm betting that around midnight they'll try again and I have dedicated two batteries of 105s and two flights of AH-64s, fuelled, armed and on standby."

"Alright then, it's your battle so I won't interfere." SACEUR had allowed. "I can't spare MLRS but I can get you a few extra rotary assets from the Danes." In the early evening a half dozen Lynx from Eskadrille 723 had arrived unexpectedly in company with two Sea Kings loaded down with TOW reloads. General Allain had not asked any awkward questions but had authorised their attachment to the Italian army's Agusta 129s operating out of forest clearings in the Herbst Wald. They both used TOW rather than Hellfire missiles anyway.

The Romanian armour was another matter though, as for one thing he had no accurate tally of the numbers involved and JSTARS guestimate was between one company and a battalion. Ten tanks or thirty, they had not acted according to standard Soviet doctrine, they had not immediately turned about and set-to in securing and widening the breach for follow-on forces.

War gaming, the fighting of battles on large table tops by enthusiasts moving models around is known simply and logically as 'war gaming'. Apparently someone believed the professionals required several degrees of separation from the hobbyist's pastime and an acronym was urgently required. It is entirely possible that somewhere in the process a tender was put out and a parliamentary committee formed to select the ablest PLC of bright and thrusting young graduates who would receive a big bung of tax payer's money for completing the awesome task of thinking up a title. However it came about though, the professional soldiers were not consulted and stubbornly refuse to say 'tactical exercise without troops' when they see the word 'TEWT' printed on a training roster, using instead the term 'table top exercise' as they have always done.

SACEUR leaned forward and rested his hands on the edge of the map table, staring at the unit symbols, already knowing each units current strength and equipment, he mentally conducted several table top exercises as he decided who, if anyone, he could detach to intercept the Romanian tanks before they could seize the autobahn junction, if in fact that is where it was heading.

There was no 'Eureka moment' during his contemplation, merely a resigned sigh as he finally decided upon whom to send as yet another Forlorn Hope.

Flechtinger Forest, Germany: 6 miles southwest of the Vormundberg.

The rain beat down without mercy anointing scarred and splintered tree trunks with its thin salve. It soaked the underclothing of a soldier via a rent in his Gortex combat smock as he made his way cautiously through what remained of Flechtinger Höhenzug, the forested ridge southwest of Magdeburg. A low profile fabric panel attached to a breast pocket fastener depicted two woven stars above a crown, showing his rank as that of Tenente Colonnello, a Lieutenant Colonel, but it was hard to see even in good light ever since a Russian sniper had narrowly missed killing him with an intended head shot, perforating the waterproof material two inches from his neck and killing a young soldier behind him instead. Although he rarely drank, a large glass of Grappa had restored his equilibrium far more ably than surgical sticking plaster had thus far achieved in restoring the smocks waterproof integrity. As to the rank panel, well that was now even more low profile than originally specified by the army board of uniform standards, owing to a palm full of camouflage cream that had been applied to the material with a shaky hand, pre-restorative Grappa.

The lieutenant colonel was now accompanied by a half section of infantrymen and the brigade adjutant, also a lieutenant colonel but one who was junior in grade. Together they made their way parallel to the top of the ridge, but remaining carefully on the reverse slope, out of the enemy's sights.

The colonel's nose wrinkled with distaste as he neared one of his brigade's eight wheeled B1 Centauro tank destroyers, the barrel of its 105mm main armament was drooping at an angle, fire scarred and blackened. Not even the rain could cool the blistered paintwork of the vehicles bodywork, but instead hissed and spat as it struck the hot metal. It was dug-in, hull down in a once well camouflaged position, but the luck of both vehicle and crew had run out. Only lack of ammunition had prevented a catastrophic explosion though the flames consumed it instead, feeding off combustibles where the rain could not reach. 120mm rounds for the main battle tanks were in ready supply, thanks to the latest convoy's arrival, but the brigades tank destroyers had been reduced to the role of mobile hardpoints in the anti-infantry role, using their exposed external 7.62mm machine guns for the previous two days.

The colonel ducked as small arms ammunition suddenly cooked off in the flames inside, the ball and tracer rounds ricocheting about the interior with the odd round escaping with a whine, whirring away into the night from out of the open commander's hatch. The stench that was issuing was that of the electrical insulation and the still smouldering rubber of the tyres, but it was combined with something else too.

He doubted he could ever eat pork again.

Fifty minutes of negotiating his way, with the occasional pause at fighting positions to speak to the troops, finally brought him to the M113 APC he was using as a command vehicle.

Entering the rear of the track and pushing through the heavy blackout curtain, he emerged in the dimly lit interior.

"Sir." said one of the radio operators in the cramped confines they had to work in. "The commanders on the line."

indicating the telephone handset to their secure 'means', protected by fourteen layered encryption.

He paused for a moment before replying.

"Bloody good range that set has if it can reach the afterlife." he observed with a hint of sarcasm, not directed at anyone in particular.

The brigade commander, his 2 i/c and the regimental commanders, their own included, had been killed several hours before at an O Group, assassinated by Russian Spetznaz troops in the guise of a Carabinieri close protection squad.

"No sir, SACEUR." interrupted his own one-time 2 i/c, Major Spittori, who was now his natural successor as CO of the 11th Bersaglieri Regiment.

"General Allain himself."

The Canadian was reputed never to delegate the issuing of a 'difficult' set of orders to subordinates.

Lt Col Lorenzo Rapagnetta, senior surviving officer of the Ariete Armoured Brigade seated himself before raising the handset to his ear. They were the only two using that secure channel and VP could be set aside.

"Good morning sir, may I respectfully enquire what I can I do for you?"

CHAPTER 2

Russia, Militia Sub-District 178.
Friday, 19th October. 2109hrs.

Barely clear of the tree tops, its throttles open, the jet aircraft caused Major Limanova, the deputy commander of Militia Sub-District 178 to duck involuntarily as it passed overhead visible as a briefly glimpsed black silhouette, bereft of navigation or anti-collision lights against the stars it eclipsed in its passage.

The shock of the moment quickly passed and he had looked to the vehicle's driver, Petrov, gawping dumbly at the skies but visible only for the glowing cigarette held between his lips.

If whoever was involved in whatever-the-hell was going on had heard them approaching, then the aircraft would have been shut down until they passed well away. It therefore stood to reason that the aircraft engine had masked the sound of the noisy AFV.

"Switch off!" he had shouted even as he broke into a run back to the vehicle, gesticulating with a throat cutting signal but the driver could barely make him out in the dark, let alone hear him.

He shone the torch at himself, half blinded by the glare he had stumbled and nearly tripping over because of it.

"Turn the damn engine off!" and the gesture got the message home where words failed.

Dropping back down into his seat through the hatch the driver had done as requested and the deputy commander stopped to listen as the sound of the aircraft rapidly diminished to nothingness, and only the wind in the trees remained.

"Sir, why did you want the engine off?" the driver asked as he re-emerged, standing on his seat.

The question caught Major Limanova off guard.

"Didn't you hear that jet take off?"

"A jet, sir?"

"You heard an aircraft run up its engines and take off?"

"No, sir."

"But you heard it fly over us...you looked up?"

"Crick in me neck sir, its cramped in this seat. I didn't hear nothing on account of that." He jerked a thumb to the right.

The driver's position on a BMP-1 was offset to the left, the same as a car or trucks, where it occupied a third of the front section of the vehicle. The BMP-1s engine pack, a big six cylinder V8, took up the other two thirds. The single exhaust on the far right where it sat flush with the body had a silencer, but this vehicle was older than its current driver. Decades of soldiers had misused the exhaust, reducing the silencers muffling matrix to its current inefficient state by raising the rectangular steel grill covering of the exhaust outlet, dropping tinned rations inside to be broiled in the can, and forcing the grill closed again with brute force, such as by jumping up and down on it.

When they had halted here the deputy commander had walked forwards with his out of date map, a compass and torch to narrow down their location as there were more supposed firebreaks in reality than his map depicted.

The fabric and horsehair crewman's helmet had irritated him, the rubber ear pieces made his skin itch and as he had knelt, away from the magnetic interference of the elderly AFV, orientating map and compass, he had raised an ear flap to scratch, and that was why he had heard the aircraft but the driver had not.

Out of date or not, the map showed a disused airstrip from the time of the Great Patriotic War, and it lay in the direction the mystery aircraft had come from.

Remounting the vehicle he reached for the radio microphone.

Moscow Air Defence Centre was no stranger to the vagaries of equipment generated false alarms or the phantom sightings of aircraft by nervous sentries, but it was unusual for a senior office to call in a sighting he had made.

Civilian air traffic was strictly controlled and the logs showed no scheduled flights or military scrambles at the time stated, and certainly there was nothing near the location given.

Likewise he had drawn a blank elsewhere as enquiries with the Kremlin confirmed that there had been no VIP traffic at that time. Anyone with sufficient pull to warrant air transport was elsewhere anyway, deep in a bunker.

Security and Intelligence Liaison would neither confirm nor deny any ongoing flight operations. Finally of course there were the ground radar stations and two orbiting A-50 Mainstays, three hundred miles southwest and northeast respectively, but replaying their records brought the deputy commander little in the way of credibility.

The duty watch officer with whom the increasingly frustrated militia officer was dealing now voiced his doubts.

"Comrade, the only air traffic in that area all day was attached to your own militia for a search operation and the air defence radar records show that it was above the airstrip you mentioned." he stated the time as related to him a few minutes before. "Did the machine not land?"

The deputy commander felt a sinking feeling; he knew where Air Defence Centre was going with this.

He replied, resignedly.

"No comrade, they stated it was too heavily overgrown to risk clipping a tree."

He could hear the watch officer on the other end kiss his teeth.

"Well comrade deputy commander what can I say, if a helicopter could not land then a jet aircraft could hardly take off, now could it?"

As days went, this had not been a good one and he could do nothing about his own commander's attitude. There was most certainly no point in informing the sub district commander of what had occurred as he would have to admit that nothing had shown up on radar, and even his own driver could not support his claim.

"Grab your rifle and equipment Petrov." he instructed, pulling on his own as he spoke.

"We're going for a walk."

For the past one hundred miles the hybrid Nighthawk, its callsign simply *'Petticoat Express'*, had been down in the weeds, staying mercifully untroubled by Moscow's formidable multi layered defences and sensors by giving the city a wide birth.

"So where the hell is the promised satellite support?" Caroline had muttered soon after take-off.

The 'At-a-glance' system was up and working but it lacked was current information to project onto the aircraft's screens. Only the previously known positions of defence sites were showing, and in the case of mobile air defence units this could have changed radically since the last update, weeks before at RAF Kinloss, in Scotland.

Shading that mirrored the level of their 'painting' by radars had been apparent of course, but the radar energy had not been sufficient to cause concern.

So far so good, thought Patricia, but had she been aware that six thousand miles away there was a battle underway in the jungle close by their first scheduled assistance she would not have been quite so relaxed.

They stayed low and relatively slow, holding to the bottom end of the aircraft's best fuel economy performance and kept Nizhny Novgorod on their nose until they could drop into the Oka river valley and open the throttles a little more.

They kept to the southern side of the valley, cutting across broad swathes of marsh and bog that the river meandered around, the land around that region being largely low lying to the north. In contrast, the southern bank of the river rose as low, wooded hills.

The vast, and massively polluted industrial centre of Dzerzhinsk slid by, shrouded in soot and smoke, five miles off their left wing. The factories and chemical plants were visible, illuminated to cope with twenty four hour production and making a mockery of blackout regulations.

As Dzerzhinsk passed away behind them Caroline raised the nose and turned south to avoid the Oka River Bridge and its defences.

The Nighthawk skimmed above the wooded hills, nosing over into the next valley, now clear of known air defence zones and heading towards its target.

ESA Launch Facility, Kourou, French Guiana

The glow out to sea evidenced the flames consuming the French corvette *Premier-Maitre L'her*, mortally wounded by the People's Liberation Army Navy diesel electric submarine *Bao*, she stubbornly clung to the surface and once the flames had consumed her sundered superstructure they began to feed on the aluminium in her hull.

She still possessed a full magazine below the waterline and as she was not drifting shore wards and therefore not a danger to the town so she was given a very wide berth, abandoned to her inevitable fate.

Life rafts dotted the ocean to the north of the corvette where wind and tide took them, sweeping them towards the former penal colony isles off the coast, and of course the dense offshore minefield.

Pleasure boat owning civilians and Kourou's few remaining fishermen where now being summoned from their beds, and directed to carry out search and rescue for survivors from the *Premier-Maitre L'her* as best they could.

The sister ship of the stricken warship, the *Commandant Blaison*, pennant number F793, had arrived but she was to seaward, conducting a hunt for the second Chinese submarine, the *Dai*.

The colony's Governor had been made aware that the *Dai* had launched a single cruise missile and the significance of that event led to a panicked dusting off of contingency plans for protecting the colony in time of nuclear attack that had been written in the aftermath of the Cuban Missile Crisis.

The *Commandant Blaison* was closed up to action stations and conducting NBC Warfare procedures as she sought to find and sink the *Dai* before she could launch a fresh attack.

The locating of the *Dai* would be one of immense difficulty given the means that remained at the disposal of the colony. Two specialist ASW maritime patrol aircraft and two ASW hulls would have had a better chance, but in the space of less than an hour that force had been reduced to half its original size.

Aboard the surviving Atlantique the trio of ASW operators had identified *Dai's* type and therefore the type of weapon deployed. They could take a map and a set of compasses and draw a semi-circle off the coast which defined that weapons known/believed maximum range and that would give them the maximum area they not only needed to search but also to keep secure. The *Dai* of course had not had time to reach that pencil line so that left a smaller semi-circle, but one that was expanding exponentially by the moment.

If she was not found and sunk by the coming of dawn they would have an awful lot of ocean to search.

The colony's pair of Breguet Atlantiques, *Poseidon Zero Four* and *Poseidon One Eight* had been hurriedly armed with the means to sink submarines earlier in the evening but not the wherewithal to find them remotely once submerged. The tail boom mounted magnetic anomaly detector requires the aircraft to directly overfly the unseen submarine in order to detect it. The sowing of lines of sonar buoys permitted a single aircraft to cover a vastly larger area, and it was akin to tying tin cans to a barbed wire fence.

The Atlantique could carry seventy two of the devices, thirty of which were pre-loaded into launch tubes offset on the left side of the belly, just aft of the cockpit. However, counter measures to submarine launched anti-aircraft missiles were not the only item used prolifically in recent weeks.

They did not have seventy two sonar buoys at Cayenne, they had seven.

Zero Four was still burning at the end of the runway at Cayenne when *One Eight* touched down and raised a welter of spray as it dashed through the puddles with both pilots applying the brakes and reversing the propellers, shortening the landing run-out well clear of the wreck of the other Atlantique. Once halted, they sat for several minutes watching the flames consume *Poseidon Zero Four*.

"Là, mais la grâce de Dieu vont I...there but for the grace of God go I" declared her captain with other crew members crowding into the cabin to crouch and peer through the windscreen at the conflagration, which until a short time before had been an identical aircraft to their own.

The crew of *Zero Four* stood over by the military end of the airfield, a fenced off cluster of huts and tarmac ramp. They had escaped death or injury but showed no outward sign of relief as they watched their aircraft's death throes.

Zero Four lay on its starboard side, upon the ruined wing and collapsed landing gear. The port wingtip was visible in the light of the flames when the thick swirling smoke was not clinging to it like a shroud.

The best efforts of the Cayenne Airport fire service could never extinguish those flames given the equipment they had. A single tender, such as theirs, was judged sufficient to carry out a rescue of the passengers and the crew of an aircraft, but a minimum of three tenders would have been required to save the airframe and engines from further damage.

The raised port wingtip first sagged as the main spar buckled in the intense heat, and then launched upwards and outwards, cartwheeling into the jungle a hundred metres away as the port wing tank finally exploded in a spectacular display of petrochemical based violence that any Hollywood SFX technician would be proud of.

Bombing up *Poseidon One Eight* and hot refuelling the aircraft, the refilling of the fuel tanks without first shutting down the engines, took place even closer to the terminal than it had before. If the airport manager had any fresh objections to these further breaches of regulations he kept them to himself.

With six depth charges and four Mk-46 torpedoes in the bomb bay, virtually all the remaining available ordnance, plus two active and five passive sonar buoys in the belly launch tubes, *One Eight* taxied further down the tarmac, disappearing into the acrid black smoke before pivoting to face back up the runway.

The enshrouding smoke was whipped away by the twin Rolls Royce Tyne turboprop engines as they ran up.

Two hundred metres behind, the flames flared, fanned by the prop wash and sending myriad sparks gusting away.

With two hundred metres less runway to play with, full tanks and a full bomb bay, the brakes remained on until the Atlantiques nose dipped, like a bull pawing at the earth. The brakes were released and the Atlantique rolled forward, the engines temperature gauges right on the limit of tolerance but they could not reduce the rpm. *One Eight* stayed stubbornly reluctant to leave terra firma until well past the point of no return, committing them to the take-off and only then reluctantly, did the nosewheel become unglued.

Poseidon One Eight left the tarmac perilously close to the runway's end and raised its undercarriage immediately, roaring just above the trees before banking left across sleeping Cayenne, and out over the Atlantic once more.

A satellite's life is dictated by its fuel supply at the time of having stabilised at its correct orbit. Ten to fifteen years of use remains before it is boosted away from earth into a scrapyard orbit, three hundred kilometres further, out once only three months' worth of normal station keeping fuel is remaining. and a commercial satellites fuel use is mainly spent on north-south station keeping in geostationary orbit.

The small communications satellite lofted towards geosynchronous orbit above the Volga River by the Italian *Vega* rocket carried a larger number of hypergolic propellant tanks for its maneouvring thrusters in order to survive the game of orbital dodge ball that had been running since day one of the war.

The *Vega's* satellite would control not only the B61 weapon for attacking the bunker, but the Nighthawk's air to air and ground attack ordnance also. But it needed a RORSAT to provide the required radar and thermal data on the targets.

Russia

Major Caroline Nunro allowed herself a glance at the watch on her wrist as if distrusting the digital time being displayed on the instrument panel before her.

"I don't know." Patricia said, anticipating the question.

The plan called for dedicated satellite support and that support simply had not materialised.

There was no way to know if there was a delay or whether...

Her comms panel lit up as the communication satellite that the Italian *Vega* had carried aloft sent an authentication query. It would not open a downlink until it was satisfied with their bona fides.

Patricia's fingers flew, inputting the correct response and then breathing a sigh of relief at the data which flooded down.

The cockpit screens and panels giving virtual views through 360 ° began to light up with updated mission specific information on static and mobile air defences. It was being fed to them in the form of an encrypted datalink from a CIA ground station in Illinois where the mission was being run. There was no voice transmission only data.

"How current is this?" Caroline queried.

"Thirty six hours." Pat replied.

"Better than a poke in the eye with a sharp stick..." Caroline responded "Can you bring up the target area as a map overlay?"

The rolling hills had given way to open ground with little in the way of habitation on their line of flight. She let the aircraft systems take over and concentrated on what was her first look at their target.

They were both silent as they took in the defences they needed to defeat, by stealth or force.

"Tatischevo, Sharkovka, Petrovsk, Engels, Saratov West and Saratov airport." Caroline read off the airfields nearby.

"Tatischevo is a deactivated ICBM base; Sharkovka is a MiG-29 base, ditto Petrovsk...." Patricia narrated the intelligence data for the area that had been collated since they had sent the information supplied by Svetlana's contact.

"...Engels is a bomber base, Tu-95 'Bears' and an aircraft museum, Saratov is a civilian airport and Saratov West is deactivated, a graveyard for old military helicopters."

"Saratov West is the closest to the target but it is thirteen miles away..." Caroline mused.

"Doubting Svetlana's contact?" Pat asked.

"We have no reason to trust them."

"The runway looks well maintained." Patricia was bringing up the satellite photos of the base taken a year before. Beside the runway, on the untended grass field were row upon row of early production troop transport Mi-8s, and many of those without rotor blades.

For a downgraded airbase though the tower and hangars looked better maintained than the other buildings.

The mine workings near Topovka were thought to be a mile deep but what was above ground just looked as you would expect a mine that had been worked out for twenty years to look like. The satellite images, being a year old, bore no signs of recent activity, or the lack thereof, to confirm or deny its alleged purpose.

"Would you have a car park next to a mine shaft?" Patricia asked.

"I've no idea why you wouldn't, if that is any help, so I guess we just waste the place and hope the information was kosher."

A Soviet nuclear bunker could reportedly survive a hundred kiloton near miss owing to them being super-hardened boxes supported on all sides by giant shock absorbers, so their B61 weapon's relatively small dialled-in 30kt yield warhead had to be delivered on target and bury itself as deep as possible. After a time delay in which the F-117X needed to put distance between itself and the target the weapon would detonate, and produce a shockwave that would destroy the bunker.

However, despite having a small shaft to aim the thing down and a narrow, defended valley with interceptors based nearby this would not be a re-run of Luke downing the Death Star.

The 5000lb weight of the weapon seemed excessive for its size, but the body had originally been part of the barrel of an 8" artillery piece and the penetrator was constructed of depleted uranium. Attached to the tail was a JDAM tail unit containing GPS, FMU-143 delay fuse, a satellite downlink for guidance, along with a solid fuel rocket to assist ground penetration.

The F-117X would have to pop-up to five thousand feet to toss-bomb the weapon but from the moment of its release, getting out of Dodge would be the young women's principle concern.

Kourou

Six thousand two hundred and eighty five miles away the *Ariane* rocket carrying the first RORSAT dedicated to *Guillotine* cleared the tower in French Guiana.

Nine thousand miles north-west of the launch site and one hundred and thirty miles above the sand sea of the Taklamakan Desert, *Èmó 16*, a Chinese 'Demon' killer satellite, initiated a fourteen second burn to alter its orbit and speed to intercept. The speeds and trajectory range of the *Ariane* for reaching the required orbits for their payloads was a matter of record and all technical details of the Vulcaine 2 engine had been freely shared, pre-war. It was therefore a cause for concern at Chinese Space Command when data on the launch arrived from a surveillance satellite tracking the *Ariane* on radar. Its trajectory was as predicted but its speed was not, in fact if anything the flight profile was that of an older engine, a Vulcaine 1.

250,000 pounds of force was being exerted against the pull of the Earth's gravity, 51,000 pounds less than the Vulcaine 2 was capable of.

Èmó 16 had accelerated from 17,000 MPH to 23,000 MPH in order to make the interception and in non-technical terms it was now seriously over-cooking it.

The *Èmó 16* carried out a radical maneouvre, pivoting about its axis whereupon its small main engine began a sustained burn. The problem the Chinese now faced was in deciding why the older engine was being employed by the French. Had ESA simply run out of their most modern engines? If that was the case then the second stage should be the twelve year old Aestus booster.

Those who were trying to solve this puzzle were rocket scientists and it did not occur to them that the substitution of a Mk 2 for a Mk 1 was simple game-playing, a deception designed to wrong foot the Chinese and buy a little more time before the inevitable happened. The calculations were made and at the appointed moment *Èmó 16* pivoted about its axis once more, held steady for 4000th of a second and self-destructed, sending 10,000 small cubes at the point in space where the *Ariane*'s second stage would be in three minutes and nine seconds.

The second stage cleared the planned point of interception a full one point four seconds ahead of the gradually expanding cloud of cubes and its powerful modern HM-7B engine cut out prior to payload separation.

Russia

"Bingo!" Pat said with feeling, punching the air within the confines of the small cockpit behind Caroline. The 'At-a-glance' system truly came to life as real-time data populated the screens.

"We ...are...in...*business!*"

"Ordnance uplink underway..." Once completed, they could guide all air-to-air and air-to-ground weapons via data-link to their satellite support. The targets would be unaware that they had been locked-up.

"Time until Vandenberg launches number two?" Caroline asked.

"Nineteen minutes, forty two seconds, and ESA should have the second *Ariane* on the way to the launch tower at Kourou. So if our luck holds out we will have continuous support for the mission's duration...perhaps for the egress too."

So much time and effort had gone into this mission, Patricia mused, so many weeks kicking their heels in the farmhouse waiting for Svetlana's end of the mission, *Guillotine*, to bear fruit. If she had been told this time last year that she would be behind the lines in a war, creeping around in the night with a silenced pistol she would have found the suggestion ludicrous, she was an electronic warfare officer and not made of the stuff of a secret agent. A life was one of discoveries, both of the unexpected and also the unsuspected it seemed.

With that thought she stared for a moment at the back of Major Nunro's helmeted head.

"What is it the Brits say? Take off in the morning, save the Free World and then home for tea and cookies!"

Caroline's head was on the business of flying, or rather monitoring the instruments to ensure the aircraft was flying itself, but she keyed the intercom with a correction.

"Biscuits."

"Whatever..." Patricia satisfied herself that Russian ground radars and Mainstay AWACs were alert for generalised threats from without, rather than a specific threat from within. The Russian air defences would be crapping bricks if they knew a stealthy aircraft had breached their security, but they continued to look beyond their borders rather than inside of it.

"So any plans for after the war?"

"That is a red jersey question, but no." there was no humour in the answer and the set of Caroline Nunro's shoulders was stiff.

"You just know that after all this that guy's magazine is going to triple its offer to get you on its centrefold." Patricia meant the remark to be light-hearted but Caroline did not take it that way.

"So go ahead and broker a deal then; myself and Svetlana in the buff and "Look who I did in the war" as a caption." Her tone was cold; the embarrassment of Pat catching her with the Russian girl earlier was now turning to anger. No matter how courageous and resourceful a combat pilot she may be, her career in the military would be finished once word got out. She hadn't liked the label 'Pinup Pilot', especially as she had turned the offer down, and 'USAF's hottest dyke' would be equally demeaning.

In complete contrast, Svetlana's reaction to their being caught in the act was one of indifference. She did not have a bashful bone in her body. But to come back to the earlier question, what was she to do after the war; did she and Svetlana have a future?

Patricia was silent for a minute; she regretted straying from the business at hand and wanted a return of the old status quo.

"You were stationed at Nellis, weren't you?"

After a frigid moment she got a reply.

"Sure, in '05."

"Ever use the base pool"? Patricia asked but continued without waiting for a response from her pilot. "There was a lifeguard, Hispanic with lots of muscles and a bunch of clichés he tried on unaccompanied females..."

"Juan long One...the Puerto Rican love muscle." Caroline interrupted "Yep, I got his "Signorita, for one night with a Goddess such as you I, Juan, would die happy!" I think one of his biceps was even larger than the other because there is no way that would work, despite the accent and the speedo bulge."

Far ahead, a symbol appeared on the screen as their RORSAT detected the Mainstay's tanker cousin lifting off from the bomber base. Patricia assigned it a target ID. It turned northeast and began climbing toward the Mainstay and the CAP.

"So what line did he try on you, Patty?"

"I have no idea, I was mesmerised by the bulge and hoping it wasn't a rolled up sock."

"You didn't?"

"I sure did."

"But he was enlisted?" breaching the rules on fraternisation with the enlisted ranks had ended many a promising officer's career.

"I was married once; back when I was an impressionable and newly commissioned officer in this here air force, married to a college professor."

"I didn't know that." admitted Caroline in a surprised tone.

"Well it's no biggie, we didn't make it to the first anniversary on account of his dedication to his profession and being too tired for me after getting home late, showering and flopping into bed exhausted."

"Uh huh?" her pilot commented, having heard similar sagas.

"One night there had been a burst water main and he couldn't hide the scent of nubile-Sophomore-intent-on-good-grades, and that 'enlisted' not only had me walking like John Wayne for a week but he was just what the closure doctor ordered." She could see Caroline struggling to find the words that would not

"...so that kind of makes us even, huh?"

They flew in silence for a while, closing on their target.

"Okay, twenty one minutes to the IP and no one knows we are here, no threats and not even a mildly curious glance in our direction. We have green lights in every place it counts. The weapons status is good to go, and we have a ten knot tailwind." Patricia stated.

"Thanks Patty." her pilot replied, but she was not referring to the upcoming bomb run.

Russia, Militia Sub-District 178: 2322hrs.

Major Limanova led the way, at first making a bee-line for the airstrip until encountering thick undergrowth in the trees which was as noisesome as it was obstructive. He gave the task of carrying the heavy P-159 man-pack radio to Petrov as he himself took point and tried to feel his way through. With Petrov stumbling along behind him, he only succeeded in becoming disorientated, tripping and falling as brambles staged his ankles twice.

Animals, large hares most likely, took fright and bolted which caused both militiamen to jump on each occasion at the sudden disturbance in the undergrowth. They thundered away, their powerful hind legs making the fall of the wide rear paws extraordinarily loud with each step, and being rather larger than rabbits they did not corner as sharply either. To the militiamen they sounded like charging bears, not fleeing rodents.

Emerging from that block of forestry had come without warning as the once starlit sky had given way to cloud. Limanova stopped in surprise at the edge of a firebreak and Petrov, his hearing hindered by the radio headset, had walked into him from behind, uttering a "Sorry, sir!" that had seemed as loud as a shout in the silent forest.

"*Shhhhh!*" Limanova hissed loudly in annoyance before realising how ridiculously like a comic opera they sounded. Ninjas they most assuredly were not, in fact an infantry recruit would have made a better job of it.

He stood for a moment as he considered their situation and then moved one of the earpieces aside to whisper in Petrov's ear.

"Listen, this is no good, stumbling about in the dark like this, so we will follow this firebreak up to a logging trail which leads nearby the old airstrip, okay?"

Petrov nodded in the dark but then asked a pertinent question.

"Which way, sir?"

Major Limanova opened his mouth to answer but realised he was not one hundred percent sure so he knelt, taking his torch from his breast pocket, his map from the thigh pocket, and there then followed a patting of pockets and a despairing look back the way they had come. At some point he had lost his compass, probably upon falling and there was absolutely no chance of finding it again until day break, well not tactically anyway, but he was damned if he was going to embarrass himself further by waving his torch around trying to find it.

Left or right?

He tossed a mental coin.

"We head to the right...you lead." he directed Petrov, but Petrov held out the radio's telephone-type handset.

"It's the boss, 'Al'fa Odin', and he sounds unhappy, sir." When didn't Lieutenant Colonel Boskoff sound unhappy? Major Limanova thought, but kept it to himself.

"Al'fa Dvukh receiving Al'fa Odin, over?"

He reached behind Petrov and undid the locking screw securing Petrov's headset lead, unplugging it before answering the commander of Militia Sub-District 178. Further embarrassment was something he could well do without right now.

"Go ahead Al'fa Odin from Al'fa Dvukh, over."

The duty watch keeper at Moscow Air Defence Centre had contacted Lt Col Boskoff regarding the major's sighting report, and now Boskoff saw fit to give his deputy an ear blistering for wasting the time of the air defence forces and more seriously, embarrassing Lt Col Boskoff.

Limanova stood his ground, explaining what had occurred and his intention to reconnoiter the old airstrip.

"Phantom aircraft indeed...you are letting you imagination get the better of you, so get your head out of your ass and get your ass back here immediately Limanova...do you hear me? Immediately!" there was the briefest of pauses, too brief in fact to give even a one syllable reply *"Al'fa Odin, out!"*

Like hell he was.

He knew with absolute certainty something illicit was taking place at the airstrip and that a jet aircraft had taken off, and he was damned well going to prove it.

The major reconnected Petrov's headset lead, and acting as if nothing were untoward he sent Petrov away on point.

Pulling the butt of his elderly AKM-74 into his shoulder he allowed Petrov to get ten feet ahead before he followed on. It was odd how less secure you felt at night the darker it grew he mused to himself, and turned to look back down the track briefly.

Everything looked the same; he concluded and turned back, immediately feeling a stab of panic as he could no longer make out his driver.

He increased his pace despite the way ahead being as black as pitch.

He walked into the back of Petrov who had a moment before walked into the back of an armoured fighting vehicle which was sat unattended in the firebreak.

It was a BMP-1, or to be more precise, it was *their* BMP-1.

They had become completely turned around and had re-emerged from the trees close to where they had originally started out an hour or so before.

"Okay, this is not as bad as it seems as I know exactly where we are now."

"You mean you didn't know before, sir?"

The major ignored the remark and with a nudge directed Petrov to continue in the direction they had been heading.

The logging trail was indeed where the map had shown it to be and Petrov followed it to the left, feeling more uneasy with every step that took them further away from the solid armour of his vehicle.

Two pairs of ears registered a slight discord in the normal sounds of the night in this forest. Neither would be able to say precisely what it was, and a layman would use the term 'sixth sense', but it was that keenness of the senses that comes with being in tune with your environment.

Neither man could see particularly well but they were after all a listening post and not of the observation variety.

The earlier radio conversation had not gone unnoticed at the airstrip command post where they had been monitoring the radio transmissions of the militia, floundering about in the woods twelve miles away to the south. It was not something the Green Beret detachment was going to begin an immediate evacuation for, but half of a field radio conversation taking place just less than a mile north had caused concern.

The listening posts rapid clicking of their transmission switch now initiated a general 'stand-to'.

Ten more minutes walking brought the major to where he believed the runway began to run parallel with the trail they were on.

Now was the time to stop and listen.

Despite the major's conviction that there was some form of illegal activity that had taken place here, he nonetheless felt the need for some form of confirmation that he was in fact right, and therefore his immediate superior, the sub-district commander, was again wrong on all counts.

He could smell the heather and the scent of the pine forest, he could hear the very faint rustle of some animal but he could discern nothing else.

They broke track with Major Limanova taking point now, but after just a dozen steps another frightened hare broke from cover by his feet and crashed directly away, straight into the killing area of the hasty ambush the Green Berets had set up on hearing their approach.

The major and Petrov hugged the ground, their eyes wide with shock at the unexpected thunder of a claymore mines detonation and accompanying automatic fire.

The violent sundering of the quiet of the forest echoed beyond its southern boundary.

"Al'fa Dvukh receiving Al'fa Odin, what the hell's going on out there?"

Major Limanova was well aware that only blind luck had spared them from a sudden and brutal death. He could smell the odour of warm urine as Petrov pissed himself.

"Al'fa Dvukh receiving Al'fa Odin, answer me Limanova! What's happening?"

The major could not help himself, he had been insulted, treated like an imbecile in front of his men and abused all day.

His self-control now snapped and he groped angrily for the radio handset.

Not thirty metres away a dozen Special Forces troops were laying waste to a small area of woodland and the roar of automatic weapons was such that he had to shout into the mouthpiece in order to be heard.

"Al'fa Odin from Al'fa Dvukh, nothing is happening, nothing at all...haven't you heard imaginary Phantoms having a firefight before? You...Fat...Stupid...Moronic...*ASSHOLE*!"

The MiG-29s had drunk deeply and returned to their previous station, and the Mainstay switched its radar to standby before departing its racetrack orbit for its own turn at tanking. The timing could have not been much better.

"Four minutes to IP, two more minutes to weapon release...everything is green back here."

The Nighthawk crested a low hill and dropped down above the Medveditsa River which it would follow to the IP at the foot of the hill valley in which their target was situated. A hard left turn at the Initial Point would be followed by them opening the throttles and performing a pop-up maneouvre two minutes later to toss the weapon towards the mine shaft.

If the shaft was indeed housing the Russian Premier's bolt hole it had very disciplined defences. The screens had no more than tinted yellow with low power radar radiation since departing the vicinity of Moscow's formidable air defence zone.

Luck was with them this nigh...

The mainstay suddenly banked right, breaking off its approach to its tanker support and a wave of pink washed over the At-A-Glance plasma screens as the Soviet AWAC turned its attention abruptly toward the national capital at the Nighthawk's 5 O-Clock.

"We've got fighters lifting off at Petrovsk and Sharkovka... and air defence radars coming up...'Tombstones', 'Clamshells'..." the screen began to populate with ground threats and the airborne variety alike. "...shit, did someone suddenly get wise to us?" Patricia meant the question for herself, but she spoke aloud.

"Or they were waiting for us, and this is all just an elaborate trap." Major Caroline Nunro muttered.

"You got to stop sleeping with spooks Caroline, it's making you paranoid...I think maybe someone just noted the orbits of the *Vega* package and the *Ariane's* RORSAT and connected the dots together, but it kinda verifies Svetlana's intel though.

Previously unknown air defence sites were appearing on the screen, most of them mobile and air portable weapon systems which could follow the Premier around as he moved from bunker to bunker.

"They seem to have 'Favorites' and 'Grumbles' for long and medium range, a trio of 'Geckos' and a 'Zeus' or six for point defence of the target site...*oops*, check the high ground at the IP!" a ZSU 23-4 and a Gecko mobile launcher sat at a little pre-war picnic spot overlooking the river. The RORSAT had them identified by their thermal signatures and radar returns. The symbols appeared on the screen accordingly, sat dead ahead.

Caroline automatically put the nose down to skim the rivers surface as close to the tree lined bank as she dared, hiding from the feared 'Zeus' in the ground clutter but this only made their own thermal fingerprint a little more obvious to the Gecko. Both systems were linked, although the heat seeking missiles could not guide on the ZSU's radar. The ZSU's turret traversed to point up-river, its quad 23mm automatic cannons dipping below the horizontal, slaved to the mobile Gecko launchers thermal sensor. A whir of servos also sounded as the Gecko's erector also rose up into the firing position. It was too faint for a lock but it grew in intensity by the millisecond.

Aboard the A-50 the general alert by Moscow Air Defence had come as a rude shock. Major Limanova's sighting report was now the subject of reappraisal by the watch keeper's immediate superior. The absence of any radar trace was now being regarded as evidence of the presence of at least one enemy stealth aircraft operating in the skies near the capital, rather than a lack of evidence of a conventional one being abroad.

The scrambling of fighters and active use of radar and thermal sensors in and around Moscow had spread rapidly to surrounding air defence zones and beyond.

Two pairs of MiG-29s north of the Volga received the Gecko's feed via the A-50 Mainstay and banked hard, heading in their direction.

"I have the Zeus and Gecko locked up via our support and if that A-50 keeps coming we will have him at extreme range in thirteen seconds."

"Okay, let's get busy." The nose came up twenty degrees, the belly launcher cycled and a single AGM-65E sped away, aiming for a spot on the small shingle covered parking area midway between the two launchers, which were only forty feet apart. The amount of ordnance they carried was limited so any opportunity to buy-one-get-one-free was welcomed by Patricia.

Caroline levelled off at two hundred feet above the river, holding steady for a few seconds. The launcher cycled a second time and an AIM-120 dropped free to light off twelve feet below them and accelerate ahead, climbing sharply and also under third party control.

Caroline jinked left, putting warmer trees in their background instead of the cooler River.

Aboard the A-50 the heat source disappeared from the operators screens five seconds before the AIM-120 impacted with the underside of the A-50's right wing. All beyond the starboard inner folded backwards and upward before shearing away. With the one remaining starboard engine on fire the huge aircraft rolled onto its back, beginning a long terminal dive with a two hundred foot tail of flame streaming behind it and its large radome still rotating.

Command and control was disrupted, although the hunters knew enough to know where to start looking.

Caroline throttled back, raised the nose ten degrees and stood the Nighthawk on its wingtip in order to make the turn into the narrower valley.

As the aircraft left the river valley it was illuminated by exploding Gecko missiles which were tearing apart the burning launch vehicle, and hazarded by the spectacular fireworks display created by cooking-off 23mm cannon ammunition in the flame enshrouded ZSU now laying on its side. Tracer flew off in all directions, including into the path of the F-117X, and worryingly there were six cannon rounds they could not see for every tracer round that they could.

Caroline held the turn, her jaw set and half expecting to feel a hammer blow resound through the airframe but they were through and clear without damage. She levelled the wings and let out a relieved breath, but that relief was premature.

"Mother of ..!" Caroline exclaimed a heartbeat later.

They should have expected that this close in the KGB ground troops, the Premier's Pretorian Guard, would also be defending the site by any means at hand. Tracer arose to meet them from scattered positions where AFVs sat in defensive berms and hull-down fighting positions. Firing blind, trying for the Golden BB shot, the 20 ruble bullet that brings down the billion dollar aircraft.

The small arms fire flicked by but the heavier guns sent apparently molten globs of green fire aimed directly between the pilot's eyes. It emerged from the darkness below as small glowing green dots that rose towards them with deceptive slowness before suddenly growing in size and velocity. It seemed that each one must inevitably smash straight through the cockpit screen, but at the last moment they curled away, flashing passed either below, to the right or to the left.

An audible alarm sounded as a super cooled sensor in their tail detected a shoulder launched heat seeking Strela missile locking on. Flares were pumped out automatically and the alarm fell silent.

Patricia saw none of this; she secured the uplink between the weapon and the *Vega*, updated the status of the Vandenberg launch and set to with the business of the bomb run.

"Twenty seconds." she keyed calmly "Weapon is hot and the uplink is established, this is as good as it gets..."

Caroline centred the icon for the mine shaft at their 12 O-Clock.

"Fighters coming down" Patricia warned. "That kerfuffle back there zeroed our location for them, we have two Zhuk radars crossing our six from the eight o-clock position at six thousand...now four thousand, those boys are hustling."

"Bad country to be diving on burner...this is where those boys find out how well built their rides are...but we will be outahere in seconds."

Behind them the Fulcrum's Klimov 33D turbofans were indeed producing over eighteen thousand pounds of thrust but the afterburners were cut as warnings sounded in their pilots ears from the Russian's ground proximity warning systems.

"Pop-up in five...four...*SHIT!*" The symbols and icons vanished from the screens as the RORSAT turned into an expanding cloud of low orbit debris. Their up to the second threat coverage vanished and the *Vega* communications satellite lost its targeting data.

"Patty, what's the status on Two and Three?"

"One minute fifty and six minutes forty five...the second *Ariane* is launching as we speak."

Caroline silently blessed the triple redundancy and the mission planner's foresight, but made a mental note to check on whether theirs was the single most expensive sortie in history.

"Warm up a pair of Sidewinders, we are going around again!" Caroline declared, pulling back on the side stick, taking them up in a half loop and rolling out at the top to loose off an AIM-9L Sidewinder at each of the MiG-29s that were now entering the valley. She laughed cruelly as they received the same greeting from the ground defenders as they had. There was the sudden appearance of a tail of flame followed by a ball of fire as the trailing aircraft of the pair, seriously damaged by friendly ground fire, flew into the hillside. A parachute opened briefly, rewarding its pilot for his quick reactions. The lead MiG-29 released flares and pulled up into a vertical jink, avoiding a direct hit by the Sidewinder targeting it but the missile's proximity fuse activated ten feet from its tail. It departed eastwards trailing smoke. The second AIM-9L flew into the already burning wreckage of its target which was scattered over the valleys steep side.

"How are we playing this?" Patricia asked.

"Those guys back in the valley have got their eye in now...no future there."

Patricia had to agree with that.

"So I suggest we try an up and over, back into the river valley to do a straight in south to north approach over the hills?"

"We will have to trust that the Vandenberg RORSAT will be overhead by then."

"No future in hanging around here either." Caroline declared.

Even without the RORSAT's downlink the plasma screens were providing ample warning of seven MiG-29 radars and over a dozen mobile air defence radars searching for them. Fortunately there were no longer any fixed air defence radar sites on the hill tops as their presence would have alerted the West that Russia had something worth targeting, somewhere in that area.

"I've got activity over at Saratov West, air traffic control radar just came up, so not so deactivated after all...and now a pair of radars lifting off, probably Hind Ds." Patricia informed her pilot. "Someone in the bunker just called for his bug-out transport to be standing by when the raid is over...we could always fox 'em into thinking we left, then take him out with an AMRAAM?"

"He'll have a regiment's worth of CAP and we have just one AIM-120 remaining." Caroline pointed out. "Which one is the premier's helo, and which one is riding shotgun?" the pilot asked rhetorically. "We stick to the plan and hope to hell there isn't a cab rank of killer 'Sats' waiting up in orbit."

Avoiding the guns in the valley entrance by cutting the corner, skimming over the hill tops and back into the wider river valley Caroline throttled back and flew east, reducing their heat signature and economising on fuel. Major Caroline Nunro was not that type of pilot who would ever complain of having too much fuel.

As the RORSAT launched from Vandenberg came over the horizon the screens again filled with information.

"Are we good?" Caroline asked.

They still had their link to the communication satellite and the RORSAT confirmed it was feeding that with targeting data. "We're good!"

This wasn't familiar terrain by any means and more than a few pilots had attempted to hug the contours only to find that the crest of the hill they thought to be the top was in fact a false summit. Forward inertia takes time to translate into a climb and many an aircraft has bellied into the earth and rock of those snares for the bold and unwary, with the controls pulled all the way back in a last instinctive act. Those rare, lucky ones, learned a valuable lesson, but the unlucky ones next ride was a hearse.

The RORSAT provided them with a moving map and their own precise height, speed and position. Patricia would find them the lowest and quickest way to the target from the back seat and Caroline would follow her instructions.

"Re-entrant coming up between two hilltops on the left...standby to turn...now!"

Once again the throttles opened after they banked into a hard left climbing turn.

"That's good, hold this angle...flat ground for a mile beyond then it rises in steps to a saddle. A mile of carefree flying and then it's all downhill from there...there's another Mainstay lifting off from Engels but it'll take him time to get up high enough to safe operating height."

Caroline lowered the nose and they skimmed the saddle, shielded from radar energy by the earth until cresting its far edge.

They were the visiting team and the defenders had the home advantage. Every attack scenario had been tried and tested during regular exercises before the war, before the West knew that the East was controlling what the satellites thought they saw. They knew all the approaches and the air defence radars had ceased 360° radiation, reverting instead to covering pre-assigned arcs, quartering the ground they knew an attacker must appear from.

Immediately upon reaching the far side of the saddle the screen flared red as powerful radar painted them.

"A Tombstones got us...Favorite's launching at ten o'clock, six miles...pop-up coming up...Five...Four...Three...Two...One!"

Getting down in the weeds was their best tactic of breaking the radars lock but they were committed now and Caroline brought them out of their shallow dive, zooming up five thousand feet like a Pheasant flushed by the beaters, presenting their least stealthy profile, flares and bundles of chaff being pumped out automatically by the Nighthawk.

"Launcher cycling...weapon away!"

Fourteen radars, the seven MiG-29s, three Tombstones and four Clamshells had them locked up, their MWS was screeching its warnings that no fewer than seventeen radar-guided missiles were in the air. Favorites, Grumbles, AA-12 Adders and AA-10 Alamos were homing in on their radar return.

Patricia's stomach churned as Caroline rolled hard with chaff bundles ejecting into their wake. She was taxing an airframe that was not built for aerobatics, sending them into a forty five degree dive on their egress heading, as steep as she dared take them. The Nighthawk's twin General Electric F404 turbofans were a tried and tested design, the same engines that powered the F/A-18 Hornet and the French Dassault Rafale A, but unlike those combat aircraft the F-117A's power plant had no afterburner ability purely and simply to reduce the stress on the airframe.

"Pull UP!... Pull UP!... Pull UP!...Pull UP!" exhorted the GPWS, replacing the Missile Warning System's jarring tone as the aircraft's attitude and proximity to the ground broke the missile locks more effectively than the chaff.

Back in the river valley, with the hills between themselves and the target Caroline wondered at what point she had simply stopped breathing. Sweat trickled down her face, the salt stinging her eyes.

"Time?" she queried.

"Eighteen seconds!"

Four more pairs of MiG-29 Fulcrums were lifting off to join the hunt and the seven already involved had gone to burner to close the engagement range between themselves and the lone attacker, asking for, and receiving permission to cross the restricted airspace above the mine.

On leaving the F-117X bomb bay the B-61 continued to climb for several seconds despite its weight. Gravity's pull began to replace forward motion but its tail fins prevented an immediate vertical plunge back to earth, guiding it towards a precise spot on the surface below.

The worked out mine's winding gear, tower and elevator were the only still functioning aspects of the old workings, the towers four legs straddled the mile deep shaft at the base of which an electric powered tramcar line ran a quarter mile to the bunkers outer blast door.

The weapon's rocket motor only fired once it was facing vertically downwards, aligned with the centre of the shaft.

Concealed lighting was illuminating the car park landing pad beside the shaft and a Hind-D was settling onto it when something large struck the tarmac and bounced, colliding with its rotor blades. The blades shattered, shards spinning off in all directions and the aircraft was flipped onto its side where its captain quickly reacted by shutting down its twin engines. Both pilots and the crew chief clambered out and having got clear found themselves beside a seven foot diameter steel wheel, part of the winding gear that had sat atop the tower. The tower that had held the three tonne wheel had collapsed in on itself, the steel girders buckled and the internal steel cross braces that had kept the towers integrity for decades had been sheared. The crew stepped over twisted girders and gingerly peered over the edge into the dark maw of the now exposed main shaft.

The second Hind-D came to a hover a hundred feet above the shaft; its landing lights provided some illumination.

The elevator, cables and a lot of twisted steel had gone, presumably falling the entire way down the shaft. How was the Premier to exit now? Was there an emergency escape route back to the surface? Unbeknownst to the crew, they were inhaling radioactive dust caused by the sundering impact of the B-61's depleted Uranium penetrator with the tower. Within two years all of them would have developed cancers, but as they stared down into the interior the delay fuse's timer ran down to zero.

The At-A-Glance screens of the F-117X polarised, protecting the eyesight of pilot and EWO from the harsh light reflected of the hillside to their right, giving the night-time valley the appearance of a sun baked hell for almost a second.

Russia, Militia Sub-District 178: 2349hrs.

"Cease fire! Cease fire!"
The words were unfamiliar to either Russian but not the accent. The firing immediately halted and Petrov attempted to gain his feet to flee as Major Limanova switched off the set. He gripped the field radio on his drivers back, and kept him firmly against the earth.

"Americans sir!" he whispered hoarsely "What are the Yankees doing here?"

"I think we can safely conclude that they are not the NATO Peace Delegation and they are not here to surrender, young man." Limanova replied.

From the sounds of rustling in the undergrowth ahead he thought they must have sent out searchers to check for bodies in the kill zone' and when they found no human ones they would send out a clearance patrol, maybe? It was time to sneak away.

Having been caught on the wrong foot by the approach of an enemy from an unexpected direction, the Green Beret commander gave consideration to sending out a patrol but quickly dismissed it. He did not have the numbers available to patrol offensively so he chose the hunker-down option.

The hasty ambush had been sprung on nothing more sinister than a bigger than normal bunny but he was positive they had just missed the intended target. A radio transmission close in to the ambush site, during the ambush, was proof enough for him. They had been compromised but he was certain the enemy had no idea what they were dealing with and would assume they were the band of deserters. The militia was still milling around in the woods at night and it would be dawn before they got their act together. Long before the first rays appeared the F-117X would have returned, refueled and departed, as indeed would he, his men and their rather attractive contact with the flashing, come-hither, green eyes who spoke English with an upper class Oxford accent and Russian like a native.

The northwest listening post reported in, having heard a diesel engine vehicle start up rather noisily and depart to the north east. He did not stop to question why they had not heard its approach though, and that could have altered his decision making.

At the edge of the forest the commander of the sub district stood in the light from the headlamps of his own BMP command vehicle, staring at a map of the area as if looking for a sign, some clue as to how to reunite his units here in the open where transport could move them to the airstrip. Raindrops landed upon the clear plastic of the map case. The star filled vista from the early evening was gone as a weather front from the west finally reached them.

His head snapped up and towards the sound of the other BMP's approach, and to describe Lieutenant Colonel Boskoff as furious was something of an understatement. He was shaking with rage as Major Limanova exited the BMP-1, and having shouldered the field radio before approaching his superior he failed to salute, let alone attempt to apologise for his outburst on the command channel, not that such a severe breach of discipline could ever be forgiven or overlooked.

"What have you to say Limanova, what have you to say for yourself?" he screamed.

There were just the four of them at the forests edge, the two officers and their drivers. He would have relieved Limanova there and then but regulations dictated another Major would have to escort his deputy into custody. The only other major was in the forest somewhere on the commander's orders, attempting to locate and rally the men but now as lost as they were, along with the captain and lieutenant who had preceded him, also with the same orders.

If the commander expected a response from his deputy he was to be disappointed.

Major Limanova placed the field radio on the ground between them and held out the telephone handset to the sub district commander.

"The District Commander would like a word."

Snatching the handset the commander listened for several moments before responding.

"Colonel...sir, I do not know what idiocy Limanova has been spouting to you but yes, we are the closest unit but it is utterly impossible to do anything in the dark, the fool got everyone lost so we must wait for the dawn...."

A rebuke from the other end silenced him and he handed the instrument back to his deputy as he had been instructed.

Limanova put the proffered instrument to his ear.

"Yes sir...yes sir...I believe I can sir...with pleasure sir."

Major Limanova lowered the handset, drew his sidearm and fired twice.

Twisting the frequency dial back to the unit command channel he holstered his pistol before speaking.

"All stations this is Lieutenant Colonel Limanova, you will all of you turn and follow your ears." He turned and waved to Petrov who activated the vehicles traffic control siren and kept it on.

CHAPTER 3

West of Brunswick, Lower Saxony, Germany.

A great deal of time, energy and thought has gone into the formulation of codes and cyphers over the centuries, almost as much effort as that which is expended by code and cypher breakers. Of course in order to set about breaking a code it is first necessary to recognise that one is in use.

In 1951 British Intelligence commissioned a study into a completely unique set of codes and cyphers for use by agents and Special Forces acting behind Warsaw Pact lines in some future confrontation. This would of course have to involve seemingly random frequency changes in order to avoid the opposition's signals intelligence recognising that an enemy was active on their side of the lines by their sending and receiving coded transmissions. Mathematicians, academic deep thinkers and members of the intelligence community, past and present, put forward their responses for consideration. One of the latter was a former officer in the Black Watch who had spent not a small amount of the previous war behind enemy lines in Greece, before returning to Hollywood to renew his acting career. He believed, from hard won experience, that the more complex a communication setup was, the more likely it was to fail. His input was to dispense with complicated codes and channel hopping and simply use the enemies own known military codes and frequencies as nobody would notice a needle in a stack of needles. Accordingly, good language skills with a mix of provincial accents were more important than memorised 'keys'.

Thirty two proposals were eventually considered but the 'Stack of Needles' was dismissed as too simplistic and a multi layered mathematics based encryption code was adopted instead. The only people to believe that the simpler method had any worth were the Glavnoye Razvedyvatel'noye Upravleniye, the GRU, who are responsible for special forces acting behind NATOs lines in some future confrontation, and they received full details of all thirty two proposals via the Cambridge spy ring before the final selection process had even begun.

The Stack of Needles theory was tucked away safely for the future and updated whenever new working versions of a NATO army's battlefield code came into their possession. For operations in Northern Germany, Batex, Codex, Son of Codex and Slidex code books were all in their turn faithfully reproduced in sufficient quantities to equip saboteurs, assassins, fifth columnists and road watchers. Even the high magnesium content of the Slidex strips was duplicated, those burnable keys which were the closest an infantryman carrying a radio set on his back ever got to that famous line on TV "This tape will self-destruct in five seconds!"

"...Whiskey Echo, Golf Juliet, Charlie X-ray, Zulu Mike, Sierra Delta, Lima Victor Bravo, roger so far, over?" the voice with a slight Liverpool accent queried in the operators headphones.

"Tango Four Four roger, over." replied the operator with a lilting Welsh accent of his own.

The hash of electronic noise marked a pronounced pause as per British Army signals doctrine for long messages, during which another station could transmit an urgent message of its own on that frequency.

None did of course.

"Tango Four Nine, Two November...Quebec India Foxtrot, Yankee Golf, Echo Tango, Victor November..."

The operator filtered out the sound of the rain pelting against the canvas roof of the short wheelbase FFR Landrover in which he sat, copying the transmitted bigrams and trigrams with a pencil that had been sharpened at both ends in case a tip should break, recording them onto a printed signals pad. At the conclusion of the transmission he opened a green plastic wallet; its sized designed to fit easily into a map pocket. There was nothing upon the wallet to identify its purpose beyond the stores code for that item printed in block capitals 'Army Code 62175'.

The first bigram and trigram in the message were not code at all, but the page number and cursor setting with which to decode their orders contained within the British army's own BATCO code book.

The most difficult part of the process for the operator was that of keeping the BATCO wallet from sliding away owing to the uneven angle at which the Landrovers body was leaning due to a broken axle. The decoded orders were written out in long hand below the original message.

Tramping across an intervening muddy firebreak in the forestry block that concealed them the operator handed the signals pad to his small team's commander in a camouflaged basher.

"My sobirayemsya nuzhny novyye kolesa .....we are going to need new wheels." observed the officer, Captain Sandovar, after he had finished reading.

TP 32, MSR 'NUT' (Up), north of Brunswick, Germany: 10 miles south-west of the Vormundberg.

The job of Pointsman remains one of the least glamorous, and yet most hazardous duties for a member of the military police in time of war. In times of peace, it is just plain boring of course, but the task is nonetheless one of extreme importance in ensuring the swift passage of supply trucks, troops, stores and equipment to the front, and empty trucks back to the docks for fresh loads.

TP 32 was provided by 352 Provost Company RMP(V) by way of the reconstituted No.2 Section of 1 Platoon, 99% of the original 2 Section having fallen prey to Spetznaz troops in British uniforms early on in the war.

352 Provost Company's Brighton and Southampton based platoons had loaned personnel to bring the section back to strength where it now manned Traffic Post 32's two checkpoints with their dragons-tooth chicanes, one at either

end of the junction where Autobahn 2 ran beneath the Brunswick Expressway.

The junction was laid out like a simple cross just east of the Mitterland Kanal. The Expressway ran north/south with its flyover straddling the east/west carriageways of Autobahn 2.

On the north-eastern side of the junction sat the small provincial Braunschweig Airport with its single tarmac runway and a large flat grassy expanse beside it for light aircraft in the summer.

During World War 2 a research centre hidden in the forest next to the perimeter had developed the Henschel Hs 293 anti-shipping glide bomb, the 'Daddy' of air to surface stand-off missiles.

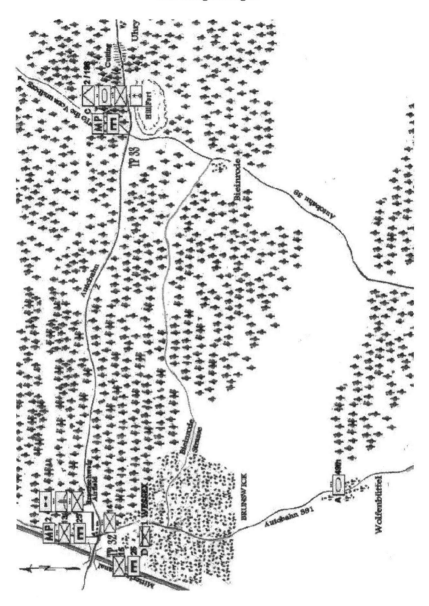

The Battle of the Autobahns 1

The airfield was currently in darkness, but for all that it was a hive of activity with US, German, British and Dutch military transport helicopter traffic coming and going, hot refuelling whilst the crews grabbed coffee next to their machines before having another underslung load of ammunition hooked on for delivery to the front lines.

Stores wise, this was the end of the line on 'NUT'. The convoys deposited their cargos at the airport before heading to the rail yards at Hanover for another load.

For a time the NATO air force's light and medium sized fixed wing transports had delivered palleted loads, but ironically it had been the great great grandsons of the Hs 293 that had comprehensively wrecked that single runway and destroyed two taxiing transports on the adjoining taxiway, a German C-160 Transall and a US Air Force C-23 Sherpa transport. Their twisted skeletons now lay abandoned where the bulldozers had shoved them.

The weather itself had soon afterwards turned to the bitter cold of a, thankfully short, nuclear winter and allowed the grass surface to be used by other Transall, Sherpa and C-130 Hercules. Once the thaw arrived of course it quickly became a quagmire, and with that the use by fixed wing aircraft had ended.

Beyond the airfields perimeter the Luftwaffe research centre was long gone, shattered by a series of US 8th Air Force raids in 1944 although the forest grew back over the decades and still remains today. There have been some incursions by farmers and housing developments since the 1970s, but the forest still extends east over the foothills to the banks of the Elbe.

South and east of the traffic post lay more forest, dark, wet and a little intimidating. An enemy could approach to within a few meters of the elevated autobahn from that direction. Trip-flares had been comprehensively sited amongst the trees and registered with fire by the heaviest weapons at the junction. Two GPMG s in the SF, Sustained Fire role, and manned by the infantry co-located with them to defend against the last of the Russian airborne troops still loose in small groups, those same ones who stubbornly refused to be mopped-up, contrary to continuous reports by the media. Thus far there had only been one triggering of a tripflare in the forest and that had introduced a bit of fresh meat into their diet, wild boar tenderised 7.62 style.

In addition to the gun groups there were two light anti-tank teams also, provided by 13 and 14 Platoons of D Company, 1 Wessex, and these covered the approaching traffic from the east and west, dug into the grassy verge beside the roadway whilst the two platoons had the additional tasks of covering the north/south running expressway.

The towpaths beside the canal had sappers from 25 Engineer Regiment RE dug in there in the infantry role to prevent any interference with their demolition charges, charges set in prefabricated bore holes that were set to drop a long section of the autobahn into the canal if called upon.

Post war construction and reconstruction in the former West Germany had been undertaken with defence in mind, for instance most of the bridges across the major rivers which had been destroyed by the advancing allies' air forces or the retreating Wehrmacht were never rebuilt, and those that had been were designed to be demolition friendly.

Along the canal to the south lay three other bridges but all quite narrow, a footbridge and two side by side single lane structures which had once upon a time carried rail tracks serving a small barge port, south of the autobahn bridge. 15 Platoon were guarding these along with another section of sappers from 25 Engineer Regiment, whilst D Company headquarters had contrived, as company headquarters are want to do, to set up in the large blue and yellow liveried premises of a well-known Swedish furniture store at a retail park half a mile south along the expressway, where conditions were reported to be hellishly comfortable.

The Bundeswehr had responsibility for the defence of the airfield abutting the north east of the autobahn and expressway junction, but it still left a mere seventy three men and women to prevent a mile and a half of key real estate from falling into enemy hands.

Two junior NCOs were shaken awake; the cold and wet rainwater running down the sleeve of a wet proof jacket assisted the process of rousing both soldiers who had only been relieved as pointsmen barely half an hour before. Lance Corporal Maggie Hebden opened one eye, frowning in irritation.

"Whoever it is, I just came off a twelve hour stag so *fuck off!*"

Her tormentor pulled the zipper of her sleeping bag roughly down its entire length, spilling out the warmth that had accumulated there.

"Route maintenance....there's signs missing apparently and a couple of packets nearly went astray down the road so get yer arse out of yer maggot *now!*" growled the section commander "The sooner it's done, the sooner you can get back to kip."

"Sorry, Staff." Maggie said and sat upright, shivering in the cold.

Just a dark shape against the canvas wall of the 9x9 they were using as a communal sleep area, the senior NCO nudged another form with the toe cap of a muddy boot, ensuring Maggie's oppo was not considering anything so foolish such as going back to sleep.

"Take 'nine three' and hook up the trailer sharpish." he said, unmoved by the angry response but not taking umbrage to it either.

"There's coffee if you're quick."

The tent flap rustled as he departed and Maggie switched on her torch in order to use the shiny bottom of a mess tin to peer critically at her reflection.

"Did anyone ever tell you that you look really sexy when you've just woken up?" Lance Corporal Tony Myers asked as he unzipped his own bag and clambered out into the cold, damp and musty smelling air.

"No?"

"They're never likely too, either."

He ducked just in time, avoiding the flying item of field dining ware.

Tony was looking north-east, his face set in a grimace against the rain, his helmets fabric cover sodden so that the rim dripped like a leaking faucet in a dozen places. He rolled back the camouflage net entrance for Maggie to drive the long wheelbase Landrover out onto the hard shoulder before reversing under the flyover to the signing trailer. They had been able use an insulated power cable running horizontally along the concrete side of the expressway's 'on ramp' to secure one edge of the camouflage nets and create a 'garage' they could drive in and out of. It made life far easier than having to roll up and stow the items every time a vehicle was used and unfurled again at the completion of the task.

Despite the constant rain the battle was easily located by the flashes of gunfire and explosions reflecting off the underside of the clouds.

Maggie left the engine running and joined him, helping manhandle the trailer, hooking it up and connecting the chunky rubber clad electric socket.

"They're still at it." He observed, referring to the direction he had been looking, the Vormundberg battle.

"And let's hope they are still going strong when the 4 Corps Yanks get here..." Maggie began, but her voice tailed off in embarrassment. People were fighting and dying over there in the distance.

They shared a mug of strong, hot and sweet compo coffee made with evaporated milk as Staff Sergeant Vernon gave them the unwelcome news that he had no exact location for where the fault was supposedly located so they had to check a twenty six mile stretch of autobahn to Lehrte, where TP 31s area of responsibility began.

The driver who had called in the complaint had been less than helpful.

"You've signs down on the approach to a junction."

"Which junction?"

"The junction with the cocked up signage, of course!" Click! Brrrrrr!

With the trailer hooked up and connected they paused to stand together at the edge of the autobahn's embankment facing the dark forest as they loaded their personal weapons, SA80s. These were of the older Block 1 model, the problem child, brought out of whatever cobweb bedecked armoury they had lain in since the MOD had given up trying to offload them.

352 Provost Coy's Block 2s had all been redistributed amongst mobilised infantry reservists.

Tony clambered over the tailgate and laid his rifle across his knees whereas Maggie slotted hers into the weapon rack behind the drivers and front passengers seats.

SOPs stated that for safety purposes vehicles should always proceed in a manner that did not conflict with the intended direction of the traffic, in other words they were supposed to drive east for a mile to the maintenance vehicle gate between the carriageways, drive west for eight miles to the junction that marked the extent of their assigned 'turf' before returning slowly in order to locate and correct the errant signage, a fifty four mile round journey.

After conducting a dynamic risk assessment that had taken less than a heartbeat Maggie decided to head west on the eastbound hard shoulder. This would avoid head-on collisions with any heavily laden Foden and get her back into her nice warm green maggot in at least half the time. However, they could have been on another planet as there was no traffic, no street lighting and not so much as a single unguarded bulb to be seen anywhere on the sodden landscape. Only the sound of to-ing and fro-ing helicopters ruined the effect.

Those few civilians who had not fled west were keeping a very low profile.

The black, wet ribbon of the autobahn stretched off into the distance as Maggie adjusted her PNGs and let out the clutch to pull away, but remained in second gear. On reaching the far side of the canal the Pointsman there moved the metal caltrops, the tyre puncturing spikes to disable vehicles attempting to run the roadblock, aside for them and Maggie gave him a friendly wave that was acknowledged with an unsmiling but perfunctory nod, the passive night goggles he wore adding to the cold and emotionless automaton effect.

"Miserable bugger isn't he?" said Tony from the back as the linked, sharpened spikes were noisily dragged back into place behind them.

"Well dancing a jig every second for being the only one still alive after the Spetsnaz came calling would not really be appropriate, now would it?" Maggie replied without looking back.

"I suppose not, but what's he got in that bergan side pouch he always has with him on point duty?" Tony asked, staring at the object of discussion as they drove past it.

"It isn't scoff, he doesn't go near it. He just sticks it on the verge by the chicane halt sign and collects it again when he's relieved."

"Did you ask him?" Maggie asked.

"No."

"Then why ask me?"

Tony was silent for a moment.

"He's still a weird fucker."

As the Landrover drew away, the checkpoint with its covering infantrymen in a trench, and the solitary military policeman on traffic point duty were quickly swallowed by the night.

Maggie had undergone her recruits cadre at Chichester, or 'Chi' as referred to by members of 'The Corps', with the lone pointsman. He had been a very affable, happy go lucky young soldier back then though a little immature, and seriously keen on a WRAC member of his unit.

The pointsman owed his life to the makers of the helmet he had been wearing; the close range headshot delivered by the female commander of the Russian team had been deflected, although the scar on his forehead would be a visible reminder until the end of his days whenever he saw his own reflection. All that having been said though, having regained consciousness in a ditch buried beneath the bodies of his colleagues and finding himself staring into the dead eyes of the young woman he had been so fond of, it would never require the presence of a mirror to remind him of the events of that night.

Having recovered from his injuries he had been returned to duty but remained aloof. The sections new commander had tried to integrate him with his new comrades but when that had failed he had been permanently posted to the solitary role of pointsman at the TP, the task he had been undertaking when the rest of the original section had killed. But he went about that duty uncomplaining of the 12-on-6-off stag roster and remained distant, even to the extent of positioning himself well away from the covering sentries of 1 Wessex.

Maggie put aside all thoughts of the pointsman and his ghosts as she concentrated on not falling asleep at the wheel.

Tony sat in the rear of the vehicle where he used a heavily filtered red lamp to pick out the 'NUT' route signs as PNGs were in very short supply and limited to one per vehicle. He occasionally shouted out when a sign needed a slight adjustment due a combination of the rain saturating the ground and the wind acting on it like a sail, canting it over at an angle or toppling it to the sodden verge in the case of those on pickets. A couple of signs affixed to street furniture required a moment to be repointed an additional twist or two of the retaining wire ties to sit them more securely by Tony, with shoulders hunched against the rain and wind, his SA80 hung reversed down his back by its harness to keep water out of the barrel.

After seven miles the road began a long climb, the dark fields either side gave way to even darker forestry plantation, and once at the top Maggie halted again to allow Tony to lift another drunkenly leaning sign, rooting it more firmly with deft use of the signing vehicles most vital tool, a 2lb hammer. Two solid blows did the trick and Tony turned back to the vehicle, but paused as something in the distance caught his eye despite the rain. He slid open the driver's side window.

"Would you look at that." he said to Maggie.

She opened the door to lean out in order to see what he was referring to as the rain pounding the windscreen was not exactly an aid to viewing, and the windscreen wipers best effort was lacking.

Off on the horizon the position of the 4 Corps lead elements was just discernable by flashes reflected off the clouds in a similar manner to that of Vormundberg's fight.

The flashes relented and vanished as another air threat was dealt with, and the progress continued, if indeed it had even paused at all. Out of the cloud base emerge a burning aircraft, falling to earth with no clue as to which side had owned it.

"Come on, let's get moving."

The road began a gentle incline but any elation that the sighting of 4 Corps had caused was diminished by the smell that became apparent, growing stronger by the moment.

Rüper auto services, named after a small village to the north, had served both truckers and the motoring public with fuel, food, a rest stop and motels for both east and west bound traffic until the war. When the coup in Poland had forced a sudden withdrawal by NATO to avoid being flanked a horde of refugees in some hundred or so vehicles had bypassed the military road blocks by using the tracks through the forestry plantation and descended upon the westbound services, desperate for fuel and food. They had been in sufficient numbers for their vehicles collective heat signature and radar return to register with the Soviet equivalent of JSTARS.

The refugees and their vehicles remain there still, hidden from view by the darkness but the nauseous petrochemical scent of napalm and that of its victims lingered on.

It was worse in daylight of course, the blackened and buckled cars and vans were nose to tail, side by side, a disordered logjam on the filling station forecourt and its approach ramp where they had attempted to extract fuel from storage tanks already emptied weeks before.

The southern services two hundred meters away had received the same treatment. The two infernos had burned unchecked, melting the tarmac of the autobahns so that in the dark on that uneven surface it is not unusual for tired drivers to think they have strayed off the road.

Perhaps this was the cause of the complaint and they could both head back to their sleeping bags?

No such luck.

A 'Nut' 'UP' arrow was pointing at an angle towards the Rüper auto services off ramp.

"Shit...some bastard has being playing silly buggers with the signs." Tony shouted, turning his head as they passed the obviously interfered with item.

Maggie halted the vehicle and pressed her camouflage face veil, worn cravat style, against her nose in an effort to block out the stench of death as Tony clambered over the tailgate. She hated this place and usually held her breath and floored the accelerator on the downhill westbound route, treating any passengers to a severe bone rattling ride as the uneven surface was akin to the 'slow-down-ripples' from hell.

Lifting her PNGs clear of her face she looked at her watch; pressing the tiny button on one side of the casing to illuminate the hands and figured she could get over an hours sleep if she kept her foot down all the way back.

Maggie looked in the wing mirror, but it was beaded with raindrops and did not reflect any light from Tony's red filtered torch so she gritted her teeth and opened the side window, grimacing in the rain as she peered back at the off ramp, but she could see no sign of Tony.

"Tony?" there was no response.

"TONY!" she paused to listen but there was just that miserable non-stop rain.

Muttering aloud, she lifted her SA80 from the weapons rack behind her, killed the engine and removed the ignition key.

Emerging into the rain she listened for a second before calling Tony's name again.

He couldn't seriously be playing a practical joke could he, knowing how she disliked this place?

Pulling the PNGs back into place and holding the rifle casually in one hand she walked cautiously to where the off ramp began. There was no sign at all of him and she now fully expected her partner to be playing a foolish prank as she started along, the blistered and melted road surface crunching beneath her feet, until she reached the nearest buckled and burnt out car, a people carrier. The naked wheel rims it was sat upon were now an integral part of the off ramps tarmac surface, sunk into the tarmacadam when the napalm had brought it to boil. The driver's door was open, restricting her view further down the ramp. As she reached the open door she glanced inside. Even in the mixed shades of green from the PNGs she could make out a skeletal foot upon the brake pedal.

Bile rose in her throat and she fought the impulse to gag.

"Tony?...I am not fucking about here, so quit screwing around or you're walking back, you bastard!"

Her foot struck something metallic that skittered away and looking down she saw it was a 3' picket with 'NUT' still affixed.

Brittle tarmac crunched behind her and she started to turn, to shout an angry remark at Tony but something slipped over her head and contracted around her throat, stifling the retort. The SA80 clattered to the ground as Maggie raised both hands to her throat and as she did so a knee pressed into the small of her back, pulling her off balance.

The cheese-wire sliced deeply into the female British soldier's fingers but he knew she was unable to even give voice to the pain and shock. The face veil about her throat to keep out the rain was a little hindering, but with a vigorous sawing motion it was but the work of a moment to cut through it and into the soft flesh beneath.

Vormundberg: Same time.

Royal Marines of A Company, 44 Commando, passed through the fighting positions of 2LI, the 2nd Battalion Light Infantry, to a pre-arranged point where guides from 2 Wessex led them safely through the lines of the men from Berkshire, Buckinghamshire and Hampshire to a muddy forest track on the reverse slope. There, medics and the marines own quartermaster sergeant waited. 1 Troop was the first to arrive, numbering only nineteen men now, and their current troop commander, a corporal, carried out the reorganisation drills and reduced the troop further, sending one marine away in the direction of the medics, protesting vocally as he limped off.

The remainder stocked up on grenades, fragmentation and smoke, refilled magazines and water bottles, attempting at the same time to boost flagging energy reserves by shovelling cold compo rations into their mouths, replacing what the nervous energy and physical effort of close quarters combat had burned off. The small metal tin openers revealed a variety of contents from Baked Beans to Fruit Salad, all were devoured cold, straight from the tin. As ever though the 'Cheese, Processed' cans, and green mini packets of 'Biscuits, Brown' were passed over by many. For some, only the onset of starvation could motivate them to eat what was more commonly known as 'Cheese Possessed'.

Sheer weight of numbers had eventually told over the Royal Marine Commandos fighting skills and fighting spirit. The loss of their sister unit, 42 Commando, with such terrible casualties had at first stunned and then enraged the men from 44. The deliberate running down of a group of survivors in the ditch by the Czech T-72 tank had been seen by many across the narrow valley in the NATO positions and widely reported.

The men topped up on ammunition and moved off, following the guides to the rear of 1CG and the 82$^{nd's}$ position.

Colour Sergeant 'Ozzie' Osgood, 1CG, made his tentative way across the rear slopes of the rain swept hill, his arms aching from carrying a stretcher loaded down with ammunition boxes collected from the RQMS in the rear. Behind Oz a young Guardsman cursed, slipping in the mud and almost dropping his end of the stretcher.

"I'm chin-strapped, sir." He wearily declared.

Oz was tired too, and not just physically.

There had been a time when he had mocked people like himself, back when he was young, stupid and working a coal face. Some men couldn't hack it at all, the knowledge of how much rock and earth was above their heads. They left immediately, or as near as dammit. But it was the occasional older man, those who had been at the colliery for fifteen, twenty years or even longer who one day just couldn't step into the cage another time. They got jobs on the surface, but few stayed with the colliery and most moved away. The wives were worst, and the kids a close second. The jibes and the whispers, the bullying in the playground.

Oz came from a long line of miners, a proud line. His grandfather had survived an explosion and rock fall, and his Dad had lived through both a fire and a flooding. There was no way the Osgood's would ever lose their bottle like that.

One day he and his Dad got into the cage together at the start of the shift, but before it was full his Dad had turned to him.

"I'm sorry our kid, I just can't do it." And he walked away.

The bravest man Oz had ever known just walked out of the cage and up to the mine manager's office to collect his wages and give his notice.

Oz wasn't in the army because he'd quit too, he was there because the pits were closed, but Oz now knew that perhaps one day his bottle would also have held all it could, just as his Dad's had.

All those tours of duty at the sharp end, in Ulster, Bosnia, the Gulf War, Iraq and now this, the big one, were telling. The stress builds up over the years, sometimes unseen, and with little or no warning something snaps. His friend, Colin Probert, had seen the fractures forming in Oz, and Colin had tried to help by easing the burden. A platoon sized fighting patrol had gone out without him, its platoon sergeant, and they hadn't come back. That had nearly finished him there and then. Colin and two men had been found alive but badly wounded; the remainder were dead, along with one of those three. The man had died on the casevac chopper, just three minutes away from the field hospital.

Oz wasn't at the sharp end anymore, but he wasn't ecstatic about being a headquarters wallah either, a 'REMF' in yank parlance.

"Seriously sir," his assistant grumbled again."Me arms are a foot longer than they were at reveille.

"Grit yer teeth bonny lad, we'll have a breather and a brew in a minute at the battalion CP, it's just over yonder."

The track plan had long been abandoned and the approved routes from his ammunition stocks to the three platoon headquarters positions was a morass now so they cut across at an angle to arrive at the rear of the sandbagged command post, ducking under the camouflage netting and hessian. It allowed a little shelter from the rain, and having lowered the heavy stretcher they squatted against the sandbag wall, giving their aching muscles some respite.

They had just settled down when Oz heard the steps of two others in the mud just around the corner at the side of the CP.

"Well Derek, what is it that you could not tell me inside?"

Oz recognised his commanding officers voice.

"Did the Adjutant speak to you on a personal matter, before he took over 3 Company, sir?"

The Guardsman beside Oz suddenly caught on that two officers were having a private discussion and Oz gestured his assistant to be quiet.

"Is this something to do with that infernal whispering between yourself and Captain Gilchrist?"

"Sir, you may have noticed another gunner officer earlier, he is a Forward Observer with 2LI..."

Although Oz could not see Pat Reed he sensed him tense.

"...it is with profound regret that I must inform you that your son Julian was killed in action this morn...." They heard the CO turn suddenly away.

There was a moment's awkward pause before the battalion's artillery rep squelched away back to the entrance to the CP.

Oz and his assistant sat in the shadows in embarrassed silence, unwilling voyeurs to their CO's grief.

After several minutes Pat forced himself to stand upright, he then shook himself and removed the water bottle from its webbing pouch to rinse his eyes. A grubby sleeve dried his face before he straightened, squared his shoulders and returned to the business of running the battalion's battle.

As soon as he was satisfied that the coast was clear, Oz turned to the young soldier.

"You breathe one word of this to anyone and I'll plant you in a shallow grave." He said with grim sincerity, "Clear?"

He received an earnest nod in reply.

"Now come on then, let's get this lot back where it'll do the most good."

With a grunt they lifted their burden once more, staggering away into the rain and the night.

The Czech 23rd MRR had sorted themselves out for another attempt to drive the stubborn British and Americans from their positions above those the 23rd had early taken, but as they were in the process of mounting their vehicles the infantry were ordered to debus and form up on foot in the immediate rear of the main battle tanks. Only the AFVs drivers remained with the vehicles as the squads departed, and then somewhat bemused they followed new orders to drive to a location a half mile to the rear, switch off, collect their weapons and don full fighting order before re-joining the squads at the double.

In similar collection points facing the slopes of the Vormundberg, mechanics moved amongst the infantry's fighting vehicles, syphoning off the precious fuel for use instead by the tanks and AAA vehicles.

As for the 23rd MRR relieving the Romanians and Hungarians in the attack, they were held back temporarily, a delay for the purpose of coordinating four attacks at once. 9th Russian MRD on the east bank of the Saale would attack westwards, 77th Guards Tank Division on the west bank of the Saale would attack eastwards at the same time as elements of the 91st Romanian Tank Regiment seized key positions west of Magdeburg in NATO's rear.

Saale River Valley, Germany: nineteen miles east of the Vormundberg: 0134hrs.

The rain came again, dumping copious amounts of misery onto the blasted hillside, flowing into the fire bay of trenches and slowly filling them about the ankles of occupants too busy to bale.

The heavy clouds robbed the Earth of any of the half-moons rays. It was stygian, relieved only by the flashes of occasional, and fitful, lightning from within and the light from fires and bursting shells reflecting off the cloud base.

The massive bombardment of the Elbe/Saale Line had severely depleted the Red Army artillery stocks and the NATO airborne forces, acting unsanctioned by their governments, were seeing to it that resupply did not come any time soon.

Once the paratroopers ran low on ammunition and explosives though, the roads to the rivers would reopen, although that was another hurdle for the Red Army to vault over once more.

The French and the Canadians had left armour in hide positions, two brigades worth, and once the main juggernaut of Red Army had unknowingly bypassed them they had emerged in the enemy rear. The NATO armour smashed everything they found of worth, stores, bridging equipment, fuel and ammunition dumps, tankers and trucks. All had been left burning.

Trucks had become the number 1 bullet magnet, and engineers, or anybody who could fix or build a pontoon bridge came a close second. For once it was safer to be an infantryman, relatively speaking, anyway.

With the fall of darkness the Hungarian 43rd MRR did not return and 2Lt Ferguson, the green commander of the Nova Scotia Highlanders Reconnaissance Platoon, was settled in at the bottom of his trench for an uncomfortable night. Sergeant Blackmore had conjured up a couple of plastic heavy duty beer crates from somewhere and these were upended, allowing them to avoid the water at the bottom of the firebay in relative comfort for an hour, taking it in turns to bail out the trench every thirty minutes.

His sergeant was currently squatting, hunched up with the collar of his combat smock pulled up to keep out the rain. Asleep with mouth partly ajar and heedless, or just too exhausted to care that the side of his face was pressed against the firebay's muddy wall. A ballistic helmet with its chin strap undone was displaced by the sleeping posture, sat at an angle upon the sergeants head, its camouflage cover sodden with the rain and the water dripping from the helmets lower edge.

Dougal Ferguson was himself in a similar posture, like a slightly better than average looking, upright, church gargoyle. Shoulders hunched to trap the field telephone handset against his left ear whilst his right enjoyed the unbroken hissing from the radio earpiece, the hash noise. About his left wrist were looped string communications cords to the trenches on either side. Three forms of communication at his disposal in his muddy hole in Germany thought Dougal, who was momentarily tempted to add a fourth by uttering an imitation of a night owl, Hollywood Western style. Dougal though was aware that so far his contribution to the platoon was not held in very great regard by his men. He was determined to change that, but he just did not know how? Everything he touched seemed to turn to mud, and his sincerest suggestions were greeted with either thinly veiled contempt, or muffled sniggers. He was not sure which was more demeaning.

The fear of failure was almost equal to the fear of death or disfiguring injury, and the low esteem he was apparently held in by the men was reducing his self-confidence to tatters.

After the departure of the Hungarians he had been ordered to send out a patrol to check on what was occurring with a suddenly reluctant enemy, and the answer was that they had simply gone, taking with them many of the dead from the battalion that the Canadians had already defeated. The land beyond the turnip field was empty of all but the tracks of caterpillar treads and tyres leading east.

The previous day the brigade had emerged from its hide position in the forest and split into four elements, a defensive firebase and three combat teams of an armour squadron mated with two mechanised infantry platoons in AFVs and an armoured reconnaissance squadron. The brigade artillery, engineers, remaining armour, and the bulk of the infantry had dug in at the firebase in preparation for a wild and furious enemy reaction. The combat teams had roved abroad in assigned sectors, smashing and trashing for twelve hours before the brigadier had called a halt to the fun and games. The combat teams fell back to the firebase but the brigadier had almost left it too late before ordering the recall. A troop of four Leopards had engaged in a fighting withdrawal with an under-strength Hungarian battalion, covering the remainder of the combat team's departure, picking off enemy tanks and AFVs, and leapfrogging backwards from cover to cover.

Unable to achieve a break in contact themselves, and in danger of being swamped by greater numbers, that old quantity versus quality equation again, the Leopards had fought a running gun battle with the Hungarian's PT-76 light tanks that culminated in a last-man-standing gun fight in the turnip field, backed by direct support from the firebase. The single surviving Leopard had required the services of an armoured recovery unit.

Ferguson's four man clearance patrol, led by Corporal Molineux, the section commander of 2 Section, had remained on the forward edge of the turnip field, out of sight of the firebase, digging in inside a hedgerow as night fell in order to provide a listening post.

The remainder of the recce platoon were dug in in less than ideal ground, as is frequently the way in woodland positions. Losses over the months had only been partially made good and with the four men out of the lines on the listening patrol it left two empty trenches.

2Lt Ferguson and Sergeant Blackmore took over the trench of 2 Section's commander whilst the platoons sniping pair occupied the other. The radios, field telephone and Claymore clickers were transferred to the trench along with the communication's cords.

The platoon's fire plan with its DFs and FPFs was written on Sgt Blackmore's range card and attached to the radio antennae by para cord. Needless to say, the young officer had not been trusted to contribute to that either.

The level of muddy water was now an inch from drowning the beer crate sanctuaries and Dougal stood carefully, hooking the telephone handset over the set itself, hung suspended by its carrying strap clear of the water on a tripflare picket.

An old mess tin served to bail out the trench, being careful not to dump the contents on the section's C9 Minimi sat on the lip of the firebay.

Bailing duty complete and Dougal paused to listen. Someone was snoring and it seemed to come from the sentry position to his left where the platoons main firepower, the GPMG, general purpose machine gun resided. Everyone was tired but that was no excuse. There was never any excuse for the sentries to be asleep. The platoon's gun position covered the approaches to the position from this side of the woods and the duty was shared on a stag roster, so called as the duty was at staggered times, a 'fresh' sentry coming on duty every hour for a two hour stint.

Dougal looked down at the sleeping Sergeant Blackmore and wondered if he should stay aloof and instead delegate his platoon sergeant? Dougal hefted his C8 assault rifle and left the trench to lie beside it, pausing to peer through the rubber eyepiece. In the same way an ordinary pair of binoculars will assist your ability to see at night, so too do the unpowered weapons sights by magnifying the available light, even if that light is poor.

Sweeping from the platoons left flank to the right flank he saw just empty open ground beyond the woods edge. Belly down, he snaked across the intervening space between the trenches.

Both men were asleep on their feet, an act achievable by the truly exhausted in the most uncomfortable of circumstances. Dougal did not know what made him raise his weapon to again use the sight but the ground beyond the trees was no longer empty, four men were moving toward this very spot in single file, moving carefully, 'ghost walking' to avoid noise and sudden, eye catching movement.

The lead man carried a weapon the same as his own Canadian army variant of the M16, and wore the same French style ballistic helmet, but the remainder were tucked in close behind him and their weapons were not visible either.

The GPMG had a starlight scope attached to the tripod in place of a C2 sight and Dougal slipped into the trench between both sleeping sentries and switched the sight on.

A low pitched whine announced that the sight was working, he pressed his face to the eyepiece and immediately the approaching men were more clearly picked out in varied shades of green. The picture was better than that of his Suit sight but the lack of any stars light meant the scene was darker than it could be. Dougal thumbed on the sights laser torch attachment.

The laser torch provides a light source similar to that of a clear starry sky, but it not only sucks batteries dry with frightening speed, it also acts as a beacon for battlefield laser detectors so should be used with extreme caution.

The young Canadian took a long look at the higher definition picture before switching the laser off.

The sentry to his left came awake as the GPMG was cocked.

"Halt!" Dougal hissed as loud as he judged necessary to be heard by the first of the four.

He saw a momentary hesitation in stride but they continued.

"It's Molineux and the listening patrol, sir." The sentry whispered, staring through own C8's Suit Sight.

Dougal had been able to see the name tag on the lead man's combat jacket and indeed it did read 'Molineux'

There were a number of reasons why the patrol could be returning, such as to report the approach of the enemy in person if their radio had gone U/S, unserviceable.

It would have been easy to allow the sentry's judgement to over-ride his own; after all he was a veteran, unlike his screw-up platoon commander.

Instead of being reassured though, Dougal felt hairs rising on the back of his neck. Ignoring the sentry, his thumb depressed the safety lug.

"HALT...hands up!"

It was seemingly implausible that all four could not have heard the challenge, and they were now almost too close.

He unlocked the tripod, allowing the weapon to be traversed and elevated manually.

"No sir, its Molineux..."

The GPMG roared, the muzzle flash illuminating the scene and the long burst ripping through the lead man and the three clustered behind.

"STOP, its Molineu...!"

"STAND TO!" Dougal shouted, seeing figures appearing in his sights out of the dead ground before them, a hundred and fifty metres beyond the edge of the wood line.

Rounds cracked passed and the sentry to his right awoke only to drop without a sound to the bottom of the trench, his helmet spinning away in a scarlet haze of blood, fragments of skull and grey lumps of brain matter.

Two PK machine guns, close cousins to the GPMG in Dougal's grasp, were firing on the gimpy's muzzle flash.

Startled awake by the burst of fire from the GPMG, Sgt Blackmore immediately looked across to where his young platoon commander should have been, but wasn't.

Where the hell was the idiot? Then of course he heard Dougal shouting *Stand-to!* and saw the cause. Blackmore made a frantic grab for the Claymore clickers.

Exhausted men, rudely awoken, and only a few of whom were quick enough to put rounds down, and then not entirely accurately as tired eyes take some moments to focus.

The desultory muzzle flashes were encouraging rather than inhibiting, and the relative lack of accuracy emboldened the Russian infantry officers.

Two infantry companies had quietly made their way into the dead ground between the turnip field and the woods, waiting in the rain as the four specialist reconnaissance troopers had attempted to enter the Canadian's lines by subterfuge.

Plan A was for the sentries to be despatched with some dexterous knife work thereby allowing the waiting infantry to follow on with bloody effect.

Plan B was to rush the positions on a narrow front, one company behind the other should the first course of action fail.

The company commander of the second company was a cautious man and ordered his company forward by half sections. It was a slow business and a tiring one, but it kept half of his men in cover and able to put down supporting fire for the remainder at any one time. It was in contrast to the leading company's advance.

Instead of employing fire and manoeuvre the lead attacking company now broke into a slow jog as folding bayonets were swung into position and locked into place, whereupon the men opened their legs, picking up speed. This became an energetic dash to close with the enemy before they could rouse themselves. There was no shouting, no war cries, just the pounding of two hundred and twenty boots against the sodden ground. The panting breath of a hundred and ten men exerting themselves into as close to a sprint as the equipment they bore would allow.

Adrenaline surged, hearts pounded...

A hundred metres...

.....fifty...

........thirty...

Those at the forefront were pounding ahead of the pack and could make out the outline of individual tree trunks on the edge of the wood.

Heads lowered and arms began to straighten, extending bayonet tipped assault rifles toward an enemy they would be amongst in just a few more strides.

Before the wood line there blossomed black clouds of smoke with the flash of detonating claymore mines at ground level. The Russian infantry charge met a wall of ball bearings that turned men into shredded, bloody rags.

The echo of the blasts reverberated in rapid succession cross fields, hills and dales, giving way to screams from the injured, the mortally wounded, the disfigured and blinded.

Over a hundred bodies lay in the open between the dead ground and the wood line. Most lay unmoving but some writhed in agony, screaming for aid, or in the case of the mortally wounded, calling out for their mothers as men who know they are dying will often do.

For a few moments the firing paused, both sides seemingly shocked by the mines effects and Sgt Blackmore was startled by a figure landing with a splash beside him.

Blackmore released the mines firing clickers and grasped his folding shovel. He was in the process of raising it up high for a killing stroke when the figure jammed one of the earpieces of the R/T set against his right ear and spoke in a raised, but controlled voice into the microphone, a contact report followed by a mortar fire control order.

"Hello Zero this is Six Nine, contact, contact, contact... one hundred, one hundred plus enemy infantry advancing to my front, out to you.....hello Five Zero Charlie, this is Six Nine, infantry in the open, shoot Foxtrot Papa Foxtrot Six Zero Alpha, over.....roger that...wait, over!"

Dougal squatted and peered at his wristwatch for several seconds before turning his head and speaking calmly to his platoon sergeant.

"You may want to put that down and take cover, Sergeant Blackmore, this could be close..." cupping his hands to his mouth he called out the warning. "..INCOMING!"

His sergeant blinked as if not recognising the confident young officer before him. Gone was the hapless and bumbling subaltern, dismissed forever with the first hostile shot.

The first belt of 81mm mortar rounds landed to the right rear of the second infantry company.

"Hello Five Zero Charlie, this is Six Nine, adjust fire, shift Left one zero zero, Down zero five zero, over!"

"Five Zero Charlie, wait...shot One Two Four, over!"

Again Dougal looked intently at the illuminated hands of his wristwatch as the second hand counted off twenty four and again shouted "Incoming!" with four seconds to spare.

With no warning whistle such as would accompany artillery rounds, the next belt was 'on' and devastating.

It did not land dead centre, it straddled the left flank platoon, blasting apart all of those on their feet at the time.

"Six Nine...adjust fire, shift Left zero five zero, Down zero five zero..."

Kneeling beside the body of the partially stripped Canadian corporal, the commander of the Russian 32nd MRD's reconnaissance battalion listened to the sound of his gamble failing. So be it, he thought, it had been worth trying as they had found the four-man listening post asleep, so there had been the chance that the same weariness was affecting their main body. Taking a position by stealth was far more economic than the alternative.

Raising his glasses he watched the companies of infantry who had accompanied his men. They were caught out in the open by mortar fire that was being walked through them in a well-controlled manner.

"Well comrade, we try the old fashioned way instead, yes?" he said resignedly, addressing the infantry's battalion commander.

To their rear, 120mm mortars fired their bedding-in rounds towards the woods as the officers returned to their respective command vehicles.

Dougal was peering cautiously over the lip of their trench, called in adjustments as if this were a table-top exercise on the Puff Range at RMCC Kingston with, as the name implies, puffs of talcum powder representing the fall-of-shot on a chicken wire and painted hessian mock-up of a landscape, instead of a real battlefield.

The enemy infantry had gone to ground; the only sensible option and the platoon's sniping pair left the trench in the rear. Running forwards, on their feet due to the absence of incoming fire, and the bursting HE providing cover from view almost as effective as that of smoke. Even the PKs that had been suppressing the platoon's 'Gimpy' SF were now silent.

Both snipers sprinted past Dougal and Sergeant Blackmore, intending to crawl the last few yards into cover.

Dougal was thrown backwards, the front wall of the trench he had been leaning against having physically jolted him off his feet.

The ground heaved; trees exploded sending wicked splinters a foot in length flying outwards, and the sound ruptured eardrums.

A small portion of the division's mortars pounded the woods but the artillery merely laid on their guns and waited.

The Canadian's mortar lines were unable to counter-battery fire the larger Russian 120mm tubes which were beyond their range.

ARTHUR, the brigade artillery's back tracking radar followed the azimuth of the incoming rounds and provided a location for the enemy mortar line that was accurate to within ten feet. The operators were sceptical though as these mortarmen were top class, not some green or third rate unit so why hadn't they scooted and a second mortar line taken over already? That was how the Russians worked, three, four and sometimes five mortar lines sharing the same fire mission, in turn they would drop three or four rounds per tube and be gone before the counter battery fire arrive. In that way the target received constant attention.

Whatever the reason for the Russian's actions the Royal Canadian Horse Artillery's M109s received the fire mission. The 155mm guns fired on it, but only a single round per gun.

The Russian counter battery was fast but it still hit an empty sack, whereas the air bursting 155mm rounds destroyed two tubes and killed or injured a dozen mortarmen.

The artillery's game of dodge-ball had begun.

The Russian mortars fire stuttered and failed but fallen trees and amputated boughs lay tangled on the floor of the wood. In amongst that wreckage was Dougal Ferguson's platoon.

Each man knows his number in his own section and the section commanders used this to call the roll.

Dougal had feared that the platoon had been wiped out. It was not as bad as that, but it was not good either.

Initially they had one dead, three wounded and four were missing. Two of the missing men were the snipers and a crater sat at the spot where Dougal had last seen them running forwards. The remaining pair had been inside their trench's shelter bay, protected from airbursts and the shrapnel from tree bursts, but a near miss had collapsed the trench on top of them. Frantic digging had uncovered the soldiers but they were as dead as if it had been a direct hit, asphyxiated by the weight of earth as much as by the lack of oxygen.

When counting the listening patrol, which had to be presumed dead, the platoon had lost just over half its strength. The three wounded were passed back to the company sergeant major for transport to the brigades medical aid centre, but the dead were left where they had been found because the artillery and mortar fire began again, prepping for the next attack.

CHAPTER 4

Ariete Task Force
Autobahn 2, 16 miles east of Brunswick, Germany.

The Recce Troop, 5th Cavalry Regiment of the Ariete Armoured Brigade led the way in their four-wheel Lince multi-role vehicles, speeding ahead of the task force.

Lt Col Lorenzo Rapagnetta had been given the task of finding and destroying the missing Romanians, the T-72 and T-90 MBTs along with their accompanying BTR-70 and BMP-2 IFVs. Pierre Allain had been clear and precise in the orders he had given, as he had also been with his explanation as to why the Ariete had been selected for the task. The ground they had been defending was more suited to an infantry heavy unit with howitzers for artillery support such as their northern neighbours, Britain's '3 Para' in the leg infantry role, and the 105mm light guns of 7 Parachute Regiment, Royal Horse Artillery on dedicated call. He was to leave the 11th Bersaglieri Regiment, two companies of the 5th Cavalry Regiment's infantry and all but a battery of the 132nd Artillery Regiment. The remainder of the brigade, its thirteen surviving Ariete main battle tanks, an infantry company mounted in Puma AFVs, three PzH 2000 155mm SP howitzers and a recce element were to reinforce the Mississippi National Guardsmen of C Company, 2/198th Armored.

SACEUR, General Allain, was positive that the enemy force, possibly a tank battalion, was driving towards the nearest of the critical autobahns. By seizing Autobahns' 2 and 39 where they met east of Brunswick, the Red Army would have fast transit routes to all of the Dutch and Belgian ports.

Lorenzo knew that SACEUR was aware of his brigade's current state, and Lorenzo was also aware of the condition of the 2/198th. Both units had been in the thick of NATOs fight with the Soviet 10th Tank Army, fighting that numerically superior monster to a standstill only to have then been struck by the fresh Third Shock Army, which then forced the Elbe.

Lt Col Lorenzo Rapagnetta's Ariete MBT's from the 32nd and 132nd Tank Regiments together numbered only slightly more than a soviet tank company mustered.

God help them all if the Romanian strength was an underestimation.

The order of march was the 5th Cavalry's Recce Troop followed by the Puma equipped infantry company, the six tanks of the 32nd, the 132nd's seven tanks. The big German built 155mm SP Howitzers and finally the ammunition train, armoured ambulance and combat engineers armoured recovery track, with his second-in-command in a Dardo infantry fighting vehicle bringing up the rear.

Lorenzo had considered commandeering the M-113 but quickly disregarded that idea. The older APCs, the boxy battle taxis, had been pensioned off gradually as their Dardo and Puma replacements were rolled off Iveco's production lines at a pitifully slow rate. The specialist mortar, anti-tank, air defence and command versions had yet to appear owing to budgetary constraints. It frequently left the army with geriatric command and heavy weapons vehicles sat on their lonesome awaiting recovery or repair as the rest of the army disappeared into the distance. Lt Colonel Rapagnetta had elected to hop aboard the infantry company commander's Puma instead.

Lorenzo was originally an infantryman before being posted to an armoured squadron on receiving his majority, and as such held to the wisdom of the footsore, 'Never walk when you can ride.' He had however declined to spend the journey in the commander's position, his perforated Gortex defied his best efforts at repair and besides, it was nice to be out of the rain. All in all it was an invigorating experience after the snow and ice of the Elbe's defence, and the rain and mud of the Flechtinger Höhenzug of course, to now be speeding along smooth tarmac and enjoying a heater's warmth without worrying about thermal signatures.

Lorenzo's plan was simply to drive hell for leather along the auto routes to Autobahn 2 which he would follow at speed to most quickly reinforce the US troops at the autobahn junction. Once there they would go-firm and his recce troop would sweep back towards the scene of the breakthrough and locate the enemy armour.

The Romanians had a head start on him even though they were moving across country, so he had little choice but make this non-tactical dash.

With luck though the enemy had simply run out of fuel, as that was being reported of other Soviet units.

"Colonnello?"

The infantry's OC was bending down in the commander's hatch.

"Si?"

"Active jamming on the 2/198th's frequency, sir."

There are several methods of interfering with radio communication, and obviously the so called 'silent' jamming is preferred as there is no immediate warning that it is taking place. Active jamming is cruder and also instantly recognized for what it is.

Lt Col Rapagnetta removed his helmet and slid the vehicles radio headset into place, listened for a moment and chuckled.

Someone with a sense of humour had tied down a microphones transmit switch and placed it before a speaker blaring out a Rap song.

"Rap is to music, what firing a handgun sideways is to marksmanship." He opined. "But it serves as a declaration of intent here."

"How so?"

"In Mississippi good music is considered to be a mournful song about how their dog died and their car broke down, not an out of key chant about how their 'Ho' was unfaithful. I can't think how they could more greatly offend a country and western fan." Lorenzo grinned, but then it faded. The time for joking was past, and it seemed SACEUR may have been correct.

"Order the recce troop to stop, switch off and report back with anything they hear. They are only about 10k from the junction, yes?"

Five kilometres ahead of the task force the recce vehicles pulled off the autobahn and onto one of the many purely functional truck stops that serve the German road system. The Lince drivers switched off and they listened.

The rain fell unrelentingly, drumming on the thin skins of the vehicles so the troop commander left his to walk a short distance away.

The rumble of battle to the north was all there was and he cursed the rain before turning back to the shelter of his Lince but he froze in mid stride. Whatever had caught his attention was not repeated for several moments but when it recurred he broke into a run, cursing again but not at the rain this time.

Pulling open his vehicle door he barked at his radio operator.

"Tell 'Six' I can hear main tank guns firing to the west!"

TP 33, MSR 'NUT' (Up), Autobahn's 2 & 39, east of Brunswick, Germany: 19 miles south-west of the Vormundberg.

For only half an hour Lieutenant Franklin Stiles, acting CO of C Company, Second Battalion, 198th Armoured Regiment, had been asleep on the folded down seats along one side of the first sergeant's M113 APC. His rest was disturbed by the tinny sound issuing from a radio headset and whatever it was it was not a message, and that fact crept into his subconscious and brought him to a state of reluctant wakefulness.

"What IS that godforsaken row?" he growled.

"It's Rap, sir." his sergeant's APC driver responded.

"It's two rabid cats, high on acid, perched on a transmit switch and screwing, is what it is."

"Weren't you ever young sir?"

"Another remark like that one and I promise you that you'll never get any older, soldier."

Lt Stiles swung his feet down and as he did so Sergeant Jeffries, the first sergeant, arrived, clunking up the rear ramp and squeezing through a blackout of groundsheets.

"I think we're being jammed sir." He stated. "I checked everyone and no one's fat ass is sat on a handset, or fooling around on one either."

"Drop down to the alternative." Stiles instructed.

"I tried that already, and battalion too, but it's the same story."

Franklin reached for the company's other means, a telephone handset connected to DEL, the German emergency military phone network.

Since the construction of the Inner German Border, the 'Iron Curtain' of Winston Churchill's famous speech in 1945, the nations of Western Europe had wisely undertaken the creation of an alternative telephone system for military use in time of war. It is sort of hard to keep that kind of thing from the general populace though. In the frequent exercises held during the Cold War when the various units needed to tie in on the DEL, finding the hidden access points could cause headaches for newbies. The solution was always to ask a local.

"Wo ist die geheimnis telefon, where is the secret telephone?" would be the question to a passing Fräulein, farmer or Postbote.

"Where it always is, at the left side of the oak tree and dig down a half metre."

Consequently it was not a secret from the Soviet Bloc intelligence services for very long.

The DEL handset was dead.

Whoever was jamming them needed a radio for each known channel, so there was a limit to what the enemy could achieve. The previous occupants of the location, 2RTR, had left behind a weirdly named DFC RANTS, the British version of their own communication equipment operating instructions, and he consulted it before changing his own sets channel to that of the

RMP traffic post to the west of them. Rap music blared out of the earpieces.

It was not inconceivable that they were the victim of random, though deliberate, interference with their radio transmissions but Mrs. Stiles 'didn't raise no fool'.

"Stand the company to, and occupy the fighting positions Sergeant."

"No evidence of anyone moving out there sir, but you are dead right, better to be safe than sorry." Sergeant Jeffries ducked back out the way he had come to pass the word verbally.

The company had had a hard war so far despite not having arrived until several weeks after the fighting had begun. Modern armoured warfare uses up machines quickly and they had found reserve equipment in both short supply and in need of several upgrades. The old Abrams had the same 80s generation technology as at the time of mothballing, in the vast tunnel complex at Husterhoeh Kaserne.

C Company 2/198th was guarding this junction because the regiment had been pulled from the line in a pretty fought-out condition, as had other units of NATO's armies, but each and every man and woman could hold their heads high and say with conviction *"If you think we look bad then you should see the other guy."* The 'Other Guy' was the Soviet's Tenth Tank Army which had started off as a two corps, tank heavy and first rate unit with 770 MBTs and 209 AFVs. '10th Tank' was now two battered divisions worth of exhausted leg infantry. The men had been passed back east, allegedly to rest and refit, but they were ordered to hand off their surviving tanks, AFVs and guns to other units instead. The command elements from battalion groups upwards had been trucked away by KGB troops for a 'debrief 'and were never heard of again.

Lieutenant Stiles and just one other were the only officers that the company had, and sergeants filled the other command slots.

With only three M1 Abrams, one of which suffered from an unreliable transmission, they had relieved an understrength squadron of the Royal Tank Regiment which was 'rested' after just forty eight hours out of the line. Its crews of comparative youngsters, each one of them with old men's eyes, had not been that much different from themselves.

Franklin now heard the M1s, and ITV start up in their camouflage net enclosures and move toward hull-down fighting positions, of which there were plenty. The British had prepared this place for defence by a tank company, not just one in name only.

The position was unoriginal inasmuch as it was recognized as a key defence point long before the time of Christ. The ancient routes that the autobahns now followed had required defence/taxation but the ground was flat at that point. According to local historians and archaeologists, the Hill fort that C Company occupied had been built from scratch, with hundreds of thousands of wicker baskets of spoil to create its height and dimensions. Time and the elements had reduced the hill to something less than its former glory and its wooden palisade had rotted away centuries ago, of course. The top of the fort was now flat and partially open to view, from the south in particular.

Those same historians had protested vigorously when the sappers and pioneers began laying the current new defences on top of the very, very old. They were set out in a triangular fashion, two hundred metres to a side with the corners at the south, east and west. There were no blocking positions to bar the way to an enemy motoring up to the junction, this was a hardpoint, an iron triangle, and from here they could engage targets approaching in any direction. An enemy had to deal with them all as a package, not in mutually supporting firing positions that could be quickly isolated by weight of numbers. Coils of barbed wire hindered the approach to the top by anyone on foot, and although laid with infantry in mind they had worked exceedingly well against protesters from the civilian population. Abandoned makeshift shelters, constructed of fertilizer bags and plastic sheeting for the most part, sat beside the foot of the fort where placards and protest banners decorated the steel barbs.

The 'Uhry Hill Fort Preservation Protest Group' camp had been abandoned before C/2/198 had arrived, however they had sent messages of good luck to the British tankers before joining the refugees fleeing west.

The junction itself was half a klick to the northwest where a section each of German Pioniertruppe, combat engineers, and Feldjäger military police were posted. There was not much interaction between the Americans and the Germans.

There was the usual shouting as camouflage nets snagged a vehicle and had to be unsnarled or the hard work of building those enclosures would be undone. That was the trouble with camouflage nets; they were nets, invented to catch stuff a very long, long, time before their adoption as tools of concealment.

The M125s merely started up, opened up the split hatch in the roof and cleared away the netting. The 81mm mortars were ready to put rounds down at any time.

Franklin tossed the CEOI to the tracks driver.

"Start trying a few channels, they can't all be unworkable. When you get someone tell them you'll be listening on their channel for them to pass the word to our battalion CP for an alternate frequency, and that we are stood-to as a precaution."

He left him to it, pulled on his helmet and load bearing equipment before grabbing his weapon.

Stepping out into the rain he could see the 11 and 13 tanks were covering the west and south but the 12 tank was stopped out in the open, its driver trying to find a gear. That damn machine had been trouble since they'd drawn it from the POMCUS at Husterhoeh. The first sergeant was on the hull of the tank, kneeling beside the driver's head, holding onto the main gun for support as he shouted advice.

The second platoon and third platoons had no serviceable tanks, and second platoon had absorbed the survivors of third platoon in the post-Elbe reorganization. Two thirds the strength of an infantry platoon and yet they were filling that role anyway, trudging wearily towards their own fighting positions, one on each side of the triangle. They were split into three squads of six men in two fire teams. Each team had their

M-16s plus an M240 machine gun and a trio of FGM-148 Javelin missiles. Franklin had used the Javelin in Iraq and he hadn't been a fan of it despite its advantages over previous weapons. An ATGW's soft under-belly had always been its operators having to stay put while the weapons were in flight. The missiles had an obvious launch signature that identified its firing position, and of course where the guys who had launched it could be found and killed. Javelin was a fire-and-forget missile, the operator placed the reticule upon the target in the same way you would focus a modern digital camera, and the tracker acknowledged target recognition by forming a box about the targets image, again in a similar way to a camera. Once fired the missile then 'soft launched', thereby being some several feet from the soldier who had loosed it off before the rocket motor fired. The firer could scoot into cover immediately, which improved his chances of survival. The downside was that you couldn't just see a target and simply engage it, because the cooling unit took a minimum of thirty seconds to do its thing before the seeker unit would work. It tracked a target thermally so on a hot day it could have trouble locating the actual target you wanted to hit. Not exactly anybody's weapon of choice in a slug-fest but these weaknesses had been identified, and future upgrades would improve its engagement time. Teething troubles were ever the problem with weapons, and probably the only one to ever work as advertised from the moment it came out of its box was the flint knife, and that knife didn't cost the same price as a Mercedes Benz convertible each time you used it.

He raised his face to the heavens, letting the rain wash away some of the tiredness and he was enjoying the sensation of raindrops on his face until the moment was ruined by an explosion.

Franklin crouched down instinctively, feeling the sudden wave of heat and a buffet from the blast. The first sergeant hit the wet earth in front of him, or at least part of him did. All four limbs and the head were missing.

There was a smell of high explosive caused by the detonation of a Sagger anti-tank missile. A pall of smoke hung around the 12 tank but it had not penetrated the armour. The driver was now frantically attempting to find a gear, any damn gear.

Realising that he was gormlessly staring from the limbless body in the mud, to the tank, and back again, Franklin dropped to the ground and began to crawl to the nearest cover.

Finally getting the transmission to engage the M1 jerked backwards into reverse, and travelled six feet before it was struck again. It shuddered to a stalling halt where it was hit a third and final time.   Super-heated gasses jetted out of the turrets open hatches and its commander rolled screaming down the side of the turret, his overalls smoking but there was no explosion, the storage bin doors had been closed when the tank was struck. However, thick black smoke poured out, followed by a lick of flame before the Halon fire extinguishers activated.

Franklin saw the driver crawl free and climb on top of the turret, assisting the injured loader and gunner, both of whom were suffering from burns. His instinct was to run over and help but Franklin had a company to run, and the crew would have to make-do by themselves for now.

A Sagger missile streaked overhead, a clear miss, and a second struck the packed earth before the 11 tank, exploding harmlessly and flinging great clods of earth in all directions.

The ITV's commander opened fire with a turret mounted M240, the red tracer identifying one of the dismounted Romanian anti-tank team's positions for the remainder to engage but he stopped firing abruptly, hurriedly dropping from sight as Romanian infantry in turn zeroed green tracer onto him.

With a splash of muddy water Franklin arrived in a second platoon hole, they were engaging the enemy with their M16s and M240.

The company did not have a FIST and in the absence of a fire control order the mortars were silent. Franklin Stiles looked for the squad leader and saw him actively engaged in the fire fight. The young man was a supermarket trainee manager and loader in the armoured branch by way of a military trade, not an infantry leader, so despite his new title he had not yet acquired the skills to go with it.

Lt Stiles peered quickly over the lip of the position, needing only a moment to locate the enemy by the muzzle flashes. The Sagger team had not fired again and had either been killed, had their heads down or they were relocating. The infantry were not sitting handily upon any of the TRPs, the target reference points on the company's defensive fire plan, and so an adjust-fire was required.

The company's infantry positions all had field telephones with landlines laid to the CP and to the mortar carriers. The mortar tubes had already pivoted on their turntables to point towards the action, the crews impatiently awaited someone to tell them where to shoot.

"Mike Three One this is India Two Alpha, adjust fire, shift Delta Foxtrot one-zero-two-zero over"

A tinny voice greeted him without ceremony, reading back his information.

"This is Mike Three One, adjust fire, shift Delta Foxtrot one-zero-two-zero out"

"Adjust from Delta Foxtrot one-zero-two-zero...Left five-zero, Up one-zero-zero. Infantry in the tree line, over"

"Adjust from Delta Foxtrot one-zero-two-zero Left five-zero Up one-zero-zero. Infantry in the tree line, out"

Behind him the range, bearing and elevation settings for DF 1020 were identified on the fire plan, and then the adjustments applied before the number 1s of each crew received the required information.

Franklin could clearly hear the shouted orders from the rear.

"Charge two, elevation eleven zero zero, bearing forty two thirty, one round HE!"

Back home in the USA the Mississippi National Guard's mortars ability had been regarded as adequate for their role. They were part-timers after all. Here in the middle of a war in Europe they had had plenty of practice in recent weeks. They weren't fair-to-middling mortarmen any longer; they were veterans and expert at their trade.

The distinctive sound of both mortars was followed immediately by the fire direction centre's verbal confirmation that rounds were in the air.

"Shot over."

"Shot out." Franklin acknowledged and stared at the treeline cautiously, the firefight had no victors yet and the red and green tracer flew back and forth.

The telephone handset clicked.

"Splash over" the FDC stated. He knew the time of flight and on a battle field with shells falling from more than one source it was important to know which explosion was your explosion.

Two bright flashes of light eclipsed the small arms fire of the Soviet troops.

"On target, fire for effect, over."

"On target, fire for effect, out."

The mortarmen responded accordingly, the number 2s putting four mortar bombs in the air per tube before the first one landed. Each mortar round was fused 'super-quick' as the targets were not dug-in for defence. The detonating round would not provide a deep crater for cover and if it struck a tree the effects against infantry were pretty vicious.

A flash of light accompanied each explosion but it took several seconds for the crump of the detonations to reach him.

Dead or just suppressed, the Soviet infantry in the wood line were no longer firing on them, but in two other places out on the night-time landscape machine guns opened fire, green tracer falling on the right flank of the American position.

The Javelins here had no worthwhile targets yet, they weren't exactly flush with the weapons anyway, but a soldier had a Javelin's CLU operating, using the thermal sight to identify targets. Franklin nudged him aside and looked for himself. The wood line where he had called in the fire mission was to the right of a fire break. It stretched away like a Roman road before him, and there, in the distance he caught the green glow of a vehicle passing briefly into view, and then a second heat source, also travelling right to left. He kept the CLU aimed at that point for a half minute longer but the movement of those two vehicles was not repeated. Was it just two, or had he merely caught the tail-end-Charlie's of a tank brigade? That would certainly ruin his next Christmas and birthday, both.

Whatever it was, it was heading west along the forest firebreaks in the same direction as Autobahn 2.

Franklin returned the CLU and handed the telephone handset to the squad leader, reminding him that his primary job was to control the fight, not to join in. He then bent double as he ran back past the APC he had left, heading for the south side positions. He was the company commander, not a rifleman, but without working radios he had to get a handle on what they were up against by seeing for himself. He was almost there when somewhere a giant took a massive swing at an anvil and he flung himself down, gasping in pain with the effect it had on his ears. An afterimage floated before his eyes and he blinked furiously to clear it. The sound had been accompanied by a flash of intense light from the 13 tanks position.

A strange halo sat above the M1 and the stink of ozone filled Lt Stile's nostrils. It was caused by a 125mm tungsten carbide sabot striking the M1 turret's sloping glacis a glancing blow.

The enemy clearly had the 13 tank's range with the very first shot, and whether or not it was beginner's luck or the skill of much practice, the decision to stay or go was a no-brainer for the Abrams commander. 13 reversed backwards rapidly, pulling back out of its attacker's view where it pivoted on its tracks, heading for a new position with a foot long scar glowing bright red on its turrets leading edge.

A Javelin missile was ejected from its launch tube, flying a short distance before the rocket motor cut in and it accelerated rapidly away. As Franklin regained his feet there was a distant flash of light as the missile killed the 13 tank's attacker.

This was a well-planned attack, allowing the infantry to dismount and attempt to take out his tanks by surprise from relatively close in before committing their own armour. Only now could he hear the sound of tanks and infantry fighting vehicles closing on his small group of defenders.

The rain wasn't helping his Mk-1 eyeballs as he squinted through his binoculars but he was pretty sure there were vehicles moving parallel to the autobahn here too, also heading west.

The western side was currently clear of enemy but that could quickly change.

A vicious firefight was taking place down at the junction. He tried to recall how many the Feldjäger and engineers numbered. Was it twenty or so?

The combat engineer's Marder was engaging targets Franklin was unable to see unaided but which included a Sagger team. He heard a missile launch and immediately the Marder's 20mm cannon opened up, with the result that the missile went ballistic. He could only hope that the cause of that had been a dead Sagger crew as the firing on both sides petered out.

The rattle of tracks and drive sprockets grew louder from the northwest and again the Marder's cannon opened fire, only to be cut short by a T-90's main gun.

The Soviet tank troop advanced now with their main guns silent but the machine guns active, hunting down the field police and combat engineers at the junction before at last appearing from beneath autobahn 39 where it straddled autobahn 2.

Behind the tanks, the infantry tore down cables and cut wires. Not all the wires were for demolition and a white flash, accompanied by a scream, drew a rueful smile from Stiles, the ramrod of a power line maintenance crew back in Madison County.

Behind him the mortars were firing almost continuously now, swivelling first one way and then the other. That at least was something that the attackers seemed to lack, that and artillery.

"Small mercies." Franklin muttered to himself. "Anymore where those came from, big fella?" he asked, looking up at the heavens, but all he got was wet.

TP 32, MSR 'NUT' (Up), Autobahn's 2 & 391, north of Brunswick, Germany: 24 miles south-west of the Vormundberg.

At TP 32, nine miles to the west of TP 33, the sound of cross-country tyres humming on the tarmac somewhere in the distance had L/Cpl Green, 352 Provost Company RMP, looking westwards before checking his watch. Their own 'rover' had only left on route maintenance a half hour before, but maybe they had found the problem quickly. Nevertheless he took the big flat bottomed Bardic lamp and turned a dial at its top to select a red filter before setting it carefully on the ground where it both illuminated the caltrop spikes, and its glare would conceal him from clear view in his shell scrape.

In the covering trench set further back they were used to the eccentric antics of the loner, but they knew the story of how the Russians had killed his colleagues and left him for dead, so they made no comment about his habits and he went about his business undisturbed.

They far preferred it when Maggie was pointsman though, she was quick with the banter and far better looking.

"Here we go." Captain Sandovar said speaking over his shoulder to the six men crammed together in the rear of the Landrover.

"We have just a little over five minutes now before our friends make their presence known. So deal with the sentries quickly and neutralize those bridge demolition charges, understood?"

The British military number plate from their short wheelbase FFR now adorned this vehicle. The signing trailer had been left behind amongst the burnt out cars and vans at the rest stop with the bodies of Maggie Hebden and Tony Myers beneath its tarpaulin.

The young man had shown courage in his refusal to divulge the password of the day, even after one ear had been removed and dangled before his eyes by Sergeant Viskova. Captain Sandovar had therefore played good guy to Viskova's sadistic bad guy and explained that they were paratroopers merely attempting to regain their own lines. In return for the password they would remove his and the young ladies boots and leave them stranded. If he refused however, well his men had not been with a woman for quite some time and his colleague was a good looking girl... he had left the threat unspoken. Of course the young soldier had not been aware that Viskova had been rather over enthusiastic in his disarming of the fair young lady and she was already extremely dead.

"Thirty two." he had said at last.

"Thirty two?" Sandovar had queried, looking into the British soldiers eyes.

There was anger but no hint of guile in the young man's return stare and Sandovar had nodded confirmation to Sergeant Viskova who had immediately cut his throat.

One Landrover pretty much looks like another and this one slowed before it entered the chicane, switching its dipped lights off so as not to illuminate or dazzle. They were all on the same side, were they not?

However, having stopped there was no sign of a traffic pointsman anywhere.

Sandovar opened his door and stepped out into the rain, using a hand to shield against the glare of the lamp as he looked about.

"Halt!" a voice said from somewhere beyond the lamp.

Sandovar squinted against the light. He could hear the Landrover's chassis creak as his men slowly lowered themselves over the tailgate and extended the telescopic body of a 66mm LAW as quietly as they could. He quickly spoke with a raised and authoritative voice to cover the noise, and to act as a distraction of course.

"Captain Brown, 101 Provost Company, where the hell are you?" and took a step forwards.

"I said 'Halt'...sir."

The challenger was not apparently intimidated by testy senior officers.

"Thirty?" the voice said at last.

"Two." Sandovar answered and took another step.

"I didn't tell you that you could move, did I sir?"

Sandovar heard the unmistakable sound of a safety catch being released.

In the covering trench the soldiers from 1 Wessex grinned at the officer's discomfort. More than once this military policeman had caught hell from officers like this, but having been shot once by someone in an officer's uniform he clearly didn't give a crap when they kicked off. It was good sport to watch.

"When you go out the gate at Chi, do you turn left or right for the Wellington Arms, and what side of the street is it?"

Captain Sandovar almost stammered a "What?" but that would have been a serious error. 'Chi' was slang for Chichester, the RMP training depot, wasn't it?

He took a guess and trusted to bluff and bluster, allowing the handle of his fighting knife to slip out of his sleeve and into the palm of his hand unseen.

"Turn right, it's on the left....and now you and I are going to have a conference without coffee, young man!"

His men were all out of the vehicle now, poised and tense, the LAW was armed and the firer need only step from behind the Landrover to take out the trench.

Captain Sandovar, the stolen Landrover and his Spetznaz team disappeared in a hail of flame, fire, black smoke and ball bearings.

Staff Sergeant Vernon had been trying without success to reach the signing vehicle owing to the jamming that had begun a half hour before. The DEL connection was apparently broken. Only the field telephones were working. He now stumbled from the TP, gaped at the western traffic point for a second before shouting.

"STAND-TO!...STAND-TO!"

It was a fairly unnecessary order as the thunderclap of sound that reverberated across the sodden landscape had carried that message already.

Rudely awoken bodies were pulling on webbing and fighting order, grabbing personal weapons and running to their assigned stand-to positions.

S/Sgt Vernon sprinted along the hard shoulder to where Simon was just rising to his knees in the shell scrape, a claymores clicker in one hand.

"Where the *fuck* did you get that?" Vernon asked.

He did not get an answer, but he did get to see Simon smiling for the first time.

What was left of the Landrover, and that wasn't much, was scattered across all the lanes of both carriageways. The twisted chassis and engine block sat on perforated, burning tyres several feet from where the vehicle had been stopped. The skinned carcass of what had once been a man was draped over the central crash barrier.

The 1 Wessex sentries were wide eyed and hyper, still shocked at what had occurred. A vehicle had turned up and an officer had given the correct answer when challenged but his pointsman had still blown him away, quite literally.

Over on the airfield they were standing-to also, but not with the same sense of urgency.

What had happened, why was there no air raid warning? With all the noise of the helicopter traffic no one noticed what was appearing out of the forest at the north east corner until the Romanian T-90s gunned their engines and charged at the wire mesh perimeter fence.

Three enemy tanks, externally clad in blocks of explosive reactive armour which gave them the appearance of scaly skinned monsters were here, behind the front lines?

The left-most T-90 struck a bar mine, a severed drive wheel flew high in the air, sections of amputated track spun away but no sooner had it ground to a halt its main gun elevated slightly and began to track its prey.

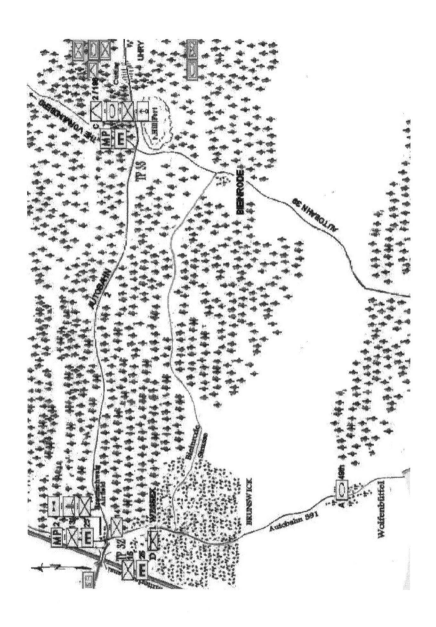

The Battle of the Autobahns 2

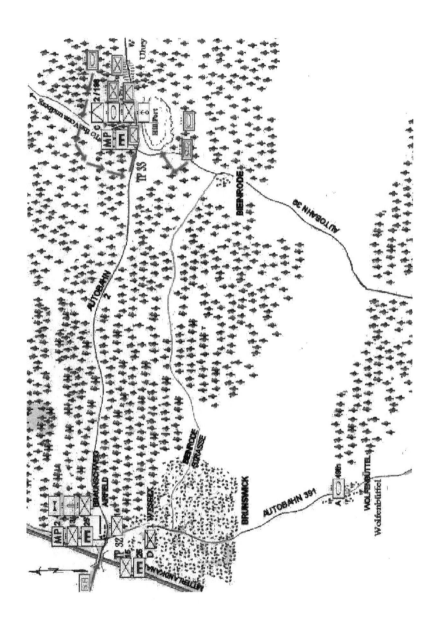

The Battle of the Autobahns 3

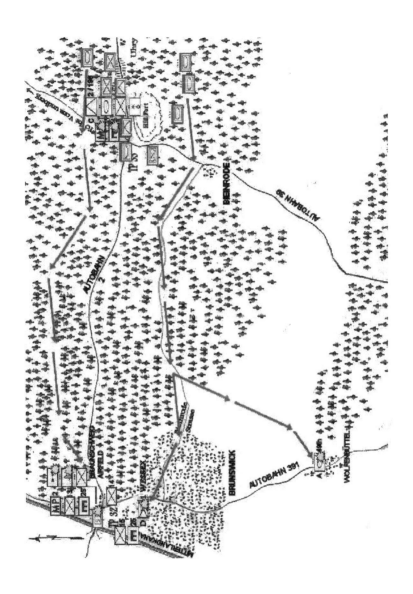

The Battle of the Autobahns 4

The crippled tank's target was a slow moving CH-53 Sea Stallion with a full cargo net of underslung artillery ammunition. There had been no wave off broadcast from the tower, no warning from the ground, and although the large machine in its German army camouflage paint scheme was moving too quickly for an accurate shot with a standard main gun round, it was a sitting target for the 125mm, beam-riding 9M119M *Refleks* missile that the main gun fired in its direction.

Essentially an anti-tank missile that was fired like a shell, the *Refleks* flew down the beam of the tanks laser range finder to its target. Although it was unsuitable against fixed wing aircraft, it worked well against the slower rotary wing variety.

The missile struck the German Sea Stallion's engine housing and detonated against main transmission, causing the heavy lift machine to immediately depart from controlled flight. It dropped like a stone with no hope of auto-rotation, falling the hundred feet onto the previously wrecked runway, landing directly upon its cargo net. The metal main rotors still rotated at a blur until they truck the tarmac and shattered, sending jagged sections for hundreds of metres in all directions. The small cluster of a half dozen airmen and women at the mobile canteen were sliced in two by a six metre length of rotor blade.

The Sea Stallions fuel tanks ruptured and the volatile contents ignited explosively.

The general reaction was initially one of shock, with ground crew, loaders and even the thirty strong Bundeswehr defence platoon left gawping instead of reacting for several vital seconds.

The control towers panoramic windows shattered into a hundred thousand shards of glass shrapnel and the roof blew off as the T-90 fired a second time.

Only now did they collectively realise the danger they were in.

Ground personnel scattered, seeking cover from the other two tanks that ploughed through the perimeter fence and without pause raced towards the flight line, machine guns and main armament firing.

It was pandemonium, and panic increased further as the Sea Stallion's cargo of 155mm artillery shells and bag charges began cooking-off in the flames.

The airfield's Spanish air defence platoon reacted positively, and achieved a faint but workable infrared lock on the stationary T-90 with a truck mounted Mistral sited at the north west corner of the airfield. It was a brave attempt but a 2.95kg charge and tungsten ball bearings may down a thin skinned aircraft but they barely scratched the Soviet tank's armour plating. Before the crew could launch a third missile the tank's commander had located their firing point and destroyed the launcher, the vehicle and the crew with a main gun round.

Autobahn 2.

East of the by now besieged Mississippi National Guardsmen of 198th Armoured Regiment at TP33, unfriendly eyes watched the Italian reconnaissance troop rejoin the autobahn and race towards the cutting below them.

"Let them pass, they are only glorified off-road jeeps."

The ambushers stayed in cover until the sound of the engines were fading.

Two kilometres east of them an unusual roadblock was in place on the westbound carriageway in the form of the 155mm howitzer gun line and ammunition train. The support vehicles had all moved off the autobahn but were close by in a temporary harbour area, beneath the flyover outside the village of Uhry.

Lt Col Rapagnetta swapped vehicles and the remainder of the task force split into platoon packets with tactical spacing between each and continued on their way.

First infantry platoon of the 5th Cavalry floored the accelerators on their young commanders orders in an attempt to catch the recce troop and they quickly drew ahead of the main body, entering the tree lined cutting at 65mph where disc shaped MON-100 directional mines attached to the trees detonated.

As a dedicated anti-personnel mine the occupants with the Pumas were safe from the shrapnel, but not so the tyres or the vehicle commanders.

All four of the APCs were hit; clods of rubber from shredded tyres bounced away as steel wheel rims raised showers of sparks. The second Puma in the packet struck the central crash barrier and flipped onto its roof where it was t-boned by the third vehicle.

Second platoon came into view moments later and having braked hard and avoided entering the ambush site it lost the platoon commanders vehicle in a catastrophic explosion. The three survivors reversed at speed and avoided falling victim to Sagger missiles such had taken out their platoon headquarters.

With the first platoon APCs crippled and immobile it was easy work to finish off the vehicles with RPG-29 rocket grenades and cut down the survivors with small arms fire.

2km is no distance at all for most modern artillery but the time of flight was exceedingly long in relative terms. At maximum elevation the cutting was engaged by the PzH 2000 howitzers firing in burst mode, each gun firing three rounds in nine seconds, the first round was fused for air burst, the second for super-quick and the third for delay. As the rounds would fall vertically the ambushers would receive no warning.

Rock and earth were still falling as the task force approached the cutting again and an Ariete flattened a section of the central crash barrier to allow access to the eastbound lanes. One side of the cutting had collapsed, sliding onto the roadway. There was no living trace of the enemy who had been there.

TP 33, MSR 'NUT' (Up), Autobahn's 2 & 39, east of Brunswick, Germany: 19 miles south-west of the Vormundberg.

The 11 tank fired but failed to kill its target despite a hit. It had already destroyed a BTR-70 from its current position and it now erred on the side of caution, changing position. The enemy's explosive reactive panels were effective, and often as many as three rounds were required from the M1's lighter 105mm main gun to secure a kill. The Javelins on the other hand had no trouble with single hit kills having been designed for that purpose. The missile had two shaped charges in tandem and even if the first's energy was dissipated by striking an ERA panel, the second charge took care of business.

A TOW missile left the ITV's dual launcher in an upward arc, its operator expertly bringing it down to strike the top of the T-72's turret that the 11 tank had targeted. The thinner armour was no challenge for the warhead and the turret parted company with the chassis.

The ITV's commander looked for more targets, peering through his periscope he swung it to the right, recognizing a clutch of waving antennae's as they passed through his vision so he swung back, lowered his angle of view and stared directly down a T-90's barrel.

Franklin heard the ITV blow up, the seven remaining missiles in its storage racks blew also, adding to the destruction with their sympathetic detonation. A fireball rose above the fighting position it had occupied, and the twisted aluminium hull began to burn.

The tanks and AFVs had appeared a few minutes after the infantry attack in the north had begun, with fewer tanks in number than the southern group, they were nevertheless dividing his fighting power.

13 fired to the south and missed, it reversed but received yet another hammer blow. The Soviet sabot screamed away into the night, a fast moving dot of light until it passed from view. The 13 tank had been struck twice now and survived, the

crew should have been feeling lucky but no one was in a betting mood.

With the loss of the ITV and the 12 tank the company was reduced to 11, 13 and half a dozen Javelins for killing tanks. Pretty soon the enemy commander was going to figure out that the Americans were now covering three sides with only two M1s and a bunch of dismounts.

The force to the north was a mechanized company with a tank platoon in support. It was closing, moving in bounds across a wide front that prevented the defenders from concentrating their limited firepower.

Over to the south, five tanks and four BTR-70s had managed to work around until they had the eastern corner of the National Guard position flanked.

Had this been a table top exercise Franklin would have admired the coordination between the enemy tanks and Sagger teams. While one engaged his positions the other moved.

Franklin had no effective way of coordinating his own unit's fire as that damn music was still foxing the airwaves.

11's turret was moving, its main gun tracking a target visible to its thermal sights but not to Lt Franklin Stiles naked eyes. It fired, and a T-90 that had just popped out from behind a clump of trees to the west exploded. Franklin punched the air triumphantly as the M1 pulled back to change position. If they could just keep sniping in this fashion they could yet win the battle. A Sagger streaked in from the south and struck the Abrams raised rump as it reversed out of the hull down position. A flash of flame and the tank was concealed from view by black smoke. When the smoke cleared the tank was hung there at the top of the fighting positions ramp, smoke issuing from its wrecked engine pack through the small molten hole in its armour and the engine compartments air vents. The crew had not bailed out though, and with a squeal of sprockets the machine rolled forwards, back into the position it had just left. It was now a stationary hardpoint, or a static target depending on which way you looked at it. Its machine guns opened fire, attempting to drive off a platoon of approaching infantry who were using the ground with skill.

The second platoon squad at the eastern corner cut loose with their M-240 and M16s before scattering in the face of an approaching tank.

A pair of heavy machineguns tore in the earth about the northern squad's holes, the fire was coming from two more MBTs, a T-72 and a T-90 that were just a hundred metres out and closing fast. The fire was pinning the squad, preventing them from rising up and engaging them with their last Javelin. The enemy tanks task was made all the easier as the holes were illuminated by the flames from the burning ITV, as was the 13 tanks rear. The M1 was oblivious of its peril, engaging a target to the south and unaware it would in moments be in the sights of three main tank guns.

Franklin found himself frozen in place, like an unwitting spectator watching a car wreck about to happen. Which of the enemy tanks would destroy the company's last serviceable M1?

The tank entering the defensive position from the east fired first, and the northern T-90 shuddered to a halt and caught fire. The T-72's turret rounded on the newcomer even as that MBT's gun came to bear. The T-72 fired before it could reload and it seemed to stagger but the round failed to penetrate and its own main gun stayed fixedly tracking. Now only fifty metres from the T-72 it fired, its round targeted on the turret ring. At that range it could not miss and the T-72 was struck at its most vulnerable spot, exploding in spectacular fashion.

Unaware that his jaw was hanging open in amazement Franklin's instinct for self-preservation did kick in as he detected the sound of an approaching freight train. The open ground to the west lit up with strobe-like flashes as 155mm shells airburst over the Romanian infantry, but Franklin did not see it, he was doing his very best to stay flat against the muddy surface.

Tank guns were firing in the night but no one was firing on the position anymore. The strange tank halted and a hatch opened.

"Buona sera, Tenente...the cavalry, it has arrived!" declared Lt Col Lorenzo Rapagnetta with a grin and a flourish.

TP 32, MSR 'NUT' (Up), Autobahn's 2 & 391, north of Brunswick, Germany:

South of the autobahns traffic point the D Company Headquarters of 1 Wessex were quartered in the premises of a large and well known furniture department. Not for them the crib of mud, folding stretcher or camp bed of green canvas that had shrunk and defied reassembly. Each man and woman of company HQ reposed upon eco-friendly renewable pine, and beneath duvets of sustainable cotton.

It was not all beer and skittles though, they were again feeding from Compo rations and boil-in-the-bag Meals Rarely Edible as their appetites' for Swedish meatballs with lingonberry jam had been tested to destruction.

1 Wessex had joined 3(UK) Mechanised Brigade after the NATO armies hurried withdrawal from north of Berlin to south of the Elbe and Saale Rivers, following the invasion of Poland.

The part-time soldiers from Bournemouth and Poole in Dorsetshire had stepped from peaceful civilian life into a maelstrom at Magdeburg, but they had held until relieved even though D Company could no longer pass muster.

D Company was detached from the battalion and now had the task of securing the bridge and autobahn junction while replacements from the UK brought them back up to strength. They were not there yet and the battle for the Vormundberg was reaching critical mass. At dawn the company was to begin preparing defensive positions west of the Mitterland Canal for the US 4 Corps and 'unspecified elements currently defending the Vormundberg', the company commander was stating during his O Group's 'Execution: General Outline' section.

The company signals rep pressed him on that vague point.

"Sir, if I know which units are going where I can save us a lot of confusion later." the Signals Platoon corporal waited with pencil poised.

"Whoever makes it out." stated the company's permanent staff instructor, unbidden from his seat at the back.

At the conclusion of the O Group the platoon commanders of 13, 14 and 15 platoons had gone into a huddle about the map board and their platoon sergeants had descended upon the CQMS, attempting to extract kit. It was always the way.

'Radar', the company clerk, entered the room with the report of gunfire and explosions north of the town. Jamming was preventing the company sergeant major from contacting any of the platoons or the Dutch tank troop in the next town to the south, along the autobahn 391. He had sent runners instead. That broke up the huddle and the scrum for replacement equipment, the platoon command elements hurrying away to rejoin their men and the company commander stepping outside to listen.

Despite the rain they all of them paused on the large and empty car park listening to machine gun fire and the crack of tank guns, and then there came the unmistakeable sound of armoured vehicles on the northbound off ramp of autobahn 391.

"They made good time!" the OC remarked as the first dark silhouettes of tanks came into view.

All three tanks opened fire with their machine guns before turning their attention to the company's soft skinned vehicles parked along the store wall beneath camouflage nets, and once they were wrecked it was the building itself that received their main guns attentions.

Sweden's flagship furniture outlet for Lower Saxony was in flames, the company and platoon command elements for D Company, 1 Wessex were all dead and the battle was only ten minutes old.

The runners did indeed make good time in reaching Wolfenbüttel to the south, and had they been despatched

twenty seconds later they would have met a troop of enemy
tanks joining the 391 from Bieinrode Strasse.

Wolfenbüttel was largely abandoned but far from in
darkness. A Romanian 91st Tank Regiment's troop of T-90s had
arrived before the 1 Wessex runners and surprised the Dutch
troops, destroying two unmanned Leopard 2s where they sat
in berms upon the town centres small park.

The Dutchmen fought back, the third Leopard knocking out
one T-90 before itself being destroyed, and a second Soviet
tank engaged in that particular fight was lost when it
attempted to drive through a glass fronted bar and outflank the
Leopard. The floor had given way, trapping it quite thoroughly
in the beer cellar where surviving Dutch tankers finished off
the trapped tank and crew with two jerry cans of petrol and a
WP grenade. The fire spread to the neighbouring shops, and so
there was quite a bit of light.

TP 32, MSR 'NUT' (Up), Autobahn's 2 & 391, north of Brunswick, Germany:

On the autobahn the appearance of the enemy armour so
soon after the solo action of L/Cpl Green, RMP, destroying a
Landrover, coupled with the jamming of the radio net was seen
as a possible indication that the Vormundberg had fallen, but
there was no time for a debate.

13 Platoon left one of its two-man AT teams in their trench
to the west but had the other engage targets of opportunity to
the north, on the airfield side.

14 Platoon's southern pair on the bottom of Autobahn 391's
fly-over was ordered to pick up their kit and double away up
the incline to find a point where they could engage tanks on the
airfield. They duly did so, arriving panting and out of breath
above Autobahn 2's westbound carriageway. The other 14
Platoon AT team had just fired a round at a charging T-90 on
the Braunschweig airfield and missed by a wide margin. The
crippled tank was beyond extreme range, although stationary,
and having seen the light anti-tank rocket fired from the

autobahn overpass the team became its next target. A main gun round screamed low over the guardrail and green tracer from its coaxial 12.7mm machinegun began to work the firing point over. It was an uneven contest and discretion being the better part of valour they backed off back to their previous covering position.

The helicopters had all been reduced to burning wrecks, the fuel bowser had blown up and the Soviet tanks were systematically destroying stacked pallets of ammunition and stores that had cost so much in effort and lives to transport across the Atlantic.

No sooner had the relocated team arrived when it became obvious that there were tanks in the town too. Machinegun and main tank gun fire was apparent from the direction of company headquarters so they picked up their half dozen LAW-80 weapons, and ran back the way they had come.

Coordination was absent at first, as were the platoon commanders and sergeants. However the army seeks to make everyone familiar with the process of leadership up to at least two command levels above their own.

Newly promoted to the rank of 'Full Screw', Corporal Baz Cotter of 3 Section, 15 Platoon, was blissfully unaware he was now the acting company commander of D Company, 1 Wessex. What Baz was aware of though was that the radios were not working due to jamming, Russian special forces had probably had a pop at taking the bridge and a 'Monkey', of all people, had handed them their arse. Now of course there was machine gun and tank fire with accompanying explosions from both the north and south.

A runner from 1 Section, along the canal tow path on the northern side of Autobahn 2, had arrived, his chinstrap for his helmet undone and hanging free. It was something many of the veterans of the Elbe were doing to distinguish themselves from the replacements from the UK. Baz was doing it too even though in hindsight it did seem a little childish. The runner informed him that there were enemy tanks on the airfield and the sapper's section commander from 25 Regiment RE was preparing to blow the autobahn bridge. This titbit earned him a 'it's-news-to-me' gesture to his questioning glance at the sappers sharing his GPMG gun pit. The two with him had wired up the pair of old narrow bridges that had once carried rail tracks, and 15 Platoon's commander had the responsibility of ordering their destruction, but the decision to blow the autobahn bridge was solely for the OC of D Company to make.

"Has he got comms with Sunray 4?" Baz asked, using the OC's generic callsign.

"Nope."

"Well remind him of four things; that firstly it's not his call to make, secondly that as 4 Corps needs to cross here he may be doing the Reds a favour, and both thirdly and fourthly it's not his call to make, so hang fire on that!"

The runner started away but a thought occurred to Baz.

"Any infantry, or any sign of IFVs?"

"No Corp', just three tanks."

"How do they expect to take and hold a bridge with just tanks?"

They both ducked instinctively as a tank's main gun fired somewhere away to the south.

"Maybe they don't think they need infantry, given as they seem to suddenly have a shit-load of tanks right on our doorstep, Corporal?" The runner then departed at a sprint back along the tow path, one hand on top of his helmet, holding it in place.

He had a point, Baz thought.

"Corporal Cotter!" a voice hailed from up on the 391's elevated section, and Baz saw the speaker was one of the section commanders from 14 Platoon."

"What?" he shouted back.

"Company headquarters is on fire" the lance corporal shouted.

Well that about proves it, thought Baz, I'm dreaming that I am back at Brecon and if I just pinch myself this worst case scenario exercise will simply vanish.

"We can see the flames from here but we can't see any of our lot making their way back from the O Group."

That gave Baz sudden pause for thought. He had been expecting the boss and Terry, the platoon sergeant, to come haring back at any moment. What if the sergeants and platoon commanders were cut off with company headquarters somewhere? Should he send a patrol out to find them?

With that last thought he realised he was the company's senior section commander and senior rank present so therefore should act like it, at least until they got back.

The sections were only six strong and two of those were on average just green and unbloodied replacements. On-the-job training was taking place with the four old sweats teaching the new guys the tricks of the trade. In many cases the result of this included a wish by those replacements that firstly, someone would whizz the odd angry shot in their general direction if it meant a cessation of reminders that they had not been 'On the Elbe', and secondly that another draft would hurry up and arrive so someone else would have to make the tea all the time.

Ariete Task Force

The first good luck then occurred a few miles east as an eight wheel BTR-60 festooned with antennae received a direct hit courtesy of the Italian recce troop calling in fire on IFVs beating a retreat from the battle at TP33. The vehicle, a dozen radios, a CD player and a compilation disc of American rap music were obliterated.

Thanks also to their recce troops the tank heavy attack to the south of TP33 and the hill fort was identified as the main threat and Lt Col Lorenzo Rapagnetta brought all but his own 'borrowed' machine around and into their rear undetected. Three BMPs and a BTR from the attackers to the north dashed in to collect their dismounted infantry and bug out. The Americans 11 tank collected a BMP just before it could disappear back into the forest and the Italian recce troop were the architects of the jamming vehicles demise along with a second BMP, with a little help from the gunners of the 155mm SP battery of course.

Baz was getting his head around the idea that his tactical thinking needed to expand to encompass nine infantry sections instead of just the one when he was hailed again by the same voice from the top of 391.

"Corporal Cotter!"

"That's my name, don't wear it out" he yelled back.

"There's good news and there's bad news...the good news is that the radios are back up...the bad news is you've got three *fuckoffbastardgreatbigtanks* heading your way. Two on the tow path and one on this road!" he pointed at the street running parallel to 391.

The LAW 80 teams were all part of the various tiny platoon headquarters but the weapons themselves did not require a rocket scientist's degree to operate it, but you had to remember that it had been designed by a left-handed rocket scientist. Operators had to work by touch as unlike the 84mm Carl Gustav it had replaced, LAW 80's selector and safety catch were on the right side of the launch tube. Although larger than both the 66mm and 84mm weapons it had replaced, it still often required several hits to secure a kill on a modern main battle tank.

13 and 14 Platoon already had LAW 80s on the north of the junction so after switching his radio back on he summoned both 15 Platoon teams on the hurry-up. The other platoons now had the task of defending the tow path to the north from tanks.

He sent one pair over the narrow road bridges with instructions to head south and find a suitable spot to have a go at the towpath tanks thinner side armour. The other team he set on the corner by a small light industrial unit to cover the road.

He tried and failed to reach company headquarters or any of the platoon commanders and so informed the other section commanders that he was taking command and they were to remain covering their assigned arcs.

"Blakie!" he shouted to his 2 i/c. Private Steve McAlwy was a bus inspector in Poole, Dorset, which earned him the nickname, whether he liked it or not, of a TV sitcom character.

"You are now section commander of 3 Section."

There was a moment's silence.

"Oh, okay."

"But I'm stopping here for now."

The two sappers were peering along the tow path into the pitch dark as the sound of tanks could now be heard approaching.

"We need to drop these little road bridges now, I reckon." Baz informed them. "Before it gets dicey around here."

"You mean it's not dicey now?"

They had a quick conversation with their own section commander before giving Baz the nod to warn the rest of the company.

The first explosion was something of an anti-climax when it happened; the cordex they had used was designed to cut through steel. It looked just like his Mum's washing line, a plastic covering protecting the powerful explosive within and Baz had watched with interest a few days before when they had wrapped it around the width of steel frame half way across, hanging under the bridge as they worked methodically. A dozen turns around each of the sixteen girders before the electrical firing cable had been laid.

"Is that it?" he had enquired at the time as they'd clambered back over the guardrail. "They had more in 'The Bridge at Remagen'."

"Well that was Hollywood wasn't it" had been the reply. "And this ain't the Bridge at Remagen, it's just a half clapped out bit of ironmongery held up by paint and weight restrictions."

Baz had looked doubtful.

"Seen any local civvies using it before they all buggered off?" the sapper had asked.

He thought about it and shook his head.

"Well there you go then." The combat engineer had replied. "If we need to blow 'em, the bridges own weight will do half the job."

A flash, a very loud bang, and lots of black smoke now accompanied the firing of the charges on the first of the single carriageway bridges. With the steel frame cut only the tarmac road bed was holding it up, but it was still standing.

"Trust me" the sapper said defensively. "A fat housefräu and her shopping trolley strolling across will have that lot down in no time." Obviously there was a dearth of Fräus, fat or otherwise.

The second bridge did indeed give up the ghost straight away. The integrity of the structure relied upon the spans and with them cut in the middle the two severed ends dropped into the canal with a great rendering of screeching, buckling metal on either bank.

The reverberations of the second demolition charge were followed by a gunshot along the canals far bank as the light anti-tank team opened fire with the LAW 80's built-in spotter rifle. It only had a magazine of five 9mm tracer rounds but what they had learned on the Elbe at Magdeburg was that the chances of getting a penetrating hit on a Soviet tank clad in blocks of ERA, the explosive reactive armour, was to find a spot that had already been hit and its armour plate exposed.

ERA cannot be cleared away with small arms fire and even if a blocks metal guard is pierced it still will not blow. Even shrapnel hits from artillery near-misses will not trigger them. Occasionally some unwise soul will have a go, and usually die trying.

Everyone listened as the spotting rifle fired a second time and the 94mm rocket followed it a heartbeat later. It hit and detonated, but two tanks, not one, opened up on the firing point with their heavy coaxial machine guns and main guns. The tanks kept coming, the round had been ineffectual.

Baz was distracted by an exploding tank round just under the autobahn bridge at 1 Section's positions and heavy calibre machine gun fire was chewing up the towpaths concrete surface, green tracer rounds ricocheting away wildly.

Both the 14 Platoon team on the 391 elevated sections and 15 Platoon's other team opened fire on the single tank on the road. Neither team bothered with spotting rounds but given the furious preparation of a second LAW80 by his team on the corner they had failed to kill it.

He was staring at them as the gunner hoisted it onto his shoulder, took aim again, and vanished in a welter of smoke and flying, shattered brickwork.

The tank round had collapsed that corner of the building and only two unmoving bodies could be seen protruding from the rubble.

Shouts from beyond the autobahn bridge and the roar of a tank engine from that direction told Baz that 1 Section was being overrun. For whatever reason, 13 and 14 Platoon's anti-tankers had not been able to engage to the north. He berated himself for pulling the team from 1 Section and they were dead now too, the only anti-tank weapons 15 Platoon had were lying beside the wall just beyond the dead team. The unseen tanks main gun fired again, striking the elevated section from where that anti-tank round had been fired from.

"Leave it to the Sappers!" one of the combat engineers shouted and with a gesture to his mate they left the gun pit and sprinted toward the unattended LAW80s. They paused to peer carefully down the street from cover before dashing into the road.

12.7mm rounds tore both men apart before they had reached the far side and they lay unmoving on the wet road.

We are terminally screwed now! Was Baz's first though. They were caught between two fires and with nothing to fight back with.

The lead tank on the towpath just began to appear when it was hit again by the team across the river. The round had hit at an angle and had probably been aimed at its engine compartment but missed. The chance of penetrating the armour is greatest if the round hits square on, and all that this one did was distract and annoy, but both tanks stopped and swivelled their turrets to aim their main guns back over their engine decks.

Baz made an instant decision to save the last two sections of 15 Platoon and join the defenders of the autobahn bridge.

"Grab the gun and tripod" he told the gun crew before shouting to the occupants of the other trenches. "2 and 3 Sections grab your weapons, collect a box of link each for the gun and follow me!"

With the gimpy being returned to the light role by the gun crew he ran across the towpath and onto the damaged road bridge, stopping to urge the men on and waiting until the last man had run past before following them.

Their Bergans had been abandoned but a British infantryman fights out of his webbing and survivors out of his smock. Each man now had an ammunition box for the GPMG and his own weapon. Not a lot to be going on with but at least when the infantry arrived they would be equipped to see them off, hopefully. First of all though, they had to negotiate this damaged bridge.

Fat Fräuliens, Baz thought, remembering the now dead sapper's words, exactly how fat and how much shopping would need to be in that trolley to finish the job the demolition charges had started, a week's worth or just fairy cake comfort food for the evening?

The Soviet tanks were still firing back across the canal when Baz reached the damaged tarmac that marked the halfway mark across the canal. The bloody thing was bouncing beneath their feet like a mattress.

In front of him the GPMG gunner was flagging. Pte 'Juanita' Thomas was one of the older members of the platoon, into his thirties and could no longer sprint like a spring chicken. Baz drew alongside him and gestured to share the load. With the gunner gripping the barrel and Baz holding the butt they ran side by side, opening their legs and gaining on the remainder.

The bridge trembled as a T-90 pivoted through 90° on the on-ramp behind them. Baz could hear both his breath and the gunners coming in gasps, and the blood pounded in his ears. Any second now it would cut them down with its machine guns.

The tank did not open fire on them, its commander had been scared, and was now more than a little angry because of that. These damned English had hit his tank twice with anti-tank weapons and he had wet himself. He wanted payback.

"Run them down!" he ordered his driver.

Tubular metal bollards and a horizontal barrier barred the way to anything larger than a medium sized SUV, although clearly the trains that had once used the bridge had far exceeding their gross weight. It was just wide enough for the heavy goods vehicles that had taken over from the trains as the form of freight transport serving the barge port.

The barrel of the main gun buckled the height barrier, and a weld in the vertical support gave out. Next, the treads pressed against the bollards, the front of the T-90 rising up briefly before the bollards concertinaed.

It was a tight fit but the driver knew his business and holding he floored the tanks accelerator but having travelled only a dozen feet the bridge seemed to snap in the middle, plunging the vehicle into the canals depths.

Both Baz and the gunner fell as the bridge gave way, but unlike the eastern half of the bridge, this end was at an angle of about 30° and they scrambled the rest of the way to the bank and from there into cover with what remained of the platoon.

The anti-tank team joined them, both men a little worse for wear after twice having to crawl for their lives as tank guns blew away their concealment.

"Phew." Someone said as the 94mm team arrived with their remaining LAW80. "Who shit himself then?" There was a very noticeable scent hanging around the pair like a cloud.

"No one has" growled one. "We've been crawling about on this bloody towpath trying to save your arses, is what we've been doing, but half of bleedin' Germany must walk their dogs along here!"

Baz allowed himself to grin at the banter for a moment and then took a look back across the canal.

Four enemy tanks now occupied the ground 15 Platoon had held, apparently unwilling to climb the embankments onto either of the autobahns without infantry support. Even the LAW80s would have no trouble achieving a kill through the area with the thinnest armour on a tank, its belly.

They hadn't exactly excelled themselves as tank killers and now the Soviets had free rein of the opposite bank and access to the demolition charges beneath the autobahn bridge, but there was nothing else he could have done, was there? He did not know what had happened to 1 Section or the sappers who had been with them either. There was no reply on the radio.

Calling up 13 and 14 Platoon he gave them a sitrep before turning his attention back to the dozen surviving members of 15 Platoon that he knew of.

The new boys were all a bit wide eyed with shock after their sudden introduction to the realities of warfare but the old sweats were looking calm even if they weren't really, and that was proving positive with the new guys. Nev Kennington, the smelly LAW gunner who had twice hit the tanks, was getting ribbed but taking it in good humour, he was just glad to still be alive.

"Okay let move off, across this field and keep the hedgerow between us and them." Baz instructed.

They all started to collect themselves and their weapons.

"Nev?"

"Yes, Corporal?"

"You take Pointer...I mean 'Point'." He added quickly.

"Piss off." Nev answered but shuffled forward, his last remaining LAW80 over his back and his SLR at the ready.

"Yeah, *Lead* off Nev" someone said.

"We'll *Dog* your steps" another voice added.

The new guys were joining in now; soldier-humour was proving a tonic.

"Leave him alone, he's had a woof night."

"Yeah, less *Stick*."

"I want a transfer." Nev grumbled and stepped off into the rainy night.

Borisovskiya forest: 230 miles SSE of St Petersburg, Russia.

It had been an eventful day for the current head of the KGB, not all of it good, but it had certainly been profitable financially and there remained the task of securing a power base for her next step.

To the rest of the organisation, the General Staff and even the Premier, Elena Torneski was nothing more than the Premier's 'Yes Bitch' and one with a timidity where violence was concerned, something of a source of amusement for them.

As she had stood with her uniformed aides beside the mine elevator awaiting their ride to Saratov West she had made several calls, the first being to a radio station but the last call had not been answered.

Major Oleg Kamavor and his three companions had sat in the rear of the Hind-D and watched Elena's temper build from the moment they had entered the aircraft at the bunker site. They had been with her for several years, ever since she had emerged from the pack as a possible contender for executive level in the KGB. Her sponsorship had raised them from dirty work as mud bespattered Spetznaz troopers on the battlefield in Chechnya, to dirty work in suits wherever she had sent them. Their boss was a good looking woman to look at, and but for her sadistic streak, vengeful nature and contempt for men as a whole he would have found her very attractive. His boss did not take rejection well and it was therefore necessary to keep their distance from the young women she took as her significant others, all of them remarkably similar in looks to the girl they had been meant to subject to rape punishment in the dacha. Transgressions by these bed partners, such as running away, were punished by Oleg and his men and it was therefore a benefit not to have formed a liking for any of them.

Torneski herself dealt with unfaithful lovers, or if they were beyond her physical reach then someone would deal with them in the precise way that she did, following her instructions to the letter.

The Antonov 72 which had lifted off from Saratov West at the premier's instruction was initially cleared westbound to the KGB-run nuclear weapon storage facility north of Kursk, where Torneski was to authorise the release of two battlefield weapons and personally supervise their transfer to the control of the front commander, General Borodovsky, for immediate use.

Ten minutes into the flight, Torneski ordered the pilots to divert to Rossiya Moskva where a Politburo Kamov KA-60 had taken them to a helipad ten minutes' drive from her dacha. Her driver, another of her sponsored talent, had collected them in her Zil.

"Now there's going to be fireworks" whispered one of his men as they'd drawn up outside.

Katriona, her latest squeeze, had not answered any of the calls on the government network cell phone Elena had given her, nor the landline at the townhouse she shared with Torneski. It could have been that the girl had left Moscow for safety reasons as the capital was a big and obvious target for a nuclear strike by the West, should things go that way, but the car owned by Katriona was sat outside the dacha, and so was another that no one recognised.

"Stay here, but wait for my call." Elena had ordered sternly.

Ten minutes later the call had come and they had trooped upstairs to the same room they had waited in days before. Elena was in the basement emptying her safe of documents, cash and the means to access her secret funds, but her shoes were outside the door where she had left them.

The mattress was still where it had been that night but there were two naked bodies upon it now, green eyed, chestnut haired young Katriona had been astride her secret male lover, confident in the belief that Elena would be away until after the war was won. She had been very new, the tattoo all the boss's girls wore was not complete, just an outline of a dogs paw on that buttock which had looked so good in tight jeans. She had not heard the door open or Elena in her stocking feet walk up behind her.

"Christ, look at the blood." one of his men had said disgustedly. "This isn't the first time she's offed one of her sluts this way...can't you sell her on strangulation, lethal injection or anything else that's easier to clean up sir?"

Oleg had sighed wearily and knelt to retrieve a single empty brass .45 casing that sat upon the varnished pine floor. No it was not the first time, but it seemed to be the favourite method by which Torneski destroyed pretty things she had no further use for, at the same time denying anyone else the pleasure of gazing into the girls beautiful faces. Katriona had been shot in the back of the head, and the heavy round had exited through her face to enter her lover's forehead.

"Just shut up before she hears you, and fetch a mop and bucket."

An air defence alert had delayed their return to Rossiya Moskva airport by the same means but they had then flown to the Deputy Premiers bunker in the forest north of Borisovskiya.

Arten Strombolovich was the perfect deputy leader, loyal but less able than the Premier, and lacking the imagination that was required to be ambitious.

Pale faced and shaken at having just received confirmation of the destruction of the Premiers bunker, he had at first voiced surprise at her presence which had only slowly turned to suspicion.

The bunker's guards, and the Deputy's bodyguard, were all her people, so once his family had been dragged from their beds and had guns at their heads he had abdicated the Premiership in her favour. New heads of the armed forces were quickly on the job and the Front Commander had been arrested and replaced.

Ariete Task Force
Autobahn 2

The 155mm PzH 2000s relocated their gun line to the top of the hill fort but the Ariete tanks were on the move west before their arrival.

So far luck had been with them, despite losing five infantry fighting vehicles and their compliments in the ambush at the cutting. That was Lorenzo's opinion anyway.

Two of his tanks had been damaged but not seriously enough to warrant immediate repair, and they had destroyed five enemy tanks plus another five IFVs. What concerned him though were the American company commander's sightings of vehicles on the forest firebreaks heading west. This was not something Pierre Allain had expected, an attempt to seize two of the vital junctions, and not just the one.

A quick radio conference with the English at the next junction had confirmed an attack by enemy tanks was ongoing,

although the Soviet armour was standing off and softening up the defenders, as it waited for the infantry that had escaped his own tanks.

Were there just four or five Soviet MBTs remaining, or was there another tank company out there?

His cavalry regiment's recce vehicles were again leading the way, but more cautiously now. Two were three hundred metres apart in the forest to the north of Autobahn 2, trying to locate which route the enemy had taken. A second pair was doing the same thing to the south. The remaining Lince was driving in a zig-zag fashion along the autobahn so as to hard-target for enemy tank and Sagger gunners.

"Six, this is Echo Two Five, over?"

Lorenzo was up in the hatch of his damaged Ariete, again getting wet despite his best intentions.

"Six, send over?"

"Echo Two Five, we've been following the firebreak the IFVs took when they bugged out, the track marks are easy to follow,

and then they are joined by more at a firebreak intersection.”
The grid reference was added.

"Six, How many, and can you tell if they were tanks or IFV's?"

"Echo Two Five, no way of telling what made them, but I reckon a squadron's worth, the ground here is pretty chewed up.”

It went along with had been deduced regarding the numbers involved in the earlier breach between 3 Para and 1 Wessex's positions.

Apparently the Soviets had got it wrong too, and had expected a NATO reaction from the north, not the east, and had committed a company against each of the junctions while having at least another company in a blocking position to the north straddling the valley road from Lehre and the Vormundberg beyond.

Consulting his map, Lt Col Rapagnetta saw the thick pine forests on the valley slopes either side of a road bordered by fields with stone walls typical of this area. A good spot for a tank company to halt a much superior force, probably from ambush. Fortunately Lorenzo had chosen the less tactical but speedier approach or they could have driven straight into that.

If he were the Soviet commander he would have relocated when the attack on TP33 failed, but would he merely reinforce the tank company attacking the junction at TP32 to ensure success quickly, or would he be covering the eastern approaches too?

Lorenzo ordered the tanks to halt briefly upon the autobahn while he carried out a hasty reorganisation, combining the tanks of the units into two groups, a full squadron and a troop of three.

To the south the Americans single remaining M1 was leading the cavalry regiment Pumas through Bieinrode and into Brunswick from that direction. His aim there was to initially demonstrate to the east, drawing out the enemy in that direction thereby allowing the infantry to reinforce the junction by swinging up from the south. The 5th Cavalry Regiment's infantrymen had the Israeli *Spike* ATGW man-pack system which the English were in dire need of at TP32.

With the reorganisation complete he led the squadron of ten into the forest and onto a parallel firebreak to the much used one and headed west with the Lince vehicle on point.

Russia

Had this been a Hollywood movie then there would somehow have been a rear-view mirror that would have been present in the cockpit to capture the back view, the awful light in their wake as they flew north. Major Caroline Nunro and Captain Patricia Dudley, USAF, were combat aircrew veterans so killing was not something new to them. It was sanitised in comparison to what an infantryman experiences and it was easy not to dwell on an aircraft they had 'splashed' having contained at least one other human being, with family and loved ones who would grieve. The ground target that they 'neutralised' may contain dozens, but they never saw them, just the explosion, a successful strike.

Tonight they had seen nothing more than the light of several suns through the filtered screens, and felt some of the ground effects, a fraction of what an air or surface burst would have had. But they flew in silence, in a kind of shock, knowing that nothing about themselves would ever be the same again, and no one who knew what they had done would look at them in quite the same way either.

Moscow was still on high alert of course and a fuel costly detour brought them to thirty miles out from the forest airstrip.

Patricia broke communications silence, using relaxed VP on the heavily encrypted channel.

"*Surf Club* receiving *Petticoat Express* on Secure Eight, over?"

Silence followed.

"*Surf Club* receiving *Petticoat Express* on Secure Eight, report my signal, over?"

There was still silence.

"This doesn't seem good." Caroline commented. "Do you think they already hightailed it out of there?"

"No way of telling."

"If they have gone then we have an hour's fuel at best before we hit the silk and hike the last thousand miles to friendly lines."

"Petticoat this is Surf, we have you strength three!"

An explosion and the sound of small arms fire in the background was evident.

"Surf this is 'coat, you guys sound kind of busier than when we left, we are five minutes out but are you waving us off?"

"We are having trouble with the neighbours but we have their measure until the ammunition runs out. The other guys came up the logging trail through the forest from the west, so approach from the north east, over."

"Roger that, out."

On the ground, Limanova had been using the two elderly IFVs to ferry the men to an RV a half mile from the airstrip. As they had appeared out of the trees, tired and fed up, their new CO had briefed them, the old CO in plain sight behind him, dead upon the wet grass. Lt Col Limanova split them into groups of fifteen for ease of transport, and these would form five man fire teams in the attack. He did not expect cheers and what the Americans called Gung Ho, and in that he was not disappointed. The forest at night was in none of the militiamen's comfort zones.

It had taken the Green Berets a little while to work out what was going on and six of the groups were delivered to the RV, crammed inside if they were lucky, or sitting on the roof getting wet if they were not. Groups 7 and 8 didn't make it, the vehicles were ambushed with venerable 66mm LAWs. Four men escaped back into the forest but Petrov was not one of them.

He had ninety men with him and another hundred awaiting transport that was now burning fiercely on the logging trail. He told them to make their way to him on foot.

Those one hundred men were complying with his order, but they made their way very slowly.

They had an old M41 82mm mortar and two men who knew how to use it but no aiming post so they would use open sights and guess the required elevation.

With a few words of encouragement they had moved off and begun their attack.

It was as black as pitch but the landing lights, infra-red strobes, though invisible with the naked eye were clear and bright on the plasma screens.

Tracer flashed back and forth on the right of the airstrip and Caroline brought them in low over the trees to minimise their exposure to the ground fire.

The Green Beret commander was waiting for them, shouting above the sound of the still running engines and the gunfire.

Svetlana was in his command bunker trying to reach her contact in the government to get the militia pulled off. She had frequencies and callsigns that Torneski was meant to monitor, but if she were listening she certainly was not responding.

The fuel bowser was not there to meet them, it was back in the trees, a less obvious target.

"I know where it is, I'll fetch it if the keys in the ignition?"

A mortar round landed over to the right, attempting by guesswork to hit or damage the aircraft they had heard land.

"Jesus!" Caroline swore.

"He can't see to aim." The Green Beret commented.

"He doesn't need to." Patricia said.

"There's a pair of my guys near the fuel truck." He told Patricia. "Be sure to shout a warning and don't forget the password, okay?"

Patricia took off , running along the edge of the lighter runway until the break in the trees. She swung left, slowing as she headed into the dark trees.

A flash robbed her of all night vision and she was flying through the air to land in brambles, her hearing was gone, shot, robbed by the 82mm mortar rounds blast and only a tree trunk being between them had saved her life.

She regained her feet and blundered about trying to find the track again. She could not see the Green Beret sentries, or hear anything, let alone a shouted challenge for a password.

The burst of automatic fire on the opposite side of the runway to that of the attack drew an immediate request for a sitrep from the CP.

The phrase Blue on Blue is rather innocuous and disguises the enormity of an incident in the same way that calling a dead civilian 'Collateral Damage' does. The unit medic arrived at a run but Captain Patricia Dudley was already quite dead.

Frustrated at the lack of progress and despairing at his men's reluctance despite there being an aircraft on the ground only a few hundred yards away. The Americans knew the ground well and had set up their defence accordingly. Lt Col Limanova had lost eight men within as many minutes of his attack starting and it ground to a halt. In his mind this was a stalemate, but in reality the professional soldiers had control of the engagement. He tried for air support to no avail and although he could find neither fault with the radio or its operator, but he was unable to raise anyone. This was thanks to silent jamming from the Americans. So involved was he with the radio and lack of communications he did not notice his force reducing in size as men slipped away, back in the direction they had come.

By the time Limanova decided on trying to get into a position where small arms could be used on the aircraft if it took off again, fire from his own militia towards the defenders was bordering on the pathetic. He left the radio operator with the mortarmen and went to investigate.

The jet aircrafts engine pitch altered and it began its take-off run. Limanova was reduced to shouting at the shadows to fire several aircraft lengths in front of it if they did actually see it.

Lt Col Limanova was on the track, kneeling and peering up into the rain, his AKM at the ready but he saw only a tail flame that suddenly appeared in mid-air, accelerating around in a great sweeping turn to dive into the ground at the same spot as his mortar and radioman. The blast deposited him several feet from where he had been standing to land in one of the many clusters of wheel ruts that had now formed large puddles on the logging trail. Earth, gravel and even parts of the radio operator and mortarmen were landing around him with a splash, a final mission critique on a now dazed Limanova's first mission as a sub district commander.

Patricia's death had demanded some kind of response, some action to mark her violent passing and the Maverick's destroying the mortar and anyone nearby would have to suffice.

The Green Berets abandoned their positions and slipped away into the night, taking with them Patricia's body to be buried in the forest at a traceable spot where she could be exhumed for proper burial by her family at some time in the future.

The shock and the grieving must wait though. They flew on, climbing to ten thousand feet to keep away from opportunists with Strela launchers, and turning due west with enough fuel, in theory, to reach NATO lines in Germany, but they had a head wind, the same one carrying the weather front from Western Europe to cover both Central and Eastern Europe.

Svetlana had been in her escape kit, camouflage coveralls over her civilian clothes and her face cammed to hide the shine for when the time came for her to evade away into the forest with the Green Berets. Her own 'G' suit had been buried after they arrived weeks before as she would not be using it again, at least that had been the thinking back then. She had retained only the thermals that Caroline called her 'pornstar suit' worn beneath jeans and sweater. So there she was, with a green and brown grease painted face and soil grubby G-suit in the back seat, wishing she had paid more attention when Patricia had once run through what her board could do.

She switched between *'Nav'* and *'Attack'* with a subsequent near cold sweat breaking out when she could not switch back. The 'Help' icon had saved the day, and that was now being employed as a tutor tool. Several hundred hours would be required for her to approach Patricia's level of skill, but she had to start somewhere. After a half hour though she was smart enough to know she wasn't smart enough.

"I am pretty much dead weight back here." She told her pilot. "I don't know if I'll be competent to do more than identify an attacker for you, Caroline?"

"Don't sweat it too much. The second seat was put in for the purpose of seeing how a command and control function would work. I could still fight the aircraft as normal, just a little slower."

Svetlana found the loadout screen. A single offensive weapon remained, and the defensive ordnance had become seriously depleted on the bombing mission too.

"One AMRAAM, that is… *Ahueyet!*…did I just touch the wrong button?" Svetlana's accent had switched from plummy Oxford English, to back alley Muscovite, and back again.

The plasma screens suddenly lost information for the second time that night. The RORSAT that had been launched out of Vandenberg airbase had apparently ducked when it should have dodged, or vice versa. The plasma screens de-populated as icons vanished.

"No, we just lost another multi-million dollar guardian angel, is all." Caroline said. "All that radar energy makes them easier to find than comsats…have you got a satellite icon on the top right of the toolbar?"

"Yes."

"Is it amber, red or green?"

"Flashing amber."

"Touch the screen and it will ask you to input an authentication code…"

"Got it."

The screens came alive once more.

"So tell me 'lana, is the war over soon?"

"As soon as a lot of gold gets paid to someone's secret bank account, and that was supposed to be following signals traffic intercepts indicating the Premier is dead after the site was nuked." Svetlana said. "You did get it, didn't you?"

"Sure did, but I can't confirm if he was there or not."

They flew on in silence, crossing the border into Belarus, then Lithuania, Poland and at last into Germany just north of a blacked out Berlin. Not quite home-free, the land below them was in enemy hands. Tentatively Svetlana typed out a request for a current situation report. The mission controllers knew where they were to an inch and she let them work out for themselves what was required.

From the air activity now becoming apparent, the war was showing no sign at all of stopping. CAP and close air support aircraft were landing and taking off, going to and from the approaching 4 Corps.

"Okay", Svetlana said, reading off a response to her situation update request. "The Elbe line fell two days ago and so did the Saale so the current defence if centred on a hill called the Vormundberg, west of Magdeburg, and our nearest safe airfield is Gutersloh."

"Forget it; we'll be flaming out before we get there." Caroline said. The headwind had been too much to cope with. "Still and all, we should be west of the Elbe when that happens so only about ten or fifteen miles to hike, by my reckoning."

Fifteen miles of enemy infested territory to reach the Vormundberg, always assuming that they had not been rolled even further west and the long hill was a new real estate acquisition of the Soviets, by the time they reached it.

Only twenty two miles to the south, an A-50 Mainstay had lifted off from Schönefeld, south east of Berlin. Its icon had it typed as soon as the RORSAT identified it and Patricia Dudley would have immediately picked up on the potential danger.

Cottbus airbase had provided the combat air patrol protection for the Schönefeld Mainstays, but the Belgian airborne brigade had put the base out of action for the foreseeable future. Consequently, the runway of the old WWII Luftwaffe base at Fürstenwalde to the east of Berlin had been hastily adopted for use by the MiG-29s.

The left side screens flared red as soon as the aircraft began radiating as it climbed through 10,000' on the way to its operational height of 38,000'.

It had them; the faint but definite return was a signature of the F-117s when caught in profile, close up.

The pair of MiG-29s were at 7 o-clock in respect of the *Petticoat Express's* position, aiming to intercept their charge. On receipt of the A-50s targeting feed the pair banked right and then left, putting themselves slightly below and a half mile behind the F-117X. Both MiGs put their radars to standby, which kind of confirmed for the Petticoat crew that the A-50 had them locked up.

"What do I do?" Svetlana asked.

"Nothing, just try not to barf in your mask."

Caroline selected their sole remaining ordnance from her position and when the *Vega* confirmed it had a solid downlink the rotating bomb bay doors cycled it out into a dark and very wet night.

The missile was under complete control of the Italian communications satellite, its sensors where also in standby mode but although it was cloaked electronically, its tail flame was still visible to the human eye.

"*KURIT' V VOZDUKHE!*" the flight leader shouted the missile launch warning into his radio. "Smoke in the air!"

The AIM-120 steered left and the Russian pilot lost sight of its tail flame. Their threat receivers were silent but both aircraft broke hard, discharging chaff and flares. They had not survived this long by taking anything for granted. Having completed a radical missile evasion manoeuvre the leader loosed off a pair of AA-8 Aphids under control of the A-50 so the super cooled IR threat sensor in the Nighthawk's tail did not trigger an alarm, it would bring them in from outside the sensors detection envelope.

The A-50 was also discharging counter measures, but it did them no good. The Vega brought in the AMRAAM for a head-on attack and for the second time that night one of the big Soviet AWACS fell victim to the Nighthawk. The forward twenty feet of the fuselage disintegrated and the aircraft crashed to earth upon the Templiner See Causeway on the outskirts of Potsdam.

With loss of guidance from the Mainstay the AA-8 Aphids IR seekers went active and Svetlana's world got turned upside down.

Caroline immediately rolled them inverted and pulled back on the side-stick, the automated defence systems spitting out flares as they dived. On her screen there flashed a red 'AIRFRAME OVERSTRESS' warning and an audible 'Whoop' in her headset until she eased off the manoeuvre but a shudder through the aircraft was a signal that something had just broken.

"Come on girl." She cooed soothingly and stroked the control panel. "Just a few miles more, honey."

The Aphids killed two flares and the MiG-29s overshot.

Caroline took them down to a thousand feet and back towards the west again.

The pair of MiGs took it in turn to go active on their radars, as much to tempt a response as it was to find the stealth aircraft. They flew a racetrack course before they too headed west, the logical destination for their enemy.

Their Zhuk-M radar came up empty, but the flight leader selected Aphids once more. The missiles sat on their pylons, the IR seekers active and discovered exactly what had broken on the Nighthawk.

A thermal shielding panel had come adrift and the weapons signalled a solid lock-on.

The MWS's pulsing tone told both Caroline and Svetlana that they had again been found as the Aphids were launched, accelerating to Mach 2.7.

Flares lit off in their wake again and the Nighthawk began a vertical jink.

A severe, school ma'amish voice intoned.

"All Flares Expended!...All Flares Expended!...All Fla..."

'AIRFRAME OVERSTRESS' flashed on the screen, the warning Whoop cut across the school ma'am, sounding twice, and the F-117X came apart at twelve hundred feet above the Ausruhen im Wald, still sixteen miles east of the Elbe.

Saale River Valley, Germany: nineteen miles east of the Vormundberg:

The crackle of flames, burning vehicles and the screams of the wounded were most evident as Dougal led Recce Platoon back yet another tactical bound.

The Nova Scotia Highlanders and the 2nd Canadian Mechanised Brigade were being reduced by the moment, hammered by a full division, the Russian 32nd MRD. The brigade commander had expected that rough weather would follow their kicking the legs out from under 3rd Shock Army's logistics, but he had never imagined anything on this scale.

He had contacted SACEUR and asked for permission to save what was left of the brigade, and so began the nightmare fighting retreat through the woods to the river Saale.

Dougal did not know at what point battalion headquarters had gone off the air, but brigade headquarters went silent around the same time, which left the Black Watch CO as senior officer with the unenviable task of getting them across the river and into the French 8th Armoured's lines where their combined numbers gave them a better chance of fighting off the Russian division.

Sergeant Blackmore brought up the rear, shouting a warning as a Leopard C2 of the Canadian VIII Hussars reversed, its main gun pointing back down the track they had taken but silent for lack of a suitable target; its machine guns though were firing short, economic bursts at the Russian infantry dogging their steps.

They had some two hundred metres to go to a harbour area where their LAV IIIs awaited.

The Leopard's main gun suddenly lowered slightly and fired at something in its thermal sight. Down the muddy track a fireball arose through the trees and small arms ammunition began cooking off in the wreckage of a BTR-70.

The platoon took up firing positions and waited for the A Company platoons to fall back through them.

In the darkness a vicious fire fight broke out as A Company hit the Russian infantry again. HE and smoke grenades were thrown to assist the Canadians to break contact and they passed through Dougal's men, carrying their wounded as they did so.

Dougal and his men lay there in the rain as the sound of A Company dimmed with distance behind them, and was replaced by cautious movement ahead in the dark woods.

A voice growled what sounded like a rebuke much further back, either an infantry officer forcing his men onwards or just as likely a KGB Political Officer urging an infantry officer to greater effort.

A flash and a bang from beside the track, just barely beyond minimum engagement distance and the Leopard staggered as a Sagger struck its right track, and in the flash of the missiles detonation he saw the Russian infantry coming through the trees.

The Leopards machine guns opened fire and Dougal's men poured it on to for several moments.

The driver's hatch of the Leopard opened and a figure pulled himself out.

"They've pulled back." The driver said. "Time to do the same, if you don't mind us coming with you, sir?"

Out of the turret came the loader and gunner, but not the commander.

"He's staying to see it's destroyed." The loader answered Dougal's query.

Dougal led them back but there was no A Company waiting for them. Perhaps they had received other orders, but either way Dougal now headed directly for where their vehicles had been camouflaged and left hidden.

After several minutes at a slow trot, their way ahead was obscured by a wall of thick, acrid black smoke from the burning tyres of a Coyote armoured reconnaissance vehicle. Dougal, coughing and his eyes smarting emerged from the smoke beyond it to find he had arrived at the harbour area. He took a pace forwards and stopped, aghast. Everywhere he looked there were smashed and burning vehicles of the Nova

Scotia Highlanders. Shell craters pitted the area, evidence that it had received the attention of a full regiment of artillery.

There was no one else about, just fallen and splintered trees, and burning LAV III IFVs.

"What now, sir?" Sergeant Blackmore asked.

Back down the track they had come along the Leopard's machine gun began firing. The vehicle commander had for reasons best known to himself decided to stay to the end.

"The river" Dougal replied "as fast as we can and over one of the ribbon bridges to join the French."

They moved out quickly, leaving the fiery vehicle graveyard behind them, slipping on the muddy track as they pushed on.

Behind them tank guns opened fire and the Leopard's machine gun sounded no more.

At last Dougal could hear the sound of running water and see flickering light through the trees. The smell of war was here too and the throb of an idling diesel engine was discernable.

The track ended suddenly and the encroaching trees gave way to the river bank with the Hungarian built ribbon bridge.

The diesel engine he could hear was directly opposite them, and a tank sat astride the ramp cut into the bank on the French side of the river.

No night viewing device was needed to identify it; the flames from a pair of burning Leclerc tanks were already illuminating the T-80 of the 77th Guards Tank Division as its machine guns opened fire.

TP 32, MSR 'NUT' (Up), north of Brunswick, Germany:

"What's it doing?" Staff Sergeant Vernon asked. He had gone to check on the eastern pointsman, Lance Corporal Tessa Newall.

The only sound now from the airfield was that of metal upon metal from the direction of the crippled T-90.

Staff Vernon was wedged into the gun pit of the 13 Platoon Wessex guys. Even given Tessa's slight build it was a little snug in there.

The gun controller was peering through the GPMG's starlight scope sight.

"An armoured recovery vehicle turned up a while ago and stopped inside the trees. The tank crew probed for more mines, and now the wrecker has come alongside and the mechanics are hitting that thing with ever bigger hammers."

"Can't you stop them with this?" he tapped the cold metal of the gimpy's top cover.

"Take a look for yourself." The infantryman told the military policeman.

S/Sgt Vernon put his eye to the sight and quickly withdrew it. A BTS-5B tracked recovery vehicle was alongside the tank, and a juicy high value target it made, but the open maw of the T-90s muzzle stared straight back.

"Off-putting, isn't it?" the gun controller said with a chuckle.

"They are conserving ammunition I reckon, but if we have a blat in their direction we'll soon know about it. We need something a bit bigger and the LAW80s don't have the legs."

"The radios are back up and there is some Italian artillery somewhere. We could give them a go?"

"No one here knows how to call in artillery fire, do you?"

"Yes actually." The staff sergeant replied. "I wasn't always a Monkey."

The map provided the Soviets grid reference and his compass the bearing from his location to the target. Unlike the remaining enemy tanks this one was not tucked in too close to safely call in fire from nine miles away, not without the risk of themselves becoming collateral damage at any rate.

The obvious problem, passing a fire control order in English to an Italian, was happily solved by the US mortar fire direction centre along at TP33 using one of its company's cooks to translate.

"Hello Mike Three One, Address Group Tango Alpha, this is Quebec One Two Bravo, address group Victor Zulu, relay to Golf One One Delta, address group Foxtrot Yankee, fire mission over?"

"Mike Three One, relay message for Golf One One Delta, address group Foxtrot Yankee, fire mission...send over?"

"Quebec One Two Bravo, fire mission grid five eight nine, zero six seven, direction zero two nine nine, tank and recovery vehicle in the open, neutralise, over."

"Mike Three One, fire mission grid five eight nine, zero six seven, direction zero two nine nine, tank and recovery vehicle in the open, neutralise, out."

There followed a delay as the company cook, a chef in a Sicilian restaurant in Bouckville, Mississippi, gave the message via field telephone to a battery commander who hailed from Genoa. Accent wise it was comparable to a resident of Somerset speaking to a Scottish Highlander, but it worked.

"Mike Three One, shot, over."

"Quebec One Two Bravo, shot, out."

Almost a minute passed before the US FDC transmitted again.

"Splash, over."

"Splash, out."

The three rounds missed by a good hundred metres and there was frantic activity as the crew of the high value asset, the armoured recovery vehicle, hurried to depart.

Calmly, the RMP NCO adjusted the fires and as the recovery vehicle carefully reversed back along the cleared path through the mines it received a near miss. But so did the gun pit as it did not take an Einstein to work out where the spotter was.

"On target, fire for effect!" Vernon shouted as the ground heaved from a sabot round that had already been loaded and ready in the guns breach. It was a far quicker process to fire an existing round than carry out a full unload. The guns twenty two pre-arranged rounds in the automatic loader were not a major task to rearrange but it still meant a delay when even seconds count.

Heavy calibre machine gun and lighter 7.62 rounds tore up the ground.

The GPMG was dismounted by its gunner braving the incoming fire to preserve it from damage, and the occupants of the gun pit huddled down to weather the storm. The next main gun round was HEF, high explosive fragmentation. Never has fifty seven seconds seemed so endless, but with the arrival of the next rounds a 155mm shell struck the engine deck and killed the crew as well as fling the turret twenty feet.

The tank was wrecked and the recovery vehicle was on its side burning.

"So you were an MFC or something, before you transferred to the RMP?" the gun controller asked, re-mounting the GPMG onto its tripod.

"No, that was the first time I ever called in a fire mission, even in practice."

They all stared at him.

"I was a civilian projectionist, and I showed old 8mm training films to RA army cadets on Tuesday evenings." The staff sergeant replied.

"Anyway, must be off."

Ariete Task Force
Autobahn 2

Echo One Five, the lead Lince with Lorenzo's tank squadron once again found the unmistakable signs of the Soviet's passage through the forest. It cut directly across their path where the enemy had turned south.

Lorenzo had them halt as his squadron caught up, and he left his tank to speak to the recce troop's commander at the young officer's request.

They squatted beside the muddy and deep indentations created by tank tracks, the rain now starting to turn them into puddles. He did not know what he and the recce troop commander were supposed to gain from the experience. He was in danger of allowing his sense of the ridiculous to take over. Had the young man sampled the mud between finger and thumb before announcing sagely that 'Long knife pale face's steel horses pass um thataway, maybe one hour, maybe two' he would not have been able to stave off the threatening laughter. It was not that he did not realise the seriousness of the situation, but lieutenant colonels get scared too and the human psyche will clutch at humour as a way to release the stress.

Indeed the young man had dipped a finger into the mud and held it for Lorenzo to smell. One of the vehicles was leaking fuel, but he scented petrol, not diesel. The Soviets were growing desperately sort of fuel if they were using the far more flammable petrol in at least some of their fuel tanks. Modern armoured vehicles were designed to run on diesel, although petrol, paraffin or even alcohol would keep them going if push came to shove, but at a cost. Crew and vehicle survivability was greatly reduced. Not for nothing had the petrol engined Sherman tanks of the previous war been nickname 'Tommy Cookers' by the German troops.

Echo One Two had its engine switched off but it coasted downhill, its driver controlling the speed with the vehicles handbrake so as not to have brake lights reveal its presence.

The Lince thermal scanners found nothing untoward between TP33 and the current position, four miles from Braunschweig airfield.

At the next truck stop, set on a slope cut into the forest, the downward incline of the autobahn ceased and the Lince engine restarted.

The absence of the enemy was perplexing. Somewhere out there was more armour of the Soviet's 91st Tank Regiment, and it had apparently come from blocking positions in the Lehre valley but now had vanished. Had they given up on the idea? If so, then why had they not appeared at the next TP where autobahn 2 crossed the canal?

Set just back in the sodden treeline behind the truck stop, a ZSU-23-4 reported the Italian recce vehicles passage. Completely reliant on battery power to operate its radios and muscle power to hand-crank the turret if necessary at that

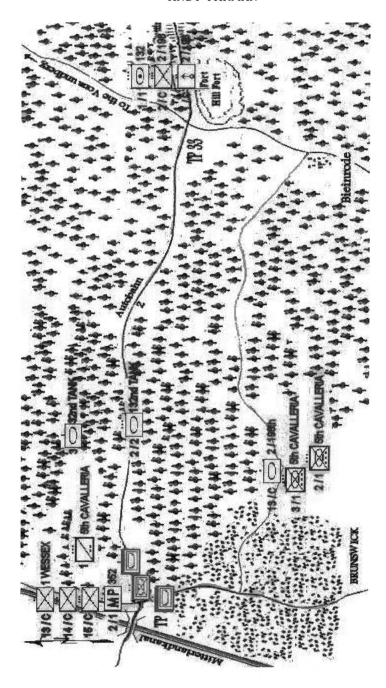

The Battle of the Autobahns 5

moment, the anti-aircraft artillery vehicle had escaped detection due to its lack of residual heat despite having been in situ less than thirty minutes. The vehicles refrigeration unit was hardly a requirement for the current area and weather the vehicle was now experiencing, and it was not an intentional stealthy addition to its manufacture either. 91ˢᵗ Tank was part of the Constanta garrison on the Black Sea coast, the 'Florida' of Eastern Europe, where high temperatures required specialist solutions for vehicles such as the Zeus. The ZSU-23-4 was a complex piece of machinery and notorious for overheating, even at the other climatic extreme on the often frigid Barents Sea coast. The engine overheated when stationary, as did the electrical systems, causing a shutdown, and it was therefore an operational necessity that the refrigeration unit be added to the Black Sea region units. The crew were aware of the unintended benefits to concealment even if the manufacturer at Mytishchi had not been.

Several minutes later the first Ariete main battle tanks hove into view.

The Soviet battalion commander listened to the reports of their appearance from the Zeus. He had been hoping for the entire force to continue its dash to TP32 as it had initially in reaching the hill fort in time to spoil his attack there.

"Driver, what is our fuel state?"

The answer cancelled any idea he may have entertained concerning the possibility of seeking out the Italian main body with an aggressive move back east to TP33, and surprising them with a meeting engagement.

Only three tanks had appeared which left him with the age old problem of guessing whether this was a lone unit or just the first of a larger force.

"All vehicles, advance to the tree line and engage the enemy."

The commander of the lead Ariete saw the heat sources appear in his thermal sight above them and to the right; seizing the commander's override he slewed the turret around to face the threat.

"GUNNER!... SABOT!...TANK.."

The enemy fired as the Ariete MBTs appeared in their sights. The lead Italian was hit three times and simply blew up. The second Ariete also received an immediate killing hit and the commanders and loaders turret hatches blew open. Like a pair of chimneys the hatches spewed smoke from the burning propellant of its own bag charges as the tank continued down the incline with its dead crew. The third Ariete had just jinked onto a new leg, the zig zag course throwing off the three gunners who had targeted it. One non-penetrating hit and two near misses had its driver suddenly reverse at an angle across the three lanes of the autobahn. It fired a sabot in reply, discharging both smoke and chaff grenades at the same time. Striking the crash barrier at speed it disappeared from view down the embankment where only swift action by its driver prevented its overturning on the steep slope.

The were no other NATO vehicles left to shoot and the T-72 to the left of the battalion commanders was pouring smoke from the turret as its crew bailed out.

He had both complete surprise and a better than three to one advantage over the Italians, so the two-for-one result was a poor one.

The second Ariete had reached the bottom of the incline and come to a halt. The fire in its turret reached the stacked HESH rounds in the lowest storage bins and explosions began tearing it apart from within.

They pulled back, retracing their route to the nearest fire break, arriving as 155mm rounds, called in by the survivor of the ambush, began landing on the edge of the lorry park. The next fall of shot landed on the right edge of the ambush position, the next in its centre and the last salvo struck the left side of the position. Expert fire control and gunnery, the Soviet commander wondered if these troops were chosen at random or were they some crack unit. He detached his last three IFVs to assist in the seizing of the autobahn over the Mitterland Kanal, and headed north with his tanks, intending to turn west again and await the remaining Arietes arrival at the bridge.

He would hit them from the rear as they counter-attacked and then he would see how good they really were.

The commander of the 13 tank did not like built up areas, it allowed a dismounted enemy to get in close, it provided countless ambush sites, and of course it robbed his M1 of its manoeuvrability.

The M1 and the Pumas avoided the shapes upon the car parks surface. Like scattered dolls, tossed away by a petulant child, the dead of D Company, 1 Wessex, lay where they had been cut down.

The giant furniture store burned out of control, flames leaping high despite the rain.

The 13 Tank and the Pumas had the benefit of eyes-on intelligence from 14 Platoon's LAW80 team on the elevated Autobahn 391.

Apparently far less concerned by the threat of the 94mm anti-tank rocket than they were by the Italian 155mm battery, the five remaining T-72s and T-90s were moving frequently but staying relatively close by to the autobahns.

The Italian commanders plan to draw out the vehicles to defend against his detached troop upon the autobahn had seemed a bust until three of the Soviet tanks went north along the tow path before dashing east beside Autobahn 2 under cover of smoke. This left the 13 tank merely outnumbered two to one, but whoever the guy was commanding the defence had a plan, apparently.

"TANK ACTION, *RIGHT!*"

A vibration on the road bed had caused some hopeful glances to the west, but the cause was not the arrival of 4 Corps but the next Soviet bid at taking the junction and bridge.

The pair of T-72s on the south side opened fire with high explosive fragmentation rounds, 12.7mm and 7.62mm machine guns.

Having climbed the embankment on to Autobahn 2 east of the airfield where they had RV'd with the IFVs. The Soviets did not wish to hanging about. Safety from the 155mm guns relied upon closing quickly with the defenders. However, the BTR's attempt to climb the steep embankment met with little success. Three T-90s sat on Autobahn 2; the BTR blocked the way for the tracked BMPs, its eight wheels unable to gain traction on the muddy slope.

Close to the bridge, the time had come to deal with the remaining pair of T-72s there.

Baz Cotter used the periscope for the GPMG's C2 sight to arrange the four crouching LAW80 operators out of view behind the crash barrier of Autobahn 2 and describe the target as he prepared a shermouli.

Each of the 94mm men had one of the weapons on their shoulders and a second weapon ready beside them.

"Okay, I can only see one of them, number two is out of sight in the loading bay of one of those little factor units. But, there is the one Nev already had a pop at and it is about one hundred metres straight ahead, and it is at a slight angle in the street." He lowered the device. "The good news is the turret isn't facing this way, the bad news is you can't see the missing ERA blocks where Nev hit because a wall is in the way, so aim for the right side of the turret, and obviously try and hit the same place."

"This had better bleedin' work or some arms dealer's customer services are getting a snotty letter from my solicitor." Nev said.

"Get ready Nev..." Baz rose up and aimed the shermouli at the tank, intending to put the flare beside the tank where they could see it without illuminating the entire junction.

He fired, and straight away it became obvious he had not thought it through that well. The thing did not simply hit the side of the tank and lie there obediently providing a source of light, it was rocket propelled and as long as the rocket was active it was not lying still for anyone. It ricocheted from the tank, to the road, to the wall, across the road and bounced off the wall there also before skidding along the road to fetch up beside the gutter.

The T-72 was back-lit by the flare and that would have to do.

Nev rose up, fired a spotting round and adjusted his aim before squeezing off the 94mm rocket, the third one to be fired by him at this same tank that night. An ERA block performed its design function, but a patch of armour was now exposed. Like a sluggish Mexican wave the AT men popped up and fired. Four 94mm rockets and no kill until Nev launched the fifth, and that finally penetrated and set off one of the tanks own rounds in the automatic loader.

The soldier beside Nev collapsed without a sound, hit in the face by a 7.62 round from the second tank which suddenly came into view.

The crash barrier provided cover from view but little else. Baz and the three survivors lay flat on the wet tarmac before crawling backwards.

The 13 tank came out of a side road and found the T-72's exposed rear filling its sights, the 105mm sabot penetrated the thinner armour behind the turret where the ammunition bins were, and it blew up.

With main gun raised to maximum elevation the 13 tank negotiated the embankment, but the Italian Pumas encountered the same problem the Soviet BTR had.

Hurriedly, a tow cable was disconnected and left to lie abandoned after a T-90s had towed the BTR up the embankment. Their gunfire support had abruptly ceased and neither T-72 was answering its radio. The BMPs gained the top of the embankment and all six fighting vehicles went straight into the attack, accelerating towards the junction and bridge, the tanks drawing ahead of the infantry fighting vehicles.

The same problem that the BTR found was also being experience by the Italian infantrymen in the 5th Cavalry Pumas.

The solution there was to debus and scramble up, hauling up the pair of Spike-MR launchers and missile canisters.

The missiles thermal seekers require no super cooling and they are capable of being launched as soon as the missile canister is attached to the launcher.

The left hand T-90 was struck on its forward glacis beside to driver's compartment by the 13 tanks sabot. ERA activated and rendered the hit ineffectual, the Soviet tank drove out of the resulting smoke and debris, returning fire.

Aboard the 13 tank a hammer blow was followed instantly by a wave of intense heat before the Halon fire extinguisher cut in. Suffering from flash burns the commander and gunner bailed out, as did the driver. The loader remained where he was, killed instantly by the penetrating round.

The right hand T-90 stopped suddenly, belching smoke and then flame, it was joined a moment later by its neighbour.

Suddenly finding itself alone and exposed the remaining tank began to jink from side to side. Its commander identified the cause of the other two vehicles demise.

"Gunner, HE, infantry anti-tank team!"

"Identified, but sabot loaded!" he reminded the commander.

There was no time waste reloading with a HE round, as the commander could see the crew were attaching a fresh canister.

"Fire!"

"On the way!"

The tungsten dart struck the tarmac beside the Spike crew, a killing result if it had been a HE round.

The Italian AT gunner fired, the tandem warhead defeated the ERA and the T-90 swung suddenly to the right, through the crash barrier to overturn on the steep bank.

Only four LAW80s remained, and with a maximum range of only 500m there were some tightening sphincters as the trio of Soviet IFVs, each with its accelerator mashed to the floor, closed on them rapidly. The BTR and BMP's 20 and 30mm cannons opened fire. Nev Kennington lay on the wet road, his body at a right angle to avoid the LAW80's back-blast when launching the 94mm rocket. He was aiming for the driver of the middle vehicle, waiting for the vehicle to come into range when it stopped and began to burn.

The attack by his last infantry, supported by a tank troop, had failed but the Abrams tank seemed to be out of action. He had eleven tanks remaining, how fast could the NATO anti-tank crews reload and how many reloads remained to them?

He would take the junction and deal with the rest of the Italians when they finally turned up.

In two files, keeping carefully to the tracks made by the first of his T-90s when they had attacked this airfield, they left the cover of the forest, the Romanian battalion commanders tank was number two in the right hand column.

"Gunner load HE...."

The lead tank shuddered to a halt with its hatches blowing off, still well within the minefield. The battalion commander had been looking intently at the junction but had not seen any obvious sign of where the shot had come from. He then noticed that the lead tank in the left hand column was also knocked out.

"Driver, go around it."

Clearly fearful of the mines but more scared of their unseen attackers the driver complied, intending to keep as close to the tank tracks as possible. He pulled out to the left, straightened up, and as he did so the left rear of the track went over a waiting bar mine.

Diesel from a ruptured fuel line would not have burnt, but the petrol in the fuel lines did, spreading to the fuel tank in moments.

Lorenzo's tankers picked off the Romanian T-90s from their positions back in the forest, targeting the enemy's engine compartments and being rewarded with single hit kills.

All eleven tanks burned with an awful ferocity.

For the second time that day, Lt Col Rapagnetta swore never to eat pork again.

CHAPTER 5

Vormundberg

L/Cpl Veneer and Guardsman Troper were members of the battalion defence platoon's most unloved, the Billy-no-Mates Section, or Air Defence, to give it its proper title. Every time they launched the enemy marked down the area for special attention. They now occupied a previously vacant location further up the hillside, their former trench having been compromised the previous day.

Drawing upon their previous experiences in the war they did not scrimp on sweat and effort. Extra sandbags were begged, borrowed or on 'permanent loan without the owner's knowledge or permission'. Their former 4 Company neighbours, all members of the 82nd Airborne, had greeted the move of the unwelcome pair in the typical heart-warming fashion of soldiers everywhere.

Abuse and catcalls had infuriated Troper as they carried out the move, and on ferrying the final item, a soggy package from his girlfriend via the British Forces Post Office, he had delivered what he believed to be the ultimate of insults to Americans everywhere.

"Yo Mother!" in best broad Lancashire accented imitation of a New York cab driver.

"What?" a mortar man from Minnesota had queried.

"You shagged my mother!" Troper qualified, turning away triumphantly.

There was a short pause as the meaning of the term shagged sank home, and howls of laughter followed.

L/Cpl Steve Veneer had shaken his head despairingly.

"You were meant to say 'I shagged YOUR mother.' You twat!"

They were now sat in the shelter bay of the new trench where Guardsman Andy Troper used his pen light to examine the contents of the package.

"That silly bitch cost me a thousand quid."

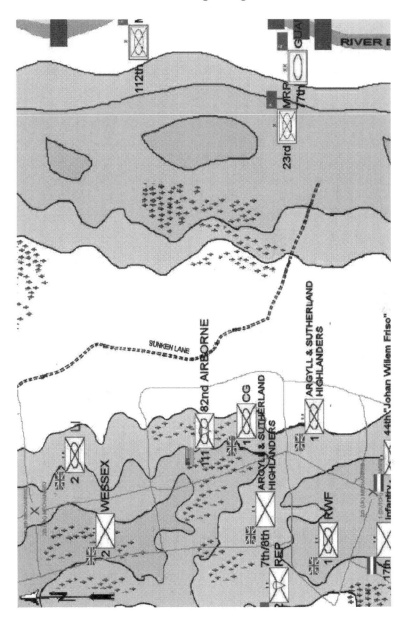

The Vormundberg UK Sector

Lance corporal Veneer reached across into the package and lifted out his mate's letter, the same one he had sent to his girlfriend.

Six fine woven rugby shirts, in the Blue-Red-Blue Divisional colours for the Guards had arrived that morning. Troper's samples were individually sealed in plastic; a large Coldstream Star on the chest of each shirt was flanked on each side by a depiction of a soldier aiming a shoulder launched AA weapon. One held a Blowpipe launcher at an angle of 45° and the other a Stinger. As a means of upping their profile and standing within the battalion the scheme had merit, but it was the execution that had been poor, so not even the most gifted marketing team could have shifted them, even at a loss. In place of the regiments motto, 'Nulli Secundus', Troper had elected to have a different form of wording to set off the garment, and it was that wording, which instead of bigging-up the section was in fact a typo that was going to cause derision in the ranks.

"A bit of punctuation and some lower case lettering in your instructions might not have gone amiss."

"Me biro was playing up in the damp." came a defensive reply.

"Spacing between words could have made all the difference too."

"It was dark."

"How many did you have made?"

"An 'undred."

"Never mind mate." Veneer said with sympathy. "Perhaps some wig manufacturer will take them off your hands after the war." He handed back the evidence that it pays to be literate. THEM SHI RTS HAVE T OHAVE THE S AME LOGOI NEACH BATC HAIR DEFENDERS.

Steve wondered if the Hair Defender rugby shirts would even sell on ebay? But he kept it to himself as Andy was having a bad day.

There had been no call on their services for almost a day. No fixed wing and no enemy helicopters either. Both soldiers had been on another hillside, above the river Wesernitz, when the

Soviets had given the battalion the full and undivided attention of a division's close air support, artillery and mortars. The day's light, to token, artillery and mortar fire which accompanied the latest attacks had been a distinct relief even if there had been no opportunity to show their ability again.

It had been quiet for a while, but they and their weapons remained ready.

The lull following the previous attack came to an end and with it the artillery and mortar fire.

The armoured juggernaut, 4 Corps, would not be stopped, and fresh orders, a renewed focus on the Vormundberg came into play.

Acting as a tripwire for the battalion, Bill and Big Stef had worked their way cautiously forward, covering only twenty five yards in the space of an hour but finding a spot where they could observe both the Czechs occupying the former positions of 7 and 8 Platoon and the far side of the valley.

All three of 3 Company's platoons had been withdrawn up the slope by Tim Gilchrist once night had fallen, digging the trenches firing bays in the soft earth but having no time to complete shelter bays. The foot of the hill belonged to the Czechs but most of the stores had been saved. The remainder had been booby trapped and destroyed in an explosion thirty minutes after their departure.

Activity in this captured position was the first indication that another attack was about to come their way.

The snipers passed up on several opportunities to kill obvious leaders, but at least they had located the positions of their next targets when the time came.

Artillery and mortar fire fell to their rear so they saw, rather than heard, when the Czech 23rd MRR's tanks broke cover and began to advance across the valley towards them.

They came on slower than usual, a mass of tanks, mixed T-76, T-80 and T-90 main battle tanks with ZSU-23-4 and BRDM-2 equipped with SA-9 air to surface missiles were dotted about in the mix.

Despite the circumstances, the almost complete lack of any remaining anti-tank mines, the way was led by T-72 and older T-60s equipped with mine ploughs.

"No APCs, no infantry fighting vehicles at all." Stef reported back to the battalion CP.

Bill nudged him with his foot. He was not looking across the valley but at the nearby trenches.

"These guys are in an awful hurry!"

Frantic activity had suddenly taken hold amongst the infantry.

"Oh crap; they're getting suited and booted for NBC, all masked up!"

After the initial, massive expenditure, of chemical weapons at the start of the war their use had petered out. Their principle means of delivery, artillery, had been choked off by the mass airborne landing in the Soviet's rear.

"They seem to know something we do not..." Stef hurriedly informed the CP of this important fact.

The snipers wore their 'noddy suits' beneath their ghillie suits, they ceased breathing as they pressed against the earth out of view to pulled on the masks. Despite the absence of chemical and biological weapons of late, they had continued changing the smock, trousers and air filters regularly. Wet weather can reduce the life span of both filters and suits by fifty percent and it had been raining solidly for two days.

The detector paper sheets that were currently upon their clothing and equipment were now changed as a precaution.

Stef produced a small booklet which declared itself in print to be 'Detector Paper, Chemical Agent, No.2, Mk 1, Liquid, One Colour'. Bill flipped across another with US stock numbers on the front, M8 Detector Paper, which allegedly identified the group a chemical agent came from, Mustard, Persistent Nerve Agents and the Non Persistent variety.

Stef affixed the small sheets to boots, upper arms, and the backs of their rubber gloves as well as to their weapons.

Back in the battalion CP the staff were hurriedly masking up. All along the Vormundberg masks and gloves were being pulled on and hoods were raised.

The buddy-buddy system came into play, crouching down in pairs to check the seal on your mate's suit and mask. Once suited and masked there were two main ways of identifying an individual; a hastily printed name in chalk or yellow crayon on a strip of black masking tape stuck to the chest of the charcoal impregnated smock, and one written on a piece of surgical tape on the masks 'forehead'.

The Operations Officer of 1st Battalion Coldstream Guards looked around for his commanding officer. Pat Reed had stepped outside with the acting adjutant a short while ago. The 2 i/c was aware of the reason, Timothy Gilchrist had informed him briefly of the death of the CO's son when Tim had been called away to take over 3 Company. The former adjutant and Pat Reed were quite close and such news would have best come from him, but as ever in war that ideal circumstance, bad news broken by a friend, is often denied to us.

With Tim now the OC of 3 Company there was another slot to be filled in the command chain, albeit temporarily. The acting adjutant had returned from his unenviable task but the CO had not. 'Ops' was the third in command of the battalion and raised the radio handset quickly.

"Hello all stations address group Hotel Zulu, this is Nine Bravo, *'Sceptic Arrow'* over."

The company, squadron and battery headquarters that were part of the battalion, or attached to it, began to answer in turn and inform their own sub units.

A figure in full NBC entered the CP, identifiable by gait and bearing as Lieutenant Colonel Patrick Reed, and the Ops officer vacated the CO's command spot.

As Pat Reed took his place the Ops officer looked into his commanding officers eyes, bloodshot with very recent outpourings of grief but now with a certain hardness, and anger, he had never seen in Pat before.

Once more the Hussars Challenger 1, 2s and Chieftains 10s occupied fighting positions. The CO wanted to open the defence with a TOT, a timed on target shoot, with all the heavy weapons available to the battalion hitting the enemy at the same instant. The different ranges and trajectories were all worked out by the artillery rep for the battalion but the target very much depended on the enemy's choice of approach route. The resulting Soviet counter battery fire meant the TOT could only happen the once because shoot and scoot would then be the name of the game. As they only had that one opportunity to inflict maximum damage and a telling shock effect they had better get it right, and those had been Pat Reed's words early in the evening.

Major Venables stared into his sights at the approaching armour, the accompanying artillery barrage now falling heavily about them, shrapnel from airbursts striking the armour.

"I could have got used to there being no artillery," his driver said over the intercom, his voice slightly muffled by the mask.

"All good things come to an end…" now it was back to business. "Okay, heads back in the game, we can forget the plough tanks as priority targets, so look for command tanks and AAA vehicles, people." Mark Venables would have preferred a battalion commander, but he saw three enemy tanks with clusters of antennae, the lead company commanders if their positions were anything to go by. It was too good an opportunity to miss, and destroying all three at once would pay a bonus in shock effect too. Keying his radio mike he began to set it up.

"Hello Tango One One Alpha and Tango One Two Charlie, this is Tango One…"

Bill checked the detector paper that was stuck liberally about himself and his equipment; it was all clear despite the barrage. Had the Czechs in the captured trenches received the wrong directive? No, they were all of them still suited, booted and alert now.

Elsewhere along the Vormundberg, detector paper and electrical devices were being checked but all remained clear. It was unlike the enemy to give more than a couple of minutes' notice to its own advance troops lest they lose the benefits of surprise.

"Where's the infantry then?" Stef asked. "Where are the IFVs?"

With that tank battalion now half way between to the sunken lane and the start line a second battalion of thirty tanks appeared out of the trees across the valley.

"How very retro." Bill murmured, having swung his sights back in that direction.

Each tank carried perhaps a dozen infantrymen clustered upon it, and twice that number crowded behind in the machines wake. A thousand man infantry battalion doing it the way their grandfathers had.

These were also in full NBC order. It had to be heavy going for those on foot as the enemy's suits retained heat just as the NATO version did.

"What is the betting they only had enough fuel for the tanks, not the grunt buses?"

"Air Red!...Air Red!" the radio blared.

To the rear, the battalions Royal Artillery air defence launched a trio of Starstreak missiles at the approaching threat, and the battalions own dedicated air defence troops stood-to with Stingers.

Two regiments of SU-25 'Frogfoot' aircraft had been assigned the sorties to deliver the underslung ordnance at two locations. No precision bombing was required; however, the munitions required these ground attack aircraft release at a greater altitude than the pilots felt safe with.

The close air support squadrons had each begun the day with fifteen airframes apiece, but with each regiment, or wing, sortieing forty eight aircraft against the US 4 Corps. By midday they were still sending four dozen aircraft up, but only by using the squadron's spares.

It was midnight now; the losses of the day had reduced the regiments to an average thirty aircraft available to continue the attack, although ground crews worked furiously to repair damaged machines back at the airfields.

A change in orders, a complete change of load-out, and all direct from the High Command apparently. It had delayed the take-off before bombing-up could commence. They were now late as a result and had to burn precious fuel in an attempt to make up the time.

They came from the north east, with the wind behind them, and the approach of both regiments divided up the defender's assets although one of the regiments had the Vormundberg as its secondary, not primary target.

Flares and chaff were discharged by the lead squadrons which dived towards the earth to evade without pressing home with their ordnance loads.

AAA has a habit of frequently relocating, as that is the surest means of their survival, and none of the firing points matched those of the previous day's attacks.

The foremost flights of the second regiment were engaged upon dedicated 'Wild Weasel', AAA suppression. Having now identified anti- aircraft units all along the Vormundberg they began launching anti-radar missiles, and looking for target's for cluster bomb munitions.

French, Dutch, British and US units south of the hamlet of Vormund were the focus of the air effort, and weapons flew both ways between the attackers and the defenders, long and medium range missiles passing each other in the sky.

Steve Veneer waited for a green light to appear in his sights and fired immediately, the Stinger launched with its accompanying smoke and audible signature, flying true, and straight into a Frogfoot's port side engine intake.
Neither Steve nor Andy Troper saw the aircraft hit, they were back below ground inside the shelter bay.

The pilot ejected, leaving the aircraft as it became a fireball and lost consciousness in the blast, falling to earth with his burning parachute trailing behind.

Unnoticed almost, twenty aircraft performed pop-up manoeuvres, tossing half of their ordnance in the direction of the long hill. The weapons did not fall all the way; altimeter fuses triggered them at five hundred feet above ground.

The flashes of the air bursting bombs were eclipsed by falling artillery shells and mortar rounds. Two attackers fell to the air defences and a third aircraft limped home, trailing smoke.

British chemists at ICI in 1952 had discovered a new organophosphate and it was initially marketed two years later as a pesticide under the trade name of Amiton. Obviously ICI were unaware of the full extent of the chemicals effects upon the human nervous system at that time. Inhalation and contact with the skin was extremely hazardous to health as even a 10mg drop on exposed skin would be quickly absorbed by the body. Muscular twitching, running nose, vomiting and a tightening of the chest soon followed before paralysis of the diaphragm muscles caused death by asphyxia. Too toxic for safe use, Amiton was withdrawn from the market but the genie was out of the bottle now. The Ministry of Defence began research on Amiton at its chemical weapons research facility at Porton Down. Once weaponised, Amiton was renamed 'VX' and assigned the code name *Purple Possum* to keep its existence hidden from the rest of the world.

But nothing remains a secret for long.

NAIAD, an easier acronym to say in a hurry than Nerve Agent Immobilised enzyme Alarm and Detector, began to sound as the warheads contents, now falling in aerosol form, triggered the alarms. But for the rain the VX would have been carried upon the wind for the entire length of the Vormundberg.

NAIAD, and its equivalent's in other NATO units screeched, one-colour chemical detector paper turned blue, Stef and Bill's M8 paper turned yellow. Only the persistent, lingering nerve agents of the 'V' family of poison weapons caused the paper to do that.

The air raid was over as quickly as it had begun, three multi-million ruble aircraft had become fiercely burning wreckage scattered over the German countryside, an elderly Chaparral had been struck by an anti-radiation missile, and Rapier launcher fell to cluster munitions whilst artillery spotters called in the fires on the sites of three shoulder fired launches.

The sniping pair passed on a brief Chem-Rep to the battalion CP and got back to the task of observing and reporting, awaiting the battalions coordinated response.

It was not long in coming.

"Sir, Company Sarn't Major Hornsby is asking for permission fire. He has a stack of fire missions for his mort..."

Pat Reed cut the signaller off in mid-sentence.
"When CSM Hornsby was Lance Sarn't Hornsby he knew what a TOT shoot was." The commanding officer snapped. "Tell him to do as he was damn well briefed to do or he'll be a full screw once more!"

Those who heard the exchange paused to glance at one another at the out of character show of temper.

"Ask Stephanski and Gaddom how far they are from the sunken lane?" Pat demanded, leaning forwards with both sets of knuckles, clad in rubber NBC gloves, bearing his weight on the map table.

The artillery rep had heard the snipers reporting infantry unprotected by their fighting vehicles and addressed the CO.

"Sir, with regard to the infantry now being in the open, perhaps we should amend the fire plan to include airburst instead of super-quick fusing?"

"The fusing is fine as is." Pat responded, without looking up.
"But sir...."

"You let me worry about fighting this battle young Captain, and you concern yourself with making sure your gunners hit what we tell them, understood?"

Having been put firmly in his place, the artilleryman was turning to return to the RA's corner of the CP when Pat spoke again.

"The lead battalion of tanks is of more concern to me right now but the mortars are wasted on heavy armour so switch them to the second echelon ."

Yes sir." He turned to go again.

"Oh and Captain."

"Sir?"

"Mix WP with the mortar fire mission." Pat instructed.

The artillery rep was well aware that the rules of war forbade the use of white phosphorus as a weapon against infantry, but they forbade the use of VX also, did they not?

"Yes Colonel, right away."

Bill watched the battalion of armour come on, untroubled by so much as a stray round, despite the slower than normal speed.

They had killed a lot of this regiment the previous day, but now they were back, reinforced with armour if not troops. Instead of three infantry battalions and one tank battalion, 23rd

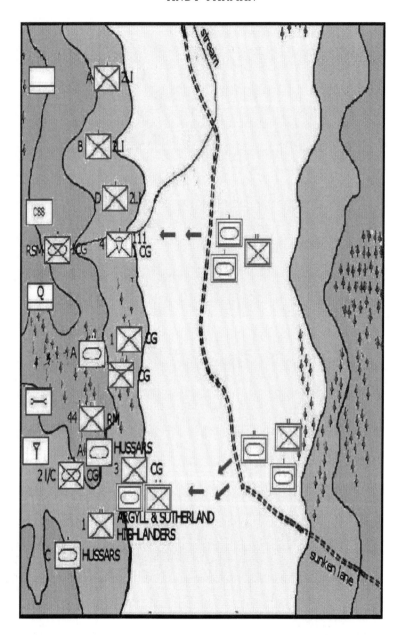

Final assault by the 23rd MRR 1

now consisted of two infantry and two tank battalions, albeit it all were below strength they still outnumbered the battalion of British Guards and US Paratroopers who they considered the weak link.

Fifty seven armoured vehicles, AAA tracks, self-propelled anti-tank guided weapons launchers and of course main battle tanks along with its remaining infantry. The 23rd Motor Rifle Regiment was driving towards less than five hundred guardsmen, paratroopers and a half dozen tanks.

They had been 1CG's first opponents in this war, months previously, on the hill above the Wesernitz river.

Barely more than a hundred guardsmen who had been on that particular hillside remained with the battalion now. Half of the original battalion had died on the Wesernitz in that first battle. Lt Col Huppert-Lowe, the then CO, and his rover group had perished in the flames of napalm hell as he attempted to restore command and control with 1 Company. The battalion CP had been destroyed soon afterwards by a random, lone 240mm mortar round. All communications and coordination had been lost and just two rifle companies, with part of Support Company, had fought their way out. The remainder, both the prisoners and wounded, the 23rd had bayoneted or shot.

Certain elements of the media, none of whom had been present, had shamelessly capitalised on the battle in order to sell copies. A photograph of the battalion on ceremonial duties, the red plumes in their bearskins photo-shopped into yellow, had adorned the front page below the headline 'They Ran!' The stain on their honour had remained with them, bolstered of late by the Defence Minister as it suited the needs of her own agenda.

Few survivors of the Wesernitz were watching now, the remainder huddled in their water-logged shelter bays as their positions were pummelled by artillery and mortar fire.

The Soviet artillery west of the Elbe had received only a limited resupply via helicopter, a trickle in comparison to their needs and it had been husbanded on the orders of General Borodovsky, the Front Commander. It was stockpiled in case 77th Tank and 32nd MRD could not reopen the logistical supply lines before the US and Canadians of 4 Corps arrived. But in the last hour had come word that Borodovsky had been replaced, as had all the leadership at High Command apparently. Every effort must now be made to overturn this final obstacle NATO had placed in their path, and drive to the coast. 4 Corps could be brushed aside before it could transition into a defensive posture. Success, not excuses, was all that the High Command wanted. Everyone was expendable.

Within the lane the remains of that first attack had new additions lying on top and here and there it was possible to use the burnt out fighting machines as a bridge, otherwise the armour had to negotiate the lanes steep sides.

"That's fifty metres, as near as dammit." Bill observed.

"Wait until they crowd up." Stef grunted, his voice muffled by the respirator.

The previous day had seen carnage along this section of the lane during the very first attack by the Red Army upon the Vormundberg hillside. Pat Reed had called in smoke, not HE, blinding the lead ranks which had driven full pelt through the hedgerow bordering the sunken lane. No anti-tank ditch could have worked so well.

The tanks now slowed.

British Army Air Corps Apache attack helicopters and Danish Lynx singled out the Zeus and Gaskin anti-aircraft vehicles for attention.

Pat Reed listened to Lance Sergeant Stephanski confirm the lead tank battalion was bunching up before the sunken lane.

He gave the order to open fire himself, raising the microphone.

"All stations address group Hotel Zulu...start killing those bastards."

The 105s fired first, followed by the battalion's mortars. The Milan, TOW and Hellfire missiles came next, and finally the

120mm rifled L11A5 and L30 guns of the Challengers and Chieftain 10s.

In the ideal Timed on Target world, each shell, each missile, each round would arrive at once, but it was close enough that they arrived within a two second time span.

Mark Venables had the commander's tank of the left hand company dead to rights and the Challenger II rocked backwards on its sprockets when he fired. It was a killing hit and he released his override, allowing his gunner to fight the tank whilst he fought what remained of his squadron.

The 105s had sowed confusion as well as knocking out one T-72 and shearing the tracks of two others. Milan rounds had killed two more, as had his own squadron's tank guns. Zeus and Gaskin vehicles burned. It was a good start but the friendly artillery had fallen silent as the gunners relocated hurriedly.

Further to the rear the shrapnel from bursting mortar rounds had swept a couple of tanks clear of their passengers and others had leapt off, rolling in the mud in an attempt extinguish the white phosphorus that had fallen upon them. In the darkness and poor visibility a few tanks ran over contorting figures in their path.

Looking right he located the second command tank, it was stopped with smoke issuing from its open hatches, the crew bailing out. He looked again, seeing that not quite all the crew had abandoned the vehicle. The company commander was knelt at his open hatch and operating a fire extinguisher on the smouldering bags of propellant inside. He seemed to be making headway as the smoke was lessening. Without warning he collapsed, like a puppet with its strings cut he toppled headlong through the open hatch. The battalion's snipers were busy about their deadly trade, and earning their rations.

The third command tank was stationary and burning fiercely despite the rain.

The Challenger fired again, targeting a T-90 cautiously moving across the dead hulks of previous attackers, it stopped dead, denying crossing point to the others in line behind it.

Having fired twice from the same location Venables driver reversed the vehicle out of the fighting position and headed for a fresh spot.

The first Soviet tanks dropped from view and reappeared on the NATO side of the sunken lane, targeting Milan firing points and the Hussars Chieftains and Challengers, attempting to suppress the defenders fire until the obstacle was negotiated. A TOW fired by a Lynx of Eskadrille 723 destroyed one of these guardians but it been forced to remain hovering until the wire guided weapon struck. A *Refleks* missile sped across the intervening space, launched from a T-80's main gun it struck the Lynx before it could withdraw from view and the helicopter exploded.

Bill used the TOT shoot for cover, the noise masking the sound of the shot as he killed the commander of the Soviet troops in the captured trenches. He and Stef then edged away, moving back into more friendly territory.

Despite the success so far, it was not going to be enough to prevent the bulk of the 23rd from reaching the hill. Close quarters combat was not something within the snipers remit and so they withdrew to higher ground.

Above them droned Soviet counter battery fire, the heavy mortars targeting the ground the Guards and 82nd's fire had been backtracked to, and the artillery shells falling in the valley behind the Vormundberg.

The Soviet fire had not slackened, it merely switched from pounding the once wooded slopes in order to fire counter battery missions before shifting back, a fact noted with relish by Major General Dave Hesher. MLRS sub munitions trashed five entire batteries of the 23rd's artillery support.

"Air Red!...Air Red!...Air Red!..." was again broadcast.

Several minutes later NAIADs on the rear slopes screeched anew as SU-25s tossed more air bursting ordnance at the hill's defenders on their way back from doing the same to 4 Corps. They did not press home an attack with conventional weapons but dived to the tree tops and headed east, throwing out flares and chaff in their wake.

By the time the 105mm guns of 40 Regiment RA fired again the last tanks of the lead Soviet battalion where clear of the sunken lane.

Firing two rounds apiece the guns were departing for a new gun line before the Soviet gunners could respond. The first battery's rounds landed harmlessly to the rear of the tanks but the second battery landed among the centre company, disabling one and destroying another.

The Hussars fired and moved, fired again and reversed quickly. The Milans of the Anti-Tank platoon lost a precious crew, killed three more Soviet MBTs in revenge, but the tanks of 23rd MRR still came on.

So involved became that fight with the leading echelon that the movements of the second echelon were only noticed late.

They had accelerated, carrying those infantry upon the tanks hulls rapidly to the foot of the hill. Half were closing up behind the first echelon, but the remainder of the second echelon's infantry borne on tanks were almost at the juncture of where the Guards left flank met the 2nd Battalion Light Infantry's right.

Pat had fully expected the 23rd's first battalion sized effort to attack in this fashion yesterday, seeking weaknesses in the flanks, but they had defeated it, utterly, before it reached half way across the valley. It would now seem that someone over there thought it too good a plan to waste.

Pat had been wrong footed by expecting the 23rd to exert its entire, remaining fighting power where they already had a toehold. The paratroopers of the 82nd were about to pay the price for that lapse.

In front of 3 Company's positions the Soviet tanks were being picked off according to a pre-arranged plan using the Apache, Lynx and Hussars. But the old adage was holding true 'No plan survives first contact with the enemy'.

"Warn 4 Company...."

"Too late sir, they are in close contact already!" the Ops Officer had the landline handset to 4 Company CP in his hand, the roar of small arms and detonation of grenades clearly audible from across the table.

They drove clear across 16 Platoon's trenches, machine guns blazing and the infantry on the decks firing downwards into the positions. They lost an elderly T-60 plough tank and a T-90 to multiple strikes from the shoulder launched LAW-80s but continue on. The remaining tanks slowed to allow the infantry to debus in the centre of 14 Platoon, the company's in-depth position. It was a good tactic as it initially inhibited the fire from 15 and 16 Platoons.

Fierce hand to hand fighting raged within 14 Platoon's lines but the enemy were not there by pure chance and those not involved in the trench fighting moved on up the hill with a company moving into the stream bed that marked the boundary between 1CG and 2LI's turf.

Behind 14 Platoon at the company CP, Lance Sergeant Gibbons, the Signals Platoon rep for 4 Company and the only Coldstreamer, fired at a Czech rifleman crowding through the entrance. The shot smashed the visor of the soldier's respirator and exited through the back of the head, sending his helmet spinning away. A grenade from outside followed moments later, hitting the sandbagged side of the doorway before landing upon the wooden pallets that lined the floor. The company's first sergeant, Jerry Anthony, flung himself on top of the grenade, smothering it with his body and dying instantly but more grenades were tossed through the doorway and their detonations were followed by automatic fire.

Despite his wounds, bleeding from ruptured eardrums and coughing up frothy blood, Captain O'Regan, the OC of 4 Company, recovered consciousness and spoke into the handset he had been using when the grenades had gone off. His NBC suit was torn and he had lost his respirator in the grenade blasts. VX in the air began to take effect and his voice, coupled with violent muscle spasms, caught the attention of a trio of infantrymen from the 23rd who were looting the dead, tossing wallets and watches into a bag of decontaminating Fullers

Earth. They crowded about the injured American, their bayonets rising and falling repeatedly.

Lightning flashed overhead, immediately followed by thunder. This was Mother Nature's doing, not mans, and the rain redoubled in intensity as if making up for the enemy shell and mortar fire that had abruptly lifted, falling elsewhere to inhibit reinforcement.

"Hello Four Six Delta this is Nine Four Bravo, over?"

"Four Six Bravo, send, over." Spider replied.

"Nine Four Bravo...shoot Eff Pee Eff Four Four Four Lima, over!"

The US Airborne company on their right with 1CG was calling in mortar and machinegun fire on its own company command post. Company headquarters are always at the rear of their sub units and everyone with a radio now knew there was a breakthrough in progress.

Spider called off the bearing and elevation for FPF444L and attached his bayonet to his personal weapon in readiness.

On the right flank of 2LI, men attached their bayonets too, and placed grenades where they could be easily reached.

The professionals and 'weekend warriors' alike, all of the trenches occupants on the right flank faced right and waited.

L/Cpl Veneer and Gdsm Troper heard the triple digit call as they were part of the company net.

Leaving their shelter bay they fixed bayonets and peered into the darkness. They had no night sights for their rifles, just the monocular qualities of the rifles SUIT sights, the Sight Unit, Individual, Trilux.

Checking their pouches they laid their fragmentation grenades and spare magazines on the shelf below the parapet of the trench. Andy Troper pulled a set of brass knuckles over his rubber 'outers', the NBC gloves.

They could hear the sound of fighting dying down below them but they did not know who the victors were, was it the US Paratroopers or the Soviets? If it were the Yanks then they would know all about it the very next day, the abuse would be heaped on with remarks about playing with aeroplanes instead of doing real soldiering.

""What the fuck are you wearing them things for? You can't shoot for shit with them on!"

"I can't shoot for shit at the best of times." Andy replied. "I've never passed an annual personal weapons test in me life."

"How come you're a Band 1, Class 1 then?"

"I normally pay you to fire on me target on range days, remember?"

"Oh? Oh yeah, right." Steve replied.

They stood silently in the fire bay, with the rain falling on them as they listened for tell-tale sounds in the night.

The charcoal impregnated hoods were not made with stereophonic clarity in mind but after five minutes a faint sound of metal upon metal was followed by other noises of human origin. The squelching sound of boots in soft mud, and an oath as someone slipped. Then of course there was the sound of something landing in the mud by their own feet.

There was no thought involved, simply reflex as each man scrambled from the from the trench with his rifle and rolled clear.

The grenade went off harmlessly but scattered their spare magazines and their own grenades too.

Mud and earth were landing wetly, and thick black smoke, the residue of high explosive, still hung over the damaged fire bay as they re-entered, rolling back in immediately, knowing they would now be rushed.

They came out of the darkness from directly in front, shouting their hatred even though the effect was muffled.

The Coldstreamers fired, and fired again, but then they were parrying away the stabbing bayonets and thrusting upwards with their own. Their breath and that of their attackers came in gasps, laced with fear and desperation. Outnumbered but fighting all the more desperately because of that.

A bayonet thrust down and pierced Andy Tropers left ammunition pouch, and he let go his own weapon and grabbed the AKM by its hot barrel, tugging its owner off balance and head first into the fire bay. He crouched over the man, punching hard with the brass knuckles, smashing the Soviet soldiers jaw in order to reach what he really wanted to hit, the throat.

Steve had killed the last man, bayoneting him in the visor, the blade penetrating the brain via the eye socket.

Andy stood, gasping for breath, the Soviet soldier making gurgling sounds and thrashing about for a moment before becoming still.

Together they hoisted the body, evicting it from the trench and stacked the dead men's weapons against the trench wall.

They had killed six, a squads worth. How many were they likely to send against a single trench?

Adrenaline and effort, and of course NBC suits inability to let excess body heat dissipate, was making them both gasp for breath as if they had run a race.

"Do you think that's all of them?"

An RPK machine gun opened fire pinning them down in the trench so that more troops could close in on them.

There were no grenades coming at them this time, the RPK kept firing until the riflemen were almost on the trench.

There were seven of them this time, firing wildly as they charged the last few yards. Steve shot two and Andy managed to get one also before the rest closed. Again it was vicious and bloody work, but they won through, justifying all the bayonet practice over the years they had served. One man retreated, but not far. He was inside grenade range as the Guardsmen cleaned house again, rolling the dead over the parapet and policing up the weapons.

The grenade could have gone unnoticed but for it striking Steve Veneer's helmet before dropping into the fire bay. Again they rolled clear but Andy was empty handed, his SLR was now destroyed along with their cache of captured weaponry.

Steve heard, rather than saw the grenadier and one of the three rounds he fired left the man screaming from his wounds until the VX claimed him.

Again the RPK opened fire, but there was a second parapet to the trench now, a soft one, and not much of a muchness as regards its bullet catchment qualities. It did however provide cover from view for L/Cpl Veneer to put some well aim shots down, using the muzzle flash of the RPK as his aiming marker.

The gun stopped firing but Steve had no way of knowing if he had hit its gunner or merely scared him off.

He crawled backwards into the trench to find Andy Troper groping about in the mud.

"You got any more rounds mate? That grenade blew everything to shit 'n gone."

Steve checked his magazine."

"I've got two rounds and then I'm out?"

They both heard the sound of more of the enemy approaching, and on the left flank as well as straight ahead this time.

Andy lifted the damaged Stinger's launcher from out of the mud. The hand-guard he been blown off along with the battery coolant unit and he held it by the Venturi end. The sight unit's forward hinge was smashed and it lolled drunkenly on the back one until Andy pulled it off and tossed it away. He gave the launch tube a trial swing, and apparently satisfied he rested it on his left shoulder, bearing it casually as if it were a cricket bat and he had the measure of the bowler before even reaching the crease.

"It's been an honour mate." He said, holding out his hand to Steve.

Keeping close to the sides of the streambed, a huddled mass of infantry from the 23rd Motor Rifle Regiment crouched in the mud, waiting for the signal to split up, to head for their next objectives. The company headquarters CP of the British Light Infantry battalion to the north of the stream, the Guards 1 Company CP, and its regimental quarter masters ammunition stores, they had all been identified by radio intercepts , 'SigInt', and aerial photographs. Antiquated though it may seem, and arduous is the task of laying D10 field telephone cable, but it will always remain more secure than radio and microwave communications. As far as the aerial photographs are concerned, well that is what track plans are supposed to prevent.

Sustained fire from GPMGs to the north, south and west began to fall further down the hill, landing on the company headquarters that had been their first objective. Mortar rounds followed, destroying the CP and twelve Soviet infantrymen in and around it, including the killers of Sean O'Regan.

The plan had originally been conceived when they still had fuel for their infantry fighting vehicles and the entire battalion would have been here now. The remainder of the battalion was still making its way on foot from the sunken lane. The tank support had made it though, at least some of it anyway.

Grinding up the hillside behind them came a pair of T-90s, not the two troops worth that they had been assured would be there for them.

The company commander assigned both tanks to the attack on the Light Infantry, reasoning that there was a known enemy company position standing in the way and he and the company political officer took their place behind the second of those comfortingly bullet-proof pieces of machinery.

The remainder split up and headed uphill in different directions.

"Why has the shelling stopped, sir?"

Oz answered his stores assistant with a question of his own.

"If someone gave you a horse as a gift bonny lad, would you count its teeth before accepting it?"

They slipped and slithered here and there on the muddy path, the cumbersome NBC overshoes lacking the traction of proper boots soles. It was steep here on this part of the path leading from their CP to the vehicle track some distance away. The vehicle track led to various rear locations, including the path to the RQ's ammunition store.

The storeman led the way, the wood and canvas stretcher now furled and carried balanced on one shoulder and his SLR over the other, muzzle downwards to keep out the rain.

From years of habit, especially as an instructor, Oz carried his own weapon with the butt in the shoulder, a full magazine attached and the cocking handle out in readiness, but his SLR was uncocked. Oz had cut off an NBC gloves rubber finger-

piece to act as a muzzle cover, and this simple device kept
water and mud out of both the muzzle and the flash
eliminators apertures.

Lightning flashed and ahead they saw a line of men coming
toward them along the same narrow path.

The young guardsman stepped to one side to let them pass,
carefully ensuring the stretcher was not going to smack anyone
in the forehead.

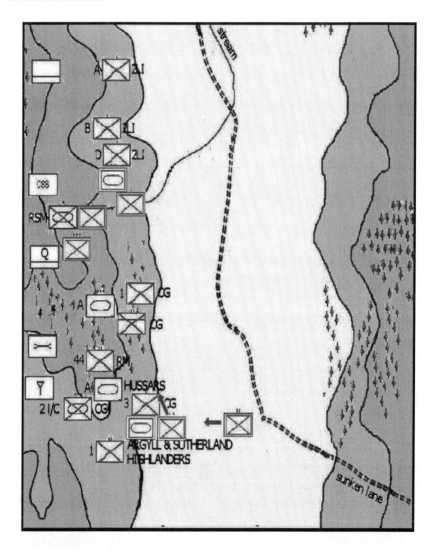

Final assault by the 23rd MRR 2

Bayonets lanced out, stabbing the 1 Company storeman through the chest multiple times. With both lungs perforated and no air remaining to shout or cry out, the soldier collapsed noiselessly, still impaled on a bayonet.

Again the lightning flashed and Oz, who was momentarily frozen to inaction, saw that these were Soviet troops, not friendlies.

Placing a boot on the dying man's throat the lead soldier used it for purchase to withdraw his bayonet and then lunge at Oz.

Muscle memory, automatic reaction, or just good training that had been drilled home at the Guards Depot, Pirbright took over and Oz cocked. He knew he had no time to aim and fire so he stepped forward into the Enguarde. The Soviet soldier used his rifle and bayonet like a stabbing spear, aiming for the colour sergeants solar plexus. The Geordie ex-coal miner parried, with powerful shoulders outmatching the strength of his opponent he knocked the others weapon off its line. Metal rang loud upon metal as the underside of the SLR's barrel struck aside that of the AKM's. Half turning he drove the SLR's butt full force into the face of the enemy soldier, shattering the eye pieces and driving him backwards into the man behind.

The Soviet troops had not fired, seeking to close with the 1 Company CP undetected.

Oz closed one eye tightly and fired twice into the packed file of men, two rapid shots, the heavy 7.62 rounds ripping through several men and the muzzle flash robbing all except himself of their night vision, and then he was gone, leaping desperately off the path and into the darkness below. Feet together and knees bent as if performing a parachute landing roll, Oz hit the dark slope, rolling with it, knuckles white as he attempted to retain his rifle. A wild burst followed, the sound of the AKM distinctively differing from that of an SLR or SA80. A shermouli rose up from a trench to the rear of the CP and the sentries, the OC's Orderly and his driver, opened fire with their GPMG.

The bayonet wielding lead man had been the Czech platoon commander, and his sergeant was bringing up the rear. When the firing began the sergeant pushed forward, halting a panicked rush back along the path. He held them at a bend where they could crouch down out of the line of fire. He saw the British machine gunners could not see the downhill slope from their current position, but he could work carefully along that way and deal with the machine gun position with grenades.

Not including the platoon commander and three men shot by Colour Sergeant Osgood, eleven men more men were dead, or as good as. Even the slightly wounded were on borrowed time in that chemical laden air.

The parachute flares that the British kept putting up were a double edged weapon, aiding both sets of antagonists. He selected the steadiest half dozen men to distract the machine gun with pot shots, and he departed. As quickly and as carefully as he could manage, he kept just beneath the level of the path and worked his way along to within grenade throwing range. Slinging his AKM the sergeant removed a grenade from a webbing pouch, and it was at that moment that Oz shot him from the shadows below.

On seeing the last of the leadership tumbling lifeless down the slope, the Czech infantry moved back the way they had come and onto the vehicle track again.

Leaderless, a short argument took place between several of the men as to what they should do next.

1 Troop, A Company of 44 Commando, now re-grouped and re-supplied, was leading the way for the Royal Marine unit, going forwards on General Hesher's orders. They were in 1CG's lines before the shelling had resumed and they now encountered the arguing Soviets on the track. It was a short,

one sided and extremely violent meeting before the marines continued forward, leaving the Czechs where they fell.

At the stream the leading T-90 engaged a low gear to climb out. The 2LI reinforcements from 2 Wessex opened fire with rifles, GPMG and grenades in case infantry were still riding upon the tanks decks.

The effect of the fire was to make the following Soviet infantry close in even more behind the tank, seeking to stay well out of harm's way.

It rose up, its wide tracks digging into the crumbling bank for purchase, grinding away the water saturated earth to find firmer ground.

Just a heartbeat separated the 94mm rockets fired by a graphic designer from Reading and an unemployed landscape gardener from Henley-on-Thames. Both reservists' weapons struck the exposed underside and penetrated. Jets of white hot molten metal cut through crewmen and set off the main gun rounds in the automatic loader. The turret unseated with the force of the explosion and the turret hatches were torn off, flying away into the rainy night like deadly Frisbees.

Awful screams sounded from the stream bed as the tank rolled backwards, crushing several men beneath its tracks and running over two others. Trapped in the stream beneath the crippled vehicle they both drowned.

Grenades arced over out of the stream bed and exploded. White Phosphorus and fragmentation grenades covered the second T-90's climb over the bank and it charged the trench manned by the men from 2 Wessex before more LAW80s could be prepared. On straddling the position it stopped and pivoted in place, turning through a complete circle, collapsing the walls of the trench and burying the men alive before moving off with its accompanying infantry in its wake.

The Hussar's guns spoke, not just Mark Venables tanks but Jimmy McAddam's and his number three troop of C Squadron too, from on the right with 1 Argyll & Sutherland Highlanders. The Highlanders anti-tank platoon also accounted for three

Soviet tanks with Milan before artillery that had been landing on the Guards and paratroopers began landing on them instead.

The Soviet guns were isolating them from the rest of 2 and 3 (UK) Mechanised Brigade. A large chunk of 2LI's area of responsibility was also receiving special attention.

Major General David Hesher looked at his own maps as contact reports from his units flooded in. His map was cover by a sheet of clear Perspex which his staff updated constantly with red chinagraph symbols for the Soviet forces and blue for his own and other Friendly forces. Civilian facilities were accorded the colour yellow and neutral forces that of green, if there had been any present of course.

The blue symbols for 4 Company HQ and 16 Platoon were removed and replaced with red ones. The process was repeated with 2 Platoon of 2LI.

The Brits were having a bad day, as were his countrymen fighting alongside the Coldstreamers, but despite the penetration on the left, the right side was going exactly as he had wished it would, at least so far.

One of his aides approached, holding in his hand a green chinagraph. There were not that many neutrals in Europe at the moment.

"Sir, from SACEUR, in the last hour Luxemburg, Iceland and Denmark have announced their withdrawal from NATO and are believed to be suing for a separate peace."

"The rot has started then." General Hesher said. "The first of rats are abandoning ship."

"There is more sir and I am also awaiting a response from the commanding officer of Eskadrille 723." He handed across the message form from General Pierre Allain.

General Hesher read it twice and looked across at his liaison officers from the Dutch and Belgian forces.

"Has anyone from your General Staffs been in contact about the possibility of your brigades extracting themselves from the line and from further combat with the Red Army?"

Colonel Van d'Kypt of the Royal Netherlands Air Force answered for them both.

"Oddly enough we were just discussing phone calls we received on that very subject." He continued. "Apparently no one on the General Staff of either of our countries could be reached, and someone claiming to be my governments defence minister called me direct."

"Mine too." Interjected Belgium's Colonel Loos.

"And?"

"He didn't know the password and so I hung up." Colonel Van d'Kypt replied.

"Password?" General Hesher asked. Secure, single source communications with automatic voice print verification between seats of government and a main headquarters made such things as passwords redundant.

"We can't do anything without a correctly authenticated password sir, but try explaining that to a dumb ass civilian." said Colonel Loos, interrupting his Dutch colleague. He went on. "My guy got quite rude and made personal comments about my parentage and lack of a future." The Belgian soldier shook his head sadly. "Naturally I also terminated the call."

"Thank you, gentlemen." General Hesher gave a little hint of a formal bow. "I mean that sincerely."

Both men returned to their work and his aide handed him yet another message slip.

Dave Hesher smiled as he read the response of the commander of the Danish helicopter squadron, Eskadrille 723, to his governments declared neutrality.

"Even if the Danish Prime Minister were thirty years younger, that position would still be a physical impossibility." He gestured to the green chinagraph pencil his aide still held.

"Toss that thing in the trash."

Pat had allowed himself to become distracted by a grief fuelled inner rage and that had blinkered his thinking. Men had died who need not have, and that was unforgivable.

He took a moment to refocus, to force away the pain and then he took a deep breath.

"The infantry still approaching from the sunken lane are now the priority target for the defensive fires. Get the mortars and SF kits on that now." If he could isolate the Soviets, just as they were doing to his men, then they could be dealt with once the attack on 3 Company was defeated.

Pat Reed did not say to himself "If" because he knew what his men were capable of.

"The tank borne infantry on the right, what is the status there?"

"We couldn't stop them sir, they and the troops already on the old 8 Platoon position are advancing up the slope as we speak, but the Hussars, ours and those with the Jocks, they are thinning out the 23rds tanks." The Ops Officer reported.

Pat looked up as if something had suddenly occurred to him "Where's the sarn't major?" Pat asked, not seeing the big American in the CP bunker.

Not far from the spot where 1CG's Padre had been butchered by Spetznaz troops in the guise of Royal Marines, a Warrior IFV sat silently in a narrow, hull-down fighting position before a steep sided cutting that the stream flowed through. Ideally they would have had claymores in the cutting but the ground was very confined here and they had to work with what they had and make the best of it. The camouflage nets that disguised the Warrior had been skilfully arranged by the vehicle commander and Arnie Moore, the Top Sergeant of the half battalion of the 82nd Airborne that had been mated to the decimated British Guards battalion months before. He became the combined units RSM following the death of WO1 Barry Stone in combat back on the Elbe. Arnie was listening to the short lived fight between the Territorial Army soldiers and the tanks down the hill.

The other members of the Warrior's crew would have been happier to have sealed up the vehicle before the chemical weapons attacks but Arnie was in the open commander's hatch. The pintle mounted 'gimpy' already charged and just the safety lug applied.

The vehicles commander, Lance Corporal Chris Holmes, came from Middlesbrough. He was generally ignored on a social level by the driver, Guardsman McCardle, who considered anyone from south of Sunderland to be a southerner. The vehicle's previous gunner had been born further north than both of them, in Wallsend, and had referred to them both as being one step removed from Cockneys. A sniper had killed the gunner back on the Elbe and his replacement came from a wee bit over to the west. He didn't understand the offside rule, leg-before-wicket, or even the difference between Union and League. The British driver and commander didn't like the stop and start of American football or 'Rounders for boys', as they termed Baseball. That kind of put a crimp on the usual source of male bonding conversation when the new gunner had first joined the crew. However, sufficient common ground had been found when it was revealed that the 82nd paratrooper was a reservist whose day job was that of a croupier in a Las Vegas casino. Given that the driver's Dad, an electrician, had once rewired a betting shop in South Shields, it served as sufficient foundation for a sound comradeship between Guardsman 'Macky' McCardle and PFC Angelo Rodriguez.

The 30mm Rarden cannon in the Warrior's small turret takes its name from its manufacturer, now defunct, the Royal Armament Research and Development establishment, Enfield, and the gunners training had been provided by the driver, with a non-technical introduction and insight into its rather user unfriendly operation.

"It's gannin ta be a reet focken pain hand cranken the fust roond, fer ya marra!" but demonstration and imitation had made up for the language barrier that exists between English speakers from opposite sides of the Atlantic. It fired two types of ammunition, APDS, armour piercing discarding sabot, and HE. By day the HE rounds were recognisable of course by their yellow tips, and the three round clips were also yellow. At night, two round holes in the clip ensured correct identification by touch. APDS had black clips, blue tips and one hole in the clip.

A problem arose they engaged a target of opportunity with less than three rounds and lost count of how many rounds had been expended. Three clips were loaded at a time but it was important to count the rounds as they were fired or a 'gap-in-feed' would necessitate a full unload of the weapon followed by a reload. After three rounds a fresh clip of three had to be loaded despite there still being two full clips ready. The mantra was 'Three rounds fired... three rounds required'.

"Divent forgit, nay single roond blats or ye'll fockoop. Three roonds at a time is easy tay count, but mind ya hay-a couple o-loose ones tay hand, reet?"

The miserable weather was never ending, or so it seemed. When was it that they had arrived here, and it had been a crisp and white hillside, was it only a week? The stream had been frozen over back then, but Arnie had seen its potential as a highway into not only their battalion's rear, but into all of those of the defenders on the Vormundberg.

Downhill, away on the left, 51mm mortars fired on a higher and higher trajectory as the enemy drew ever closer. Grenades exploded, anti-tank weapons launched with a bang and the T-90's gun fired HEF at the dug-in light infantrymen. The fighting grew in intensity.

During the Great War, which some know simply as WW1, hand grenades came into their own as trench warfare weapons. The casing and explosive fill may vary but the essential concept has changed little.

The grenades now flew thick and fast between attackers and defenders. Wounded victims screamed in agony, dying victims called for their mothers. Here and there the butchery in the darkness was revealed for a split second by a muzzle flash or yet another grenades detonation.

Hand to hand combat, the adversaries indistinguishable from one another where they rolled in the mud. Bayonets and fighting knives stabbed and slashed, rifle butts clubbed and entrenching tools rose and fell, hacking at an enemy's eyes within the gas mask or respirator that protected them, slicing into throats or necks. And all the time the rain fell like a curse.

Shut down and without power, with batteries at a premium, the Warriors night viewing devices were turned off but Arnie was relying on a more basic system. Even without respirators and hoods that muffled the senses, it would have been difficult to see or hear. Nature was assisting him now and again with a helpful lighting flash, but it meant he also had to stick a patch over one eye to preserve his own night vision. An M8 strip of detector paper filled the bill there. Exposing a thin strip of adhesive backing he had stuck it over the right visor to be his shooting eyes makeshift blackout until the time came.

Lighting strobed now, and he saw the paths either side of the stream were clear for some thirty plus metres, all the way to where it disappeared into dead ground. The stream immediately before the Warrior had created a cutting twenty feet deep in the soft earth over the passage of centuries. Its grassy sides rose at an angle that offered a challenging scramble to fit and young ramblers in peacetime.

Thunder rumbled, and out of habit Arnie had counted the interval, just as he always had since his father had explained to him how he could judge the distance to a storm that way, forty years before.

When the lighting flashed a second time Arnie didn't have to wait for any thunder to see the storm was almost upon them.

Soviet troops filled the stream cutting.

In the time it took for him to disengage the GPMG's safety lug and nudge Rodriguez with his boot in warning, the leading man's left foot had snagged a length of fishing line. Pinned to the ground on one side of the stream was a flare pot, without the flare picket or spring assembly; D10 cable and ground spikes from a discarded IPK, individual protection kit, held it firmly to the wet ground. Opposite the flare pot, on the other side of the stream, a fragmentation grenade had been placed in an old compo baked beans can. Arnie had replaced the timed fuse with a blasting cap so the moment the grenade was dragged from the can, releasing the spring arm, it detonated.

The explosion covered the loud crack of the flare pot activating, its detonator blowing off the end-cap and exposing the white phosphorus filler to the air. Illuminated in the harsh white glare and stunned by the grenade blast, only the quickest were beginning to react when the Rarden and the 'gimpy' opened fire. The 30mm cannon was loaded with HE and on the rare event it passed through a body without hitting a bone, the round exploded elsewhere, such as the man stood behind, but the tissue damage and shock would be fatal more often than not anyway. More usually the round exploded in the body, adding bone fragments to the shrapnel it produced.

Firing in short bursts and double-taping, Arnie used the GPMG to pick off the enemy who attempted to escape up the steep sides of the cutting. Spent cases fell from the spring loaded aperture in the underside of the body, rattling noisily on the turret before rolling off its sides, or down through the open hatch to bounce off the floor of the troop compartment with a loud metallic ring.

With the two Americans occupying 'his' turret, Chris Holmes exited out of the rear of the vehicle with his SLR and added well aimed rifle fire to that of the automatic cannon and machine gun.

The Rarden did bloody work on the close packed troops but despite that there was return fire coming their way, cracking overhead or ricocheting off the welded aluminium hull. These were not green troops and they employed fire and manoeuvre to back off the way they had come, down into the dead ground, leaving a cutting that was littered with their dead and wounded. The persistent nerve agent, VX, was already beginning to account for those injured men.

In the dead ground a hasty reorganisation immediately took place. The senior surviving officer tried for artillery support but none was available. The supply of artillery rounds was again critical.

The Czech officer believed they had met a defensive position and was planning accordingly, he did not even consider the possibility that it was a deliberate ambush.

The GPMG was silent now, its barrel glowing red. Arnie Moore groped about on the cold wet top of the turret for three lengths of D10 cable which had slipped away due to the recoil of the 30mm cannon, something he had not calculated for. Brushing away the pile of expended metal links which had created the belt of ammunition, his rubber gloves closed on two of them, the third could not be found. No plan survives first contact, and he squeezed the first clicker but nothing happened, the command wire had been severed in the shelling. The second claymore did explode, killing a dozen men, including one of two groups of three that the officer had just delegated the task of tank hunting. All but two of the men carrying RPG-29s had been left lying in the stream or cutting, these remaining two men he had teamed up with a pair of riflemen each.

The blast had now cut his remaining force down to a handful, too few to continue with the plan until the rest of the battalion caught up, but perhaps he still had enough men to exact some revenge now?

The stream ran red, and surprise had allowed them to do grievous harm to the enemy, but that surprise was gone now, they had shot their bolt and it was time to go.
"Corporal Holmes? Give a hand with the cam net, we're going!" Arnie shouted, trying manfully to drag aside the camouflage net without leaving the turret, but failing. No assistance was forthcoming from the vehicle commander and he looked over the side of the turret. The trip flare was sputtering, its light beginning to fail as it burnt out, but there was enough light to see the dead eyes through the respirator eye pieces, staring up at the night sky.

With a final flicker the flare was extinguished, and with the return of the dark the incoming small arms fire increased.

A grenade, flung hard but landing a little short, detonated and shrapnel struck the armoured sides of the fighting vehicle.

The Warriors Rolls Royce Perkins V8 growled and the cannons thermal sight was powered up. Angelo allowed the grenadier to creep forward and attempt another throw; the second and third rounds were wasted.

"Where's Corporal Holmes, sir?" Macky asked on the intercom.

"Dead, back us up!"

The hull down fighting position had been filling with rainwater for several hours, completely covering the Warrior's tracks, and a mini tidal wave was sent to the rear as the IFV left the position. The Warrior took with it the camouflage net, and Arnie had to lower himself back inside and reach for his knife as the net was now stretched across the hatch opening. The nets edges had become entangled in the tracks and it was clinging tightly to the vehicles body from front to rear. It would need to be cut completely free later.

Now clear of the waterlogged position Macky halted, engaged forward gear and began turning to the right, upslope, to take them back towards the centre of the battalion's lines.

Arnie was about to begin cutting the netting away from the hatch when he was thrown off his feet, and a wave of heat washed over him. Thick, choking smoke filled the fighting vehicles interior and flames flickered at the front of the troop compartment. The Warrior rolled backwards into the stream and came up with a jolt against its opposite bank. Arnie's ears rang from an explosion but he could still hear Guardsman McCardle who was screaming in the intercom.

Rodriguez was trying to open the rear troop door but it was jammed against the stream bank.

With each breath, soot was clogging the filter of his respirator. Rodriguez was frantically trying to force the troop door and the driver's screams became more strident.

Arnie Moore pulled the jack plug from his helmets headset. He was damned if he was dying like this. He hacked and slashed at the net before grabbing the gunners arm, pulling him to the hatch and they struggled out, up onto the top of the turret.

Rounds cracked by his head, the paratroopers lunged over the turrets edge to lie behind it and Arnie lost his grip on his knife as he did so, but he was out of the line of fire. He couldn't reach the pintle mounting, and both his M4 and Angelo's were still in the weapons rack inside the IFV. Smoke was pouring out of the open hatch now and Arnie had only Colin Probert's Yarin automatic.

The last RPG-26 had not been a wasted shot, and with a sense of satisfaction the Czech officer knelt beside a PK machine gun on top of the cutting, directing its fire and ordering two men forward with grenades to finish the crew of the British IFV while the PK kept them pinned down.

A half mile away, the T-90 leading the attack on 2LI's flank was struck by a Hellfire missile and blew up. Its killer headed back uphill towards the safety of the reverse slopes before beginning a fresh stalk, this time on the enemy in 2CG's 4 Company area. Its gunner saw the distinctive green tracer of Soviet small arms fire, just left of their line of flight. A one second burst from the Apache's 30mm cleansed the top of the cutting of the last of the Czech 23rd infantry in 4 Company's lines.

Macky was screaming shrilly now, the fire had reached the drivers compartment and was visible to the two Americans through the armoured glass of the hatch as if the driver had lit a candle inside, a flickering yellow light silhouetting the Guardsman's head from behind. The camouflage net was pulled tight across his hatch; he could only open it a few inches despite the strength lent him by desperation, his gloved fingers visible as they gripped the hatches underside. They both pulled and heaved at the net but it required more than brute force.

Arnie tried to remember where the knife had fallen, splashing back through the stream and clambering once more atop of the vehicle, risking the cutting of his own NBC suit and gloves as he desperately groped about the netting on the roof. He couldn't find it, couldn't see a damned thing in the dark and the rain.

Flame, firelight reflecting off the streams waters revealed the knife's location; its blade gleamed on the side of the bank. Arnie slowly climbed down and retrieved it before re-joining Rodriguez. The illumination was being provided by flames issuing through the narrow gap in the drivers hatch. Macky McCardle was no longer screaming but Arnie had to firmly grasp Rodriguez by the arm and lead him away, towards the sound of fighting on the battalions other flank.

The 23rd's armour was being reduced; just five T-90 and T-76 remained on the right whilst the six on the left flank were still awaiting the infantry on foot, unaware they had withdrawn back to the sunken lane having been caught in the open by the mortars. Counter battery fire had been requested, and promised, but it had not materialised, in fact the barrage was gradually falling silent for lack of ammunition once more. They moved left along the lane, scrambling over burnt out vehicles and detouring around freshly destroyed and still burning ones until they met up with the remaining trudging infantry from 23rd MRR and together they shook out into formation to begin the final stretch from the lane to the Vormundberg itself.

Gunfire support for the infantry attack on 3 Company was now a quarter of what it . The armour could not climb the slope 7 and 8 Platoons had withdrawn up earlier in the day thanks to the shovel and pick work that had increased the gradient, but they still tried.

The troops who had held the toehold in those platoons old trenches had gone up the slope instead, along with the infantry who had ridden upon the tank decks.

No more than fifty members of 3 Company remained combat effective. That was the estimate of regimental intelligence and the battalion political officer, which was the same thing. For once though, it was a pretty accurate assessment.

The Czech infantry hugged the slope as their own tanks attempted to suppress the enemy tank fire one last time. A British Chieftain exploded and apparently satisfied, they finally began firing high explosive fragmentation at the infantry dug in above them.

The British Challenger II was rotating its position between three firing points, but sensibly its commander was keeping quite random the spot where they would reappear. But three is three and not thirty, so it was not a great exercise in patience for the gunner of the Hind-D to hold a vacant position in his crosshairs and wait.

After three minutes, C Squadron of the Kings Royal Hussars lost its OC as Jimmy McAddam and his crew suffered a minute of unbelievable agony trapped in their burning vehicle before the flames reached the main gun rounds.

A second lieutenant just two weeks out of training called up A Squadron's OC, Major Mark Venables and identified himself as the new commander of C Squadron. Apart from acknowledging him and wishing him luck there was not much else Mark could do. One One Charlie was burning furiously, its chassis rocking with the internal explosions that were shaking it. The squadron commander's tank passed it, and the next prepared position, as that was being illuminated by 11C.

His gunner suddenly slewed the turret to the right, away from the valley.

"Stop!" Major Venables saw what had attracted his attention, and grabbed the override, preventing him engaging a hovering Apache in the dead ground where the reverse slope began.

The Danish commander of Eskadrille 723 had spotted movement across the valley and had identified it as a target he was ill equipped to tackle. He summoned assistance but witnessed the destruction of a Chieftain before a Brit Apache arrived.

The Hind-D was stalking its next target, losing it in the smoke from the burning Chieftain and edging sideways to re-acquire, keeping behind cover.

The Danish Lynx had no communications with the British tank and neither had the Army Air Corps so they just used it as bait and waited for the Russian to show himself.

Completely unaware of the danger Mark Venables vehicle headed on for a new position, pulling into it slowly.

The Hind-D rose and fired a beam riding Atak-V anti-tank missile, the Apache locked on and fired a Hellfire anti-tank missile which would miss if the Russian made any radical manoeuvres. The Russian held steady, guiding the weapon unerringly towards the Challenger II. The Hellfire was faster and when it struck, the Hind swung left with the missile turning to follow the still active laser.

Mark saw something flit across his vision, but as it was not aimed at him he got on with the job at hand, but they would only fire once before relocating.

M203 Grenades began to land, fired by 9 Platoon, and this triggered the Czech's advance. Rather than stay on the receiving end of random fire they closed in with the source, confident in their six-to-one advantage.

The sole surviving section of 8 Platoon occupied shell scrapes at the nearest point of the advance and they threw smoke mixed with HE and withdrew with 7 and 9 Platoons providing covering fire.

Encouraged, the Soviet infantry forged forwards but 3 Company was not pulling back another inch, and the ground did not allow the full weight of the enemy to fall on them at once. Most of the infantry were still on the steep slope below the position.

The close quarter's sound of steel upon steel rang out, and only the occasional shot told those who were only within earshot that it was not the ghosts of Germanic tribesmen battling the shades of Publius Quinctilius Varus's legions.

"Hello 3, this is 9, fetch Sunray, over."

"3, negative, Sunray 39 has gone forward to support 32, over."
"Ops!" Pat Reed shouted, reaching for an SLR. This was the crunch, and his battalion would live or die depending on the events of the next half hour. He had been told to expect reinforcement from 44 Commando but they had not appeared, and had probably been isolated from the Guards position by the Soviet barrage.

There was nothing more he could do that the next most experienced officer present could not.

"Sir?"

"The battalion is yours for a while. I am going to take a stroll across to 3 Company."

His driver, orderly and radio operator pulled on webbing and came across to join him.

His 'Rover Group' was a little on the light side now. Sergeant Higgins and the half section from Defence Platoon, aka the Corps of Drums in peacetime, were dead and Arnie Moore had been missing for several hours.

The RSM and Rodriguez entered the CP at that moment and Pat paused to take in the muddy duo.

"I don't know whether to quip 'Look what the cat dragged in' or 'Someone has been in the wars'?" Pat grumbled as he had half expected to discover that the American paratrooper had become a casualty of the shelling. Despite his tone he was in fact warmed to see the RSM safe and well.

"Grab a rifle and bayonet sarn't major, you too young man." He added for PFC Rodriguez benefit

As Arnie crossed the bunker for one of the British rifles and bayonets he looked for new filters while he was at it.

"Any fresh respirator filters?" Arnie asked. "Mines about done in."

The Operations officer held out two, one for Arnie and one for Rodriguez.

"Watch him carefully RSM." The Ops officer said just loud enough not to be overheard, and nodding towards the commanding officer.

"His boy was killed."

Arnie had met Julian Reed during the advance to contact with the Soviet airborne forces. A very likeable young man and one who was clearly respected by his troops. Arnie thanked God that he and his wife had started their family late, and all were well below military age.

The first hint of dawn, muted by the cloud and rain, an almost imperceptible lightening of the horizon at their backs as they headed toward 3 Company.

The sound of fighting came to the small group as they worked their way along the muddy tracks and Pat picked up the pace. The dark crater where the original 3 Company headquarters had died was on the right; Tim Gilchrist had first occupied it with a single radio operator for want of anything better being available when assuming command, but that was before the rain had come in earnest. It was more pond than protection now. They had co-located in the 9 Platoon HQ trench as the platoon commander had been a casualty earlier. The wrecked and burnt out Defence Platoon Warrior was on its side on the track beside another crater, where Sgt Higgins and the four Drummers had been killed.

The fighting masked their approach and Pat almost walked into a kneeling group of men at the side of the track preparing grenades. By the outline of their helmets they were Soviet, not British or American. They had managed to work their way around to the rear of 9 Platoon and were about to tilt the odds even more in the attackers favour.

Pat thumbed off the safety catch, and one head turned on hearing the metallic click. Lighting flashed and Pat looked upon his enemy, then shot the man in the face.

It was Arnie's place to bring up the rear, to chivvy along and ensure the tail-end-Charlie's kept up, but his offer to lead this time had been refused and so he had slotted himself behind the CO instead.

Lt Col Pat Reed shot the first man and then a second and third, but he had not moved his position, he was stood upright and illuminated by his own weapon's muzzle flash.

A hand grasped the yoke at the back of the CO's webbing, and yanked him roughly backwards, a burst of fire narrowly missing him. By the time Pat regained his feet the enemy squad, all six of them, were dead.

Arnie Moore made no apology, but gave no clue that he was responsible for the CO's tumble either. He shouted to the nearest 9 Platoon trench, identifying himself and the rest as the CO's Rover Group and warning them to watch their rear.

"Now." Pat shouted to his radio operator. "Tell Jim Popham to go now!"

Jim Popham's small force of Warrior IFVs moved into view and opened fire from the flank.

In order to engage the IFVs the tanks left the cover of the hillside, moving back into the churned mud soup that was the valley floor where they were again 'in-play' from fire from the Highlanders Milan teams and C Squadron.

The infantry attack slowed, faltered, and only the officers were keeping the men from withdrawing.

Bill allowed the rifle to point naturally at the target, the sight rising and falling with his breathing. At the bottom of the breath he squeezed, the butt kicked back and he followed through.

"Next one" Stef muttered. "Three clicks left, he's got no rank tabs but he's got a radio operator dogging his heels."

This one was canny, he didn't stay still even when he was stationary, his head and torso were in constant motion and Bill spent a while trying to predict his next movement. It was like trying to hit a balloon tethered in a gusty wind, his head would not stay still.

"Sod this, it's boring." He grumbled at last, raising himself on his toes to alter his position fractionally before relaxing once more. He fired, and the radio operator fell on top of the wily officer, pinning him to the ground. A second's pause as another minor realignment of position took place and Bill shot the officer in the head.

"Who's next?"

"A guy who just realised he is now the battalion commander…go six clicks right, the one with the big grin on his mug."

Bill shot him too.

The two leading Warriors blew up, hit by tank fire and an RPG respectively; the latter struck the turret and set off the stored HE and APDS clips. The wrecks blocked the way for the remainder and Pat's planned Hammer and Anvil withered and died. Only Jim Popham's Warrior was able to fire into the flank, aiming between the burning vehicles.

"With me!" Pat Reed shouted, and ran past Arnie Moore towards the trench fight.

"God give me strength!" the RSM grumbled. "Someone break the CO's legs before he gets himself killed, f'christ sakes!" Arnie added with an oath.

The enemy had the skeletal 8 Platoon's two trenches and one of 7 Platoon's. Stabbing down with bayonets, clubbing brutally with rifle butts at the defenders in the remaining trenches.

Voice muffled by his respirator Pat screamed hatred at these men who had killed his son and were now killing his battalion. He charged forwards without waiting to see if anyone followed.

A big sergeant rammed his bayonet through a respirator and into the face of a young American paratrooper, firing a shot to release the blade now wedged in a cheekbone, he grinned at the effects. Pat's bayonet took him straight through the sternum and the force of the charge knocked him from his feet. The man to the sergeant's right turned and raised his rifle and bayonet high. Pat's side was unguarded but Arnie Moore's blade took the man in the throat. Arnie's helmet took most, but not all, of the force of a rifle butt and he fell to his knees. He looked up and saw the weapon reversed and dawn's first rays upon the blade. Another rifle butt took his attacker in the throat and Arnie felt the ground vibrate as pounding boots thudded past him, driving into the Czech infantry, driving the men in front back into those behind.

Upon reflection, it was the most disciplined killing frenzy the American had ever seen.

The Royal Marines of 44 Commando gave no quarter, they slaughtered without remorse, avenging their comrades of 'Forty Two' and leaving bodies in their wake, dead and dying as they retook 3 Company's latest position and drove the Soviets back onto the steep slope they had so recently climbed. Men ran past him, tired men, the gun groups catching up with the riflemen who were now firing downhill.

The sun's rays revealed the blasted hillside degree by degree, announcing an end to the longest of all nights.

Arnie looked for the CO and saw Pat kneeling and firing, but not at the beaten enemy on the slope, he was aiming at the infantry approaching the foot of the Vormundberg.

The Royal Marines raised their aim and the gun groups, still breathing heavily set down their GPMGs and got down behind them. A winded man is not the best shot, but there were plenty of targets down there, struggling through earth turned to molasses by countless armoured vehicles churning tracks in the previous twenty hours or so.

81mm and 51mm mortars began to land on the valley floor and those who had just reached the five tanks, all of them burning or oozing smoke, tried to use them for cover.

There was return fire but the rising sun was in their eyes.

Lt Col Reed removed the magazine off his SLR and checked his pouches for a fresh magazine, but he had used all four. Arnie took the magazine off his own rifle and handed it across.

Pat Reed took the proffered magazine with a perfunctual nod and continued with the killing.

It ended of course, not with the complete massacre of the hated 23rd Motor Rifle Regiment but in acknowledgement by those on the hillside that they still possessed humanity. Men were surrendering, waving opened field dressings, the only items in their equipment that were white.

Perhaps a hundred survived, perhaps less. Either way, the 23rd was effectively no more.

"Colonel Reed?" a voice called out enquiringly from behind them.

Pat raised an arm and on turning saw the battalion's artillery rep approaching, and pointing.

"Look sir, above the far crest!"

Across the valley, on the top of the hill where the enemy had first appeared the previous day there now emerged more, climbing out of the river valley beyond.

"Fuck!" swore Pat. *"Fuck! Fuck! Fuck!*...haven't we done enough, haven't we?"

The best part of two first class Divisions approached, the 77th Tank Division and the 32nd Motor Rifle Division, two hundred and twenty eight main battle tanks, eighty two infantry fighting vehicles, plus artillery and the myriad support units required to maintain and run the divisions.

They had trampled the French armoured and Canadian mechanised brigades into the mud on the banks of the river to reopen the supply line, and now they would deal with the worn out defenders of the Vormundberg without hardly a pause.

"No sir, look up!" the artilleryman said. "Above the hill!"

Thin contrails, hundreds of objects were plunging out of the cloud base above the hill and the valley beyond, MLRS and 155mm 'smart' ordnance began winking like countless flashbulbs before reaching the ground.

They stood watching those twinkling lights, the defenders from all the nations upon the Vormundberg, the seemingly harmless light show in the distance, but then the sound reached them. It pummelled their ears as not just one, but all of the grid squares from the crest back to the river were 'removed'.

4 Corps had won the race.

CHAPTER 6

Germany: West of Potsdam.
Saturday 20th October. 1034hrs.

The pain roused Svetlana, dragging her back to the realm of consciousness where she took stock of her situation with little clue as to how she came to be where she was. She was swing from side to side in the breeze, the motion accompanied by the creaking of a branch above her head.

She saw that dawn was some hours past and that the rain had recently stopped. She could hear the drops that still fell from the branches to land on the soaked ground.

The pain radiated outwards from her lower back but when she tried to reach around with her right arm to examine the area, she could not in fact feel that arm at all. In a panic she groped with her left arm, searching for the right limb. She moaned in pain as the slightest movement increased the agony in her back. The arm was not there but there was no blood on her left hand either, surely they would have been if it had been ripped off? That thought sparked a memory, one of being in a cramped but warm cockpit one moment, and hurtling through the night and the rain the next, as if her seat had been shot out of a cannon.

A pretty close analogy as it happens.

Caroline had saved her, ejecting them both just as the abused airframe had said 'Enough' and given up the ghost.

She looked up and saw her arm had become trapped in the lines of the parachute when she had hit the tree and the canopy had collapsed. She retrieved the pale limb with difficult and not a little pain. The loss of feeling had been due to restricted circulation as if she had slept upon it, and she sobbed with agony as full blood flow was restored.

Regaining terra firma was difficult and she suspected a bruised coccyx was the cause. Before her first flight with Caroline back at RAF Kinloss, a seemingly long time ago, she recalled the stunningly attractive American pilot leaning over her and strapping her in whilst explaining the drills for abandoning the aircraft and the importance of posture at the moment of ejection. Svetlana's libido had got in the way and she had become distracted by the possibility of kissing that mouth rather than listening to the instructions that were coming out of it.

She now leaned against the tree and listened. There was just the wind and the sound of the trees, nothing else. So, she thought to herself, Elena had kept her word by stopping the war, rather than just pocketing the financial inducement and continuing it once she had seized the leadership. That was something she had expressed her reservations about to Scott Tafler, whether Elena Torneski could be trusted to settle for US backing of leadership of the Russian Federation, and a whole lot of money, or to go for broke and a new Soviet Union, one that encompassed all of Europe.

"Where are you, Caroline?" she muttered to herself and looking around, seeing nothing but trees, she added a rider to that question. "And where the hell am I, for that matter?"

Major Nunro had landed in a small clearing, landing with a thump that knocked the breath out of her. This had been her second parachute descent but this time it had not been the result of a shoot-down, technically anyway.

On her escape and evasion course and subsequent refresher training, the instructors had all stressed the vital importance of burying the parachute, of denying a hunter team a start point. If it was that damned important though, she had always reasoned, then why were the aircrew provided with nothing more substantial than a survival knife with a blunt tip, to prevent the accidental puncturing of one's life raft, always an important consideration in a forest.

It had still been dark when she had dragged the parachute shrouds into the undergrowth inside the treeline, bundling them into some bushes and out of sight.

Putting distance between herself and the area of a shoot-down had been the next step, if she had followed the drills, but she was not going anywhere without the Russian girl. She found a large and elderly oak tree on the edge of the clearing and sat under one of its great boughs, out of the rain and waited for the dawn, listening to the sound of battle over the horizon.

As the sun had arisen the rain had tailed off, disappearing east with the cloud. Daylight revealed her surrounds, including the white shrouds of the bundled parachute. Being an X aircraft, an experimental testbed, it had not been necessary to install the green variety. Soggy, dead bracken that she added did not make a whole bunch of difference. If someone was looking for her from the air, they would see it.

Her survival vest contained a SAR Beacon but she had it switched off. The majority of downed aircrew who are captured have used the device early on and still within the area of the shoot-down. Svetlana had no vest or beacon so she would find her and they would both beat feet before Caroline used hers to summon a rescue.

She had no clue as to where Svetlana had landed, she had to assume they were not far apart as they had been sat with only feet separating them at the time of ejection, but walking in ever increasing circles about the clearing for two full hours had not reunited them.

The distant gunfire tailed off over a period of perhaps thirty minutes, although the odd shot sounded here and there.

The sound of metal upon metal brought her up short and she dropped to the ground, peering around a tree trunk for the source of the noise. She saw nothing at first, not until a mere twelve feet away a camouflage net was lift by a Soviet tanker in black coveralls, and behind him she glimpsed the unmistakeable track and drive wheels of an armoured fighting vehicle of some description. Shocked, she looked around and saw more of the nets and realised she had walked into a harbour area. Backing away she almost stumbled over two reposed figures behind a machine gun, quite obviously sentries but from their gaunt appearance they had fallen asleep at the switch through exhaustion. She had walked past them, into the area without even seeing them.

Having crept away, looking frequently behind she relaxed, walked around the bole of a large tree and straight into the view of three uniformed KGB soldiers with a German Shepherd dog on a long lead. From their reactions they had apparently been tracking her.

Fight or flight? She had her 9mm Beretta in a shoulder holster but against three men with assault rifles it would be a short fight indeed. She turned and ran; the men shouted and released the dog.

Limping from tree trunk to tree trunk for support, Svetlana had begun to wonder if she had in fact broken the small tailbone. The pain was almost enough to induce vomit.

She kept the sun at her back and hobbled west, gritting her teeth and refusing to stop and rest as she did not know if she could find the strength to move again.

It was after an hour that she saw something white in the undergrowth and discovered a badly camouflaged parachute, presumably Caroline's. There was no sign of the pilot, no giveaway flash of blonde hair amongst the trees and so she continued on, heading west.

The shouts of more than one man and the bark of a dog came to her through the trees an hour later, and then a scream, a loud cry of fear that she recognised as coming from the American. Vomit arose as she hurried toward the sound, but she spat out the bile without stopping.

Caroline was face down on the forest floor, blood leaking from a scalp wound where she had been pistol whipped unconscious. A large dog, its teeth bared, stood beside her as three soldiers, KGB troops by their insignia, tugged down her G-suit down over her hips. The pilot had a boot pressed between her shoulder blades by the dog's handler, holding her in place as his companions next undid their trousers. Quite obviously a gang rape, and probably a murder would follow if Svetlana took no action.

The dog's handler had Caroline's Beretta stuck in his belt and his own AKM held loosely in his right hand. The other two had laid their own weapons against a tree. The dog handler was the greatest threat and Svetlana leant against a trunk, aimed and fired the automatic taken from the field policeman weeks before. Two quick aimed shots took him in the chest and throat, and then she moved her point of aim to the right, to the KGB trooper nearest the two AKMs. It was a miscalculation on her part for as the handler crumpled his dog leapt towards her. She swung back and fired again, hitting the animal in the chest as it launched itself at her throat. The dog slammed into her, and Svetlana fell back with a cry of agony but retained a grip on the handgun. Bile filled her mouth again having jarred the injury on landing. The troopers had reached their weapons but a voice barked out a command in accented Russian, ordering them to stand down. Svetlana could not see the newcomer but with arrogance typical of the KGB one spat deliberately, contemptuously at the speaker before raising his weapon in Svetlana's direction. A shot rang out and blood spurted from the side of his head before he could fire and he dropped, still holding the assault rifle. Turning and aiming, the third trooper then hesitated, staring down the barrel of the gun that had killed his companion. The sound of pounding feet approaching was followed by more shouting of commands by several voices at once, in

Hungarian this time, but the trooper got the message, dropping his weapon and raising his hands.

"If you shoot at me, my men will kill you." A voice said in very halting English from beyond the tree she had been leaning against. However, she retained a grip on her handgun, raising it towards the sound of the voice.

"You should be aware that the war, at least in Europe, is over." The speaker added. "I think it would be a shame for us both to die after the fighting has finished, don't you agree?"

A soldier knelt beside Caroline and she altered her aim, pointing at him. He looked to his right, directly at her and then at the gun before ignoring them both and tending to Caroline. Clearly a medic was not going to be putting himself in harm's way as part of a deception. Applying the safety catch she tossed her handgun away where the unseen speaker could see it.

An older man appeared and made safe the handgun he was holding before assisting her to her feet.

The surviving KGB trooper was escorted away, past the two dead men and one equally dead dog.

"Thank you." It was all she could think of saying at that time.

"You are most welcome, young lady." responded Colonel Leo Lužar.

Arkansas Valley Nebraska, USA.

When 4 Corps had arrived and removed the spear tip from 3rd Shock Army's advance, the Red Army had found itself in a worse position than it had a week before. The banks of the Elbe and Saale were back in NATO hands, held by fresh troops and fully equipped units, unlike before.

Their Premier was dead; the man who had designed and orchestrated the Third World War was now a bunch of irradiated atoms a mile underground with a man-made depression in the earth's surface, a quarter miles across, as a grave marker.

A new leader had emerged, apologising via video conferencing with the President for the hours it had taken to rein in the Red Army, Navy and Air Forces.

The President sat in a darkened room, presumably to deny any possible clue as to its location. Premier Elena Torneski sat in front of a flag of the Russian Federation, which served the same purpose, and for an hour they spoke, with the President extracting various assurances from her as to a withdrawal to pre-war lines.

Torneski's position was far from secure but international support could change that.

As the conferencing link was ended the lights came up in the Presidents room to reveal that he had been far from alone.

"Okay." Said the President. "Thoughts and observations?"

"Am I the only one who noticed that the brakes only came on *after* they lost the race for the autobahns?" said Ben Dupre, the FBI Director. "And what's with that hair?"

The President looked down at her file and the few photos that they had of this comparative unknown, and compared it with another photograph of a different Russian national.

The President turned in his seat to look at Ben and nod emphatically in agreement.

"Absolutely." He stated before looking at his CIA Director "That would seem to be one for you psychoanalysts, Mr Jones."

Terry Jones did not take notes however. The CIA's expertise in such matters was unsurpassed and already in hand regarding Premier Torneski. The organisations predecessor, the ambiguously names Office of Strategic Services, the OSS, employed the offices of one Walter C Langer to help them second guess a certain dictator. In 1943 Mr Langer, despite not holding a degree in psychiatry, duly submitted what became the benchmark for all future works in that field. The report entitled 'The Mind of Adolf Hitler' opened a window onto one sick puppy. Since then all world leaders, friend, foe and neutral alike have had dossiers that included psychoanalysis by the experts at Langley. The President himself would be somewhat put out to learn that such a report existed on Theodore Kirkland, the current POTUS, as is the case for all occupants of the Oval Office.

"Just because dog owners seem to take on certain physical similarities to their pets does not necessarily make them bad people." Joseph Levi, his Chief Science Advisor, observed.

"It is the 'necessarily' bit that has me concerned" The President said with a frown, which gave over to a faint smile. "That's why I don't own a dog, Joseph."

Elena Torneski had dyed her blonde hair the colour of chestnut and now wore it in the fashion of their own principle intelligence asset on *Operation Guillotine*.

"Now that we have agreed upon reopening diplomatic exchange via embassies and a return of pre-war media reporting norms, I can find out more about the new Premier but I cannot give any time frame for that data to be available." Terry Jones put in. "I should, however, have a handle on why the order to the Red Army to cease hostilities took so long to implement.

The President now had another conferencing call waiting with Perry Letteridge and Barry Forsyth, the Australian and New Zealand Prime Ministers. That call would be followed by yet another online conference with the European leaders, including those whose nerve had failed them. As tempting as it was to cut them out of any future exchanges their armies' men and women had blithely ignored orders to stand down and as such it would be inappropriate to tar them with the same brush as the elected leaderships of their nations.

The Axis partnership of the New Soviet Union and the People's Republic of China was dissolved, and NATO could now bring all its forces to bear on the remaining theatre of operations, the Pacific.

"Ask General Shaw..." The President faltered, but then continued "I mean, General Carmine, to be ready for a full session on our situation in the Pacific, our surviving forces in Australia, next of kin notifications too for those who had been in Sydney, and his assessment on the condition of NATO's European armies." he instructed an aide before turning again to Terry Jones.

"Any word on Henry?"

The expression on Terry's face was warning enough that no good news was coming on that front.

"Mr President, Jacqueline Shaw suffered a stroke, a big one, shortly after learning that Matthew and Natalie had been in Sydney. She is at Bob Wilson in San Diego and Henry is at her side." Terry Jones did not add that Henry was also nursing a bottle. The President had enough to deal with at the moment.

"Prognosis?"

"The 'Golden Hour' was long gone before she was found, apparently."

The Golden Hour was that small window in which doctors and surgeons could repair the damage without there being any lasting effects.

The President closed his eyes for a moment, regretting the exchange that had soured his relationship with someone who had become an anchor of support.

"Thank you Mr Jones, and now I think we need to press on with the Australian and New Zealand Premiers."

The Vormundberg.

After watching the destruction of the Red Army's two point divisions the first ground units of 4 Corps had rolled into the view of the Vormundberg defenders. Moving immediately into the attack, the armoured cavalry had destroyed the forces still west of the rivers, those too slow to run away or surrender. The Red Army itself did not stop fighting until the mid-morning.

In the afternoon, the Supreme Allied Commander, Europe, General Pierre Allain, had arrived by helicopter accompanied by Alexander Baxter, the 4 Corps commander, and Major General David Hesher, commander of the ad hoc collection of units that had formed the last line of defence. They had landed on the top of the Vormundberg, on a freshly decontaminated acre where the still smoking wreckage of the final Soviet attack lay spread out before them. The Canadian summoned all the brigade and battalion level commanders, addressing them with little attempt at formality.

"You will be gratified to learn that my headquarters has been working tirelessly on your behalf for the past seventy two hours." Pierre Allain informed them in earnest tones. "The finest military minds in the world were set a single task and it has now born fruit." Although they were suffering fatigue he could see he had their interest.

"We have named you all 'The International Division'."

It took a moment to sink in, but the tired, and in some cases nearly exhausted warriors in their filthy, stained chemical warfare protection suits had been able to laugh.

"Gentlemen." stated General Baxter on stepping forward to address Dave Hesher and his officers. "You are relieved."

It had of course not been a simple matter of just folding their tents and departing. There were the wounded to treat, the few that had not succumbed to chemical agents due to loss of their protective clothing's integrity. There were the dead and the missing to list, and the living to marshal up and organise, and all within a contaminated environment.

The dead were collected and gently laid out; their ID tags checked and double checked to confirm their identity in life, and their personal effects were then listed, bagged and tagged but not for onward transmission to next of kin. The bodies were bound for the final decontamination, a field crematorium, and the belongings to a furnace for closely supervised destruction, all having been exposed to the deadliest of chemical WMDs yet devised. Only their weapons and remaining ammunition were salvageable.

Captain Timothy Gilchrest was eventually found amongst the dead of 8 Platoon, and he had not gone meekly into the night. Beside his body were those of six members of the 23rd MRR that he had sent on ahead, right before a grenade had ended resistance from his trench.

Lance Corporal Steven Veneer and Guardsman Andy Troper joined the long line of those who had fought back desperately when 4 Company was being overrun. Shunned by the 82nd Paratroopers of that company in life, the Coldstreamers now joined them on the hillside, silently waiting processing before being slipped into body bags and removed. Their Stinger launcher would be decontaminated and eventually put on display in the Sergeants and Warrant Officers Mess at Wellington Barracks; although it would never be established which man had used it as a club once their ammunition ran out.

Just three of the dead heroes amongst all the others, the remaining one thousand nine hundred and seven dead and forever missing of The International Division.

Paderborn Garrison, Germany.
Sunday 21st October, 0023hrs

Jim Popham's men were no longer his in name only. Promoted in the field by General Hesher, his surviving men would form the core of a new battalion, the 111th Airborne Infantry. They accompanied 1CG to Alanbrooke Barracks, Paderborn, arriving after midnight and slept where they could find space.

Major Mark Venables led the last three serviceable vehicles of his squadron to the tank sheds where he and his crew fell asleep in their seats just minutes after shutting the engine down.

Pat had become very quiet after the fighting had ended, almost morose. He wanted to grieve for his son but the right time for that would be once he was reunited with Annabelle, who would probably not yet have been informed of their son Julian's death.

Jim Popham found a bottle of scotch somewhere and sat with Pat in the first vacant bunk they found in the Officer's Mess. His plan was to get Reed drunk and tie one on himself at the same time, but alcohol and exhaustion is not an ideal recipe for a drinking session and neither man was able to finish the first drink, sinking into a sound sleep instead.

At 0600hrs a sergeant from Garrison Headquarters was searching the corridors and rooms of the Officer's Mess for Pat Reed, his torch eventually illuminating the name tag on the CO's combat smock. Pat had fallen asleep fully clothed atop the bed.

Pat's raised voice had awoken Jim Popham in the armchair where he had crashed, too tired to find anything more appropriate. He could have slept at the end of the runway at LAX and been as equally dead to the world. The Englishman's fury though, had brought him to full wakefulness.

Red eyed and beside himself, Pat he was verbally venting his anger on the messenger, in the absence of the messages originator, whom he would happily have disembowelled with a blunt spoon.

"No rest, not even fresh uniforms?" he roared. "I will swing for that bitch, so help me God!"

The men were roused, prodded and cajoled into wakefulness and then put to work. Twelve of the battalion's Warriors and all three of A Squadron's MBTs were stripped of all ammunition and working parties returned it to the magazines. The vehicles were then loaded onto tank transporters that were already waiting on the square along with 17 Logistical Transport Company's Bedford 4 tonners.

The men of 1st Battalion Coldstream Guards and A Squadron of The Kings Royal Hussars lined up on the barracks square for the legal declaration. Empty magazines at their feet, webbing pouches open and personal weapons with their working parts held to the rear.

"I have no live rounds, empty cases or any other munitions in my possession, sir." Was a verbal statement legally required by all seventy two remaining members of the guard's battalion and twelve tank crewmen. The battalion attached, the REME, Royal Artillery and Army Catering Corps elements were not included in the movement order Pat had been handed.

"Ease springs!" commanded Pat Reed from their front when everyone's pouches had been checked and weapons shown clear.

"Get aboard the transport and get as comfortable as you can, we have a long drive ahead of us."

"This is one screwed up way to run an army, Pat." Jim Popham said as they shook hands before Lt Col Reed climbed into the passenger side of the lead 4 tonner. The convoy moved off, taking the battalion back home to Wellington Barracks via a press event on Horse Guards Parade at a ridiculous hour, and all to be accomplished by a road march and ferry from Zeebrugge.

Bayswater, London: 0800hrs.

A frantic scramble by the government's spin doctors in order to formulate a suitable statement had been followed by an even more frantic scramble to return to the capital and make it. The reason for the rushed return had been the Royal Family arriving back in London within hours of the ceasefire in Europe being announced. That Her Majesty had beaten her government back to the city by over twenty four hours was a fact not lost on the media, or the public.

"This is simply intolerable and unacceptable!" snapped Danyella Foxten-Billings. "Who the hell do they think they are?"

"Just leave it dear, I am assured that a feeding frenzy involving certain other governments is about to begin and this rags headline will be merely wrapping someone's fish and chips tomorrow, so come back to bed." It was not by chance that the PM knew this. The defection from NATO by certain nations during its eleventh hour was about to become public knowledge because he had ordered the leak himself. It was a tried and tested tactic, giving the media a bigger bone to chew on. The government's slow return to Westminster would indeed be soon forgotten.

Danyella though had the bit between her teeth.

"Like timid dormice the cabinet awaited the last echoes of gunfire to fade before emerging from cover." She quoted indignantly. "I was visiting the troops...how dare they!"

"You were visiting *some* troops, and on Salisbury Plain, at that." the Prime Minister corrected her. "It is not quite the same, and you must expect the press to notice these things. All of them and not just the ones you invite along."

"Is it too much for one to expect a little support?" she snapped back, before tossing the newspaper aside in disgust.

A sour look marred her features at his words as they were obviously not what she had wanted to hear, so he was clearly not going to be enjoying her body again that day.

"Churchill won over the doubters by playing up to the services." She replied, ignoring the central message of his words.

"Yes, well he was the nation's leader, and that has a kudos all of its own."

"I'm working on that." she thought, although wisely keeping it to herself.

"You also need to kick a few doors in at the MOD and find out quite how half of NATO's airborne forces took part in an operation that we in government knew nothing of, let alone authorised, and also managed to stage it out of our airfields."

"Actually." She replied. "I have already released a statement claiming ownership of the plan."

His jaw dropped.

"Well if none of the other governments knew then no one else can claim otherwise, now can they?"

He was not ready to concede her the point, but if it worked then it would possibly be an election winning item. He said no more on the matter but he would get to the bottom of it himself, quietly of course.

He changed the subject as he dressed.

"How are things going with that dreadful little soldier of yours?"

She noted the tone of his voice, just as she had noted that he had now taken to wearing a condom when they were together.

"He is our star witness and the means to bring about a complete change in the forces. He requires special handling." She reminded him, but immediately regretted the choice of words.

"No more ridiculous additional expense with different cap badges and ceremonial uniforms, and therefore no future soapbox for barely literate veterans to criticise or boast from." She added quickly.

"There are those who would argue that regimental pride held the line."

She was silent for a moment, thinking of an apt reply but having found none she shrugged.

"No doubt the dreadful little men will be bragging about how *they* won the war the very moment they step ashore at Dover."

"I suspect they will be beaten to the punch by those stepping off Eurostar at St Pancras."

Her jaw set even further. He had such an annoying habit of one-upping her remarks and observations.

She shifted her stance to carry her weight on one leg, it thrust out one hip and accentuated the curve of her spine, a pose that never failed to make Simon Manson's eyes widen in appreciation. A little sexual adoration, even from such a dullard, was preferable to being made to feel intellectually wanting by her party's leader.

Nothing goes unnoticed by the police close protection officers where their 'Principal' is concerned, but two things are ever consistent with a certain breed of cabinet minister, a snobbish level of contempt for the men and women who protect them, and the odd assumption that everything the ministers do will forever remain secret. Harry Chapman's best friend was on the PM's 'Prot Team' and the SIS had bugged the back-up cars used by the PM's close protection officers so Danyella's little adventures with the newly promoted Lt Col Simon Manson, amongst others, remained a secret from the PM for a remarkably short time.

For the British Premier's part he honestly hoped her planned media sensation worked, or her time in office would be ended and come the cabinet reshuffle in a week's time she would be returned to the back benches from whence she had come.

Wellington Barracks, London. 1029hrs.

Annabelle Reed, Janet Probert and Sarah Osgood had met up at Waterloo Station and walked the remaining way to the barracks. Young Karen Probert was there also, escorting her mother, her arm protectively gripping Janet's. The London Underground lines were unreliable due to the same fuel shortages that had brought about a reduced bus service.

The bomb site that had formerly been St Thomas's Hospital sat to the left of Westminster Bridge Road. Flowers, some fresh and some withered, sat beside the wall on the bridges approach. Cellophane encased photographs of loved ones lost on that awful day were tied to the trees alongside the hospitals wall. Patients, doctors and nurses, cooks, cleaners, porters and clerical staff, their images inevitably smiling back at the camera, captured during some happy occasion. *'Lest We Forget'*, *'R.I.P'* and *'In Loving Memory'* were the most used phrases upon these memorials.

To the women's right, once they were upon the bridge, the severely damaged London Eye sat behind barriers and cordon tape, a victim of the same raid that had taken such a huge toll in life all along the river.

Petty France had been closed off to the public between Buckingham Gate and Broadway soon after the war had started, so they walked past the preserved ruin of the Guards Chapel on Birdcage Walk, itself a victim of a missile attack in 1944. Through the leafless trees of St James Park the fire damaged Buckingham Palace managed to look unbowed in the sunshine.

Warrior IFVs of the 2nd Battalion Coldstream Guards were being washed down after training on Salisbury Plain, and then repainted as if in preparation for the 'Major General's' as the annual inspection of each battalion was known. In contrast, the barracks itself looked shoddy and shop-worn once you got beyond the edifice and entered those areas where tourist's eyes were not permitted.

Major Pulver, a silver haired officer who had come out of retirement to command the 1st Battalion's rear party, was waiting for them in his office but he had little to add beyond what they already knew. CSM Probert and all the wounded were being detained without bail on undisclosed charges at some location which was also undisclosed. A 'Special Wartime Powers Act' gave the government carte blanche in many areas and at a rather more draconian level than would be tolerated in peacetime. A security company favoured by the government had received a waiver against conscription for its employees and had in effect become a private police force with powers of both arrest and of Stop and Search. The reasoning behind this was of course to make up the short fall caused by the conscription of police officers. Rather lopsided logic, but it that had done no harm at all to the share price of T5S, the security company formerly known as Team 5 Solutions.

Janet sat and listened in silence, doped up on prescribed medication following her nervous breakdown, but Karen listened intently and would ensure she was fully aware of all that had occurred once she was well enough.

"The only person I could think of who can perhaps help is Lt Col Manson." Major Pulver said, keeping a poker face. "He is fairly thick with the Defence Minister, and indeed I believe she is in his office as we speak."

Everyone in the regimental 'family', serving or otherwise, knew of Simon Manson's return in disgrace from the battlefield, but none understood exactly why he had been promoted rather than cashiered.

They thanked Major Pulver and departed for 2CG's Battalion Headquarters, arriving as the Right Honourable Danyella Foxten-Billings was leaving the CO's office. She wore a smart suit with a pencil skirt, tight enough to reveal the outline of the stockings and suspender belt worn beneath. The Italian designer heels she also wore were calculated to both throw out her chest as well as give her an arched back to show off her behind.

Danyella paused in mid stride, pointedly ignoring Sarah, Janet and Karen but looking the wife of the 1CG commanding officer up and down with a critical eye.

"If you are going to come up to town Annabelle, you could at least make an effort."

Sarah was well used to the bitchiness of the groups of wives each battalion seems to possess, those who made a career of being hags, so her jaw did not drop on hearing her friend so deliberately insulted.

"See, you can put mink on a skank, but it will still be a skank in a mink, Pet." she said conversationally to Karen as the cabinet minister swept by. Her escorting close protection officers, Harry Chapman and Paddy Singh bit their lips in order not to laugh at both Sarah's remark and the effect it had on the defence minister, whose neck was now flushed.

"How do you know her then?" Sarah asked Annabelle as the Minister disappeared down the stairs.

"She was a couple of years behind me at school." Annabelle replied. "A wonderfully cut skirt though wasn't it?" she observed in a slightly raised voice. "You couldn't even see the knee pads!"

The return broadside, masterfully delivered, arrived clearly and distinctly along with the accompanying laughter as Danyella reached the bottom of the stairs. Her neck was no longer flushed, it was crimson.

Annabelle led the way along the corridor to the orderly room, passing the RSM's office where Annabelle glanced inside and made eye contact with Regimental Sergeant Major Ray Tessler, also newly promoted, but neither made any acknowledgement of the other.

The orderly room sergeant tried the CO's extension and explained that Mrs Reed and some wives from 1CG were asking to speak to him, but he replaced the receiver and conveyed Lieutenant Colonel Manson's regrets, but he was extremely busy and he hoped they understood.

Ten minutes after they had left, RSM Tessler was summoned to the CO's office with a note pad where the final details of a media event that the CO had worked out with the defence minister were revealed. The battalion was to be 'put on the gate' effective immediately, meaning that all soldiers beneath warrant officer rank were confined to barracks. He, Ray Tessler, was to brief the CSMs of each company but none of the pertinent facts were to appear on the companies Daily Details until so ordered by the CO.

Returning to his office Ray called the various company offices and set up an O Group for an hour hence. After a trip to the photo copying machine he pulled on a civvy jacket over his working dress, slipped a copy of the briefing into an inside pocket and informed the orderly room sergeant he was popping out to the shop.

Ignoring the NAAFI shop RSM Tessler headed out of the gate at the Petty France entrance to visit the local newsagent. Ray collided with a police officer who was exiting, and likewise wearing a civilian jacket over his uniform shirt and trousers, or 'Half Blues' as it is known. Mumbling apology's to each other they went their separate ways, Ray to the back of the queue for the counter and Sir Richard Tennant back to his office.

It is always of immense value to proper coppers to know how thieves, burglars, car thieves and fraudsters, among others, ply their trade. However, it had been twenty years since a master pickpocket had shown Sergeant Richard Tennant of the Oxford Street 'Dip' Squad the techniques and sleight of hand by which he fleeced a mark. Twenty years is a long time for rust to set in if a skill is not practiced regularly, and Ray had felt the hand that had relieved him of the copy, but of course Ray had given no indication that he had just been 'Dipped'.

Dover.
Sunday 21st October, 2356hrs.

As always, Her Majesty's Revenue and Customs Inspectors were awaiting the ferry, even at midnight. As the convoy reformed on the quayside a clutch of inspectors descended on the tank transporters, searching for the usual items soldiers attempt to smuggle back, usually alcohol, cigarettes and pornography.

The 4 ton trucks had camouflage nets rolled up and secured, tube-like, along each side in readiness for easy use. Once untied, gravity would do the rest.

Just two Inspectors searched these vehicles, one to each side of the line of vehicles and armed with iron bars they walked along the line, continually whacking the rolled camouflage nets with the iron bars and occasionally being rewarded with the muffled sound of breaking glass, followed by the leaking of the broken bottles contents onto the tarmac and a muttered oath from one or more of the soldiers in the back.

They did not bother to debus the men for a thorough search, they reasoned that they had been through enough. If bottles upon which no duty had been paid made if through then good luck to them.

Once the Customs men were done a BMW bearing the markings of the Metropolitan Police pulled in to the head of the convoy and a middle-aged constable emerged from it, offering Lt Col Reed a more comfortable ride.

The officer looked somehow familiar and it took a moment before it twigged. He looked at the name badge on the officer's jacket, the lack of rank badges on his shoulders and at the twinkle in the officer's eyes.

"Yes thank, I will." And allowed 'Constable' Tennant to graciously hold open the back door of the police car and close it behind him. There was another passenger in the back of the car, one who had been Commandant at the Royal Military Academy when Pat was a cadet. He had a lot to say.

London SE1.
Monday 22nd October, 0330hrs.

Twin 15" guns that had been fired in anger during the Second Word War sat as silent witness now as the transporters were unloaded in Lambeth Road outside the Imperial War Museum. It was a relatively short journey from there to Horse Guards Parade, where Pat's orders stipulated they were to arrive at the dot of 0400hrs.

An early morning dog walker stopped to chat but made a face and departed again.

"Pardon me boys, but you smell a bit ripe."

Back in Germany when it had been suggested that even if new uniforms were not being provided they should at least wash and dry the ones they had. Pat was not having it though, he wanted his men washed and shaved but if they wanted to play silly devils then he would go the whole hog.

In spite of instructions to continue the journey with only fuelling stops, before reaching the M25 motorway that encircles London, the police BMW had led them to Crowborough Camp in Sussex where a cooked breakfast had awaited them. A reorganisation had taken place and Pat issued orders accordingly before the journey, via the quiet road beside the museum, had been continued.

The press were briefed, not by the MOD Media Office, but by Danyella's own PR officer, which in itself had the veteran reporters exchanging glances. If this was a simple symbolic ceremony, a hand-over of vehicles from the 1st Battalion combat veterans to the newly reformed 2nd Battalion, why was Downing Street even involved, and why was it happening before dawn?

There was only one spectator in sight, lounging against the Guards War Memorial with a radio in one hand and a cigarette in the other.

The cap badges on their berets caught the light from street lamps illuminated for the benefit of the press who took their early photographs of the 2nd Battalion drawn up on Horse Guards Parade. Three companies worth of their vehicles behind them, with an obvious gap that was to be filled by the 1st Battalions vehicles, the stated purpose of this exercise.

The cameras were rolling as on the stroke of 0400hrs a stony faced Lt Col Pat Reed, stood in the commander's hatch of his Warrior IFV, drove off Horse Guards Road and onto the parade ground. It led the small convoy of armoured vehicles, a company's worth, and the single surviving troop of A Squadron, The Kings Royal Hussars.

1st Battalion, its tiny remainder, lined up its vehicles facing Lt Col Manson and his men and shut down, debussing smartly and falling in with their weapons in three ranks. The Hussars left a lasting impression on the parade square with their tracks, as the two Challenger IIs and a thirty year old Chieftain 10 stopped, pivoted to face left, and halted.

There could not have been a greater contrast between the two units. The men of one, small in number and dressed in dirty, often torn and blood stained combat dress, with fighting vehicles to match, and the other at full strength, well rested and smartly turned out.

A microphone was in place on the saluting dais for the Defence Minister, the waiting press corps attentive and her expression that of the cat that had got the cream.

She began by apologising to the assembled reporters for a deception she had been forced to employ, but there would be no ceremony, just a reckoning, and the exposure of men who had dishonoured their flag. Rogue elements within the armed forces and their disobedience to orders, their arrogant refusal to accept the laws of the land had, with deep regret, necessitated her actions. How else indeed but a trick could have brought back the most blatant of the offenders, bringing them back to where justice could be administered, and the guilty punished.

She glanced over then at Pat Reed and his men. They stood stock still as if again on sentry outside Buckingham Palace, beyond the park. They did not appear to have reacted to her words in any way?

Probably she had used too many long words for them to understand.

The Defence Minister then read out the charges, the allegation that anti-personnel mines had been used at Wesernitz in violation of government agreements with the international community, of cowardice in the face of the enemy, again at Wesernitz, and of failing or refusing to accept the surrender of men of the Russian airborne forces at Leipzig/Halle airport, a capital offence under the Geneva Convention's rules of war.

The men did not budge or move an inch.

As neither the civil or military police could be trusted she gestured with a wave to the smoking man with a radio. He crushed out the cigarette against the memorial to the Guards dead of the previous two world wars, and spoke into his radio. Two hundred members of T5S emerged from out of concealment inside St James Park, armed with riot batons and walking forward across Horse Guards Road en masse to disarm and arrest the 1st Battalion.

The man on the extreme left was the first soldier any of the T5S contractors reached, but he was not quaking in fear, he was grinning. The contractor grasped the barrel of the soldier's rifle and attempted to wrest it from him, but Colour Sergeant Osgood was not a man to give anything up easily unless he was of a mind to. At that point it dawned upon the man before Oz that none of these men were wearing berets as they had been briefed would be the case, their heads were encased in Kevlar and their faces were painted for war. The glint of light off the belt of mixed link on a GPMG at the next soldiers feet had him realise that all the weapons had magazines attached, the tanks were buttoned up with the crews still inside and the soldier whose rifle he gripped was now openly laughing at him.

Oz head-butted the contractor, the edge of his helmet flattening the man's nose and the neat, orderly ranks, dissolved as the seventy two members of the battalion went for the two hundred private security contractors.

Danyella gaped and took a step backwards as the contractors at the rear wisely turned and ran.

The press of course were not running, they were not going anywhere. This was good copy.

"Make them stop!" she shouted at her protection officers, who appeared not to hear.

"Make them stop!" she yelled again, at her PR officer this time.

The girl first looked at the fighting men meting out barrack room justice to the contractors, and then back at her employer as if she were crazy.

"No, you idiot!" Danyella shrieked, pointing at the photographers and TV news crew "Them!"

If she could not regain control of what the media were going to report then she would be finished.

The Defence Minister turned, intending to leave the rostrum and smash a few cameras if that is what it took, but blocking her way was Annabelle Reed, eyes bloodshot and puffy from crying, the notification of her son's death only broken to her a few hours before by Sarah Osgood and Captain Deacon. Annabelle's fist did not quite render the same level of damage as an Osgood head-butt; however the result was impressive nonetheless.

Five minutes later and a dozen contractors lay unconscious on the parade ground, discarded T5S uniform hats and riot batons lay littered about where their owners had abandoned them and fled.

Simon Manson was still standing before his battalion, not quite believing what he had seen.

"Fall out and mount up!" Pat Reed commanded, his voice carrying easily across the square, and with an awful start Lt Col Manson realised that the order had been directed at the 2nd Battalion as well as Reed's own men. To his complete horror his men were obeying.

"Sarn't Major Tessler!" he shouted. "Control those men!"

"Go fuck yer self." Ray replied and joined the 2 i/c of the 2nd Battalion in his Warrior.

Pat Reed led his sobbing wife gently away and the fighting vehicles departed with a purpose, separating at the road and making for different objectives. Simon Manson stood alone in the middle of the square, and Danyelle Foxten-Billings was sat on the dais, bleeding from the broken nose.

And the Press?

Well they were just loving it.

Downing Street.
0407hrs.

The Defence Minister had left an all-night meeting of the Cabinet at 10 Downing Street to preside over her media event on Horse Guards, just a couple of hundred yards away. The meeting continued without her, a junior minister making notes of all that transpired in her absence. The post-war retention of some of the laws contained within the wartime special powers act, the encompassing of MP's expenditure under the official secrets act and the permanent replacement of many public services with private contractors. The pressing issue however, was whether or not to end the war effort now that the immediate danger was gone? The PM already knew his Defence Ministers view on that, so the shaking heads around the table when the question was voiced negated the need to call for a vote.

A creaking sound could suddenly be heard from the doorway. All heads turned in that direction. The door and frame had been replaced and reinforced following the arrest of a certain PM just prior to the wars commencement. Despite this measure they could see the doorframes visibly bow away from the door. A loud bang then followed and the door crashed open.

A host of uniformed policemen stood behind Sir Richard Tennant, the Commissioner of the Metropolitan Police, who entered and dropped a red painted door ram onto the carpet in the room with a 'thud'. He grimaced and reached behind to knead his back.

"To be quite honest." He addressed the assembled Ministers. "If I have to keep doing this, I'm going to put my back out one of these days."

Wandsworth.

0510hrs.

Amongst other areas, T5S (Custodial) had taken over the running of Wandsworth Prison from HM Prisons, a service for which they received payment from public funds in accordance with the size of the prison population and the status of individual inmates. Overcrowding had become the norm.

A panicky telephone call to the Senior Contractor resulted in a hurried assembly of some of their most lucrative prisoners, the ones who had been kept incommunicado on remand. They were subject to a subsequent bundling into prison vans for dispersal to other prisons, those also run by T5S (Custodial), not HMP of course. There were more of these prisoners than there was room in the two vehicles that were available at the time. With the vans full the gates were opened and the vehicles departed, each in a different direction along Heathfield Road. The northbound prison van was negotiating the narrow bridge across the railway lines beside which the prison was situated and the southbound van jumping hooded red lights at road works by Alma Terrace. Something caught the eye of the van driver on the bridge, something traversing at speed the tidy suburban back gardens lining the railway cutting. A Warrior infantry fighting vehicle appeared, emerging through a garden fence with much accompanying splintered wood flying willy-nilly. It rocked to a sudden halt astride the road, blocking the exit off the bridge. The vehicle commander grinned maliciously at the driver of the van. Engaging reverse gear and backing away as fast as he could manage, the van driver attempted to escape them, however Major Mark Venables had also taken a short cut.

The Serious Crime Group's surveillance teams had been keeping tabs on the whereabouts of certain remand prisoners for several weeks. O.Ps covered all entrances to the prison, the telephones, landline and mobile alike, were all tapped, and thanks to the efforts of the Special Reconnaissance Regiment's late night visit a month before, they could also see and hear what transpired in key areas without the contractors being aware. When preparations to emergency evacuate those same remand inmates were detected, the operation went into high gear, as did the approaching would-be liberators who were still on the South Circular Road.

The vehicles left the highway at the first opportunity to race directly across Wandsworth Common to the Victorian built prison.

The surface of the Common was torn up, flying high, churned up by the caterpillar tracks of a dozen armoured vehicles and spat out behind, a turf and earth wake behind the speeding tanks and IFVs. Early morning traffic on Trinity Road skidded to a halt, with a resulting fender bender at the sight. A Challenger II left the Common and tore across the road without stopping, smashing through a hedge and into the prison's staff car park. It flattened several contractors' private cars to then emerge at the bridges other exit, bursting through a second hedge and skidding to a halt, boxing the prison van in.

The southbound van fared no better, and all of this took place as the Senior Contractor watched from his office window. Despite this experience, entry to the prison was refused, its doors firmly locked and barred.

Mark Venables employed his special key to change that, the one weighing 62.5 tonnes.

Colin Probert had lost a disturbing amount of weight since Oz had seen him in the forest, close to death following the night battle with the Russian paratroopers. He lay pale and wasted upon the bed in his cell in the solitary confinement wing. A rattling of keys had continued for a full minute before the correct key was found and the door swung open.

"How you doing, marra?"

Colin had been dumbstruck. He had been steeling himself for an eventual one-sided trial and never seeing the light of day, or his family, for many years. In his weakened state he could not help it, tears welled up.

"Less of that mate, Janet needs you strong, so let's be getting you home."

With its missing soldiers recovered, the armoured vehicles departed, heading for the next objective.

Arkansas Valley Nebraska, USA. Two days later.

'Mutiny Monday' was the term coined by a CNN newsreader to describe events in Europe.

At the same time as European governments were being replaced, the New Soviet Union fell apart. The unseating of governments installed against the will of the populations saw more violence than those taking place amongst NATO countries. The cabinet members of the puppet Polish government attempted to flee Warsaw by car, their convoy protected by their own armed security. Twelve Warsaw residents were killed by the security detail at a makeshift roadblock. The security men joined their principals, hung by the neck from lampposts by an angry crowd numbering thousands.

The UK had been the first NATO member state to overthrow its elected government but Denmark and Spain went the same way before that particular day was done. The remainder followed with alacrity.

A complete sea change had taken place across the Atlantic, at least as far as its politicians went.

The shedding of Soviet control once more was of course welcome. The Red Army fragmented, its divisions returning to their own countries. No standing force of great significance would be required to ensure the ceasefire was honoured.

The next video conference the President made with Europeans had required the names of the countries new representatives being stuck to the monitors.

In the hours before that conference it had been tense, as the President was faced with the very real prospect of America fighting on alone, or suing for peace with the Chinese.

He sat facing strangers, although not all were unknowns. A former SACEUR headed the British Council, as they called themselves.

"I will get straight to the point." The President said, addressing them all. "The United States of America takes a very dim view of the events which have transpired over the previous forty eight hours."

They listened, looking back at him, their expressions neutral.

"May I ask what the intentions are of you Europeans with regard to the war?" he continued with only the barest of pauses. "Now that your own borders are again secure, is it your intention to make peace with the People's Republic of China?"

"Mr President." The retired British general began. "By mutual agreement I am speaking for all of us on this side of the Atlantic, and we fully expected a deep concern to be expressed by the USA." He paused, taking a sip of water before continuing. "We regret we will be unable to continue..."

Here it comes, thought the President, we are unable to continue the war but we are grateful for the assistance of the United States, etc etc....

"...until we have reorganised and reconstituted our units, those that fought in Germany and in the Atlantic. Some battalions and regiments must amalgamate and some air force squadrons will disappear temporarily from the order of battle, their equipment and personnel absorbed into other units..."

The President sat up a little straighter.

"...but we are assembling the necessary shipping, and we will each have one mechanised brigade ready for transportation and deployment to the Far East by the end of this week, a Corps in total, and others to follow later."

The Europeans were not calling it a day, Australia and New Zealand were not being written off, and America was not finding itself standing alone.

To be continued in the fifth and final book

'Crossing the Rubicon'

TRIVIA

Volume Three and Four side tracked me with the details of commercial and military satellite operation. There are a fair few dead satellites up there but as it would cost more to refuel them than to replace them. Their technology has been superseded anyway and therefore there are two disposal options, up or down. Down requires vastly more fuel to accomplish safely than boosting to a higher orbit but there are two places that spacecraft go to die. A graveyard orbit of about 403km above the Earth and a cemetery, of sorts, 3900 km South-East of Wellington, New Zealand at the following coordinates <u>43°34'48"S 142°43'12"W</u>. Even if you could dive that deep it would not be advisable to visit. Aside from the exposed nuclear reactors of military satellites that were guided to splashdowns there, it is a toxic dumpsite for chemical weapons and old Soviet nuclear reactors.

I found the potential for new stories lying about everywhere I happened to research. For instance, there was a tiny coral atoll in the Pacific, six hundred miles from anywhere, but a hundred feet deep in inedible crabs, bad tempered sea birds and nitrogen rich Guano. (Bird poo.)

That atoll became at various times, a pirate base, a significant fertilizer resource, a retreat, a military base, the scene of several shipwrecks, and also of serial rape and murder.

The atoll's sole financial asset is long gone, but the crabs remain. (Isn't that just like life?)

Île de la Passion

French Guiana was a place I knew virtually nothing of until an attack upon the ESA facility by either China or Russia seemed to be a necessity. It is a place that was much fought over by the old European empires.

When Wolfe brought an end to the French rule in North America, France was in a quandary as to where to relocate those colonists who wanted to leave. Return to France was not an option for a bunch of losers, but they were good Catholics in the clutches of the heathen Protestant British, they had to have their souls protected if nothing else. French Guiana was the eventual site for those who had lost 'New France' to end their days.

Has anyone seen 'Papillon'?

Henri Charrière, 'Papillon', was a prisoner in the colony but not on Devils Island, that was a fabrication. Only people convicted of treason went to Devils Island.(Good movie though!)

There are whole websites dedicated to fans of Henri Charrière, and discussion groups debating the type of crimes the fans would consider committing in order for them to be incarcerated and live out their fantasy of being a Henri Charrière, and escaping from somewhere on coconuts. Suggestions that, *1/* The book was intended as a novel, and not a memoir, *2/* That Henri is dead (Born in 1904 so he'd be pushing 110 at the time of writing), or *3/* That he really was a murderer and deserved to be a convict, can lead to expulsion from the various groups.

Papillon makes life imprisonment *Cool!*

The odd case of the destroyed tooling.

The F14 Tomcat was without doubt a phenomenal war bird and one that arguably still had a decade or so left of useful life. Aircraft, like champion boxers, one day meet the young hungry wannabe who hands them their ass. No one stays at the top indefinitely. The mystery is however, why did Dick Cheyney order the F14D production halted when it was still on top of its game, and why was it so important to have the tooling destroyed so none could ever be built again, without a huge cost implication?

The ignominious end of the Aussie 'Pig'.

The F111D of the Royal Australian Air Force was quite iconic but getting a little long in the tooth. Of the forty three aircraft in the fleet, eight have crashed since 1973, twelve have been sold to museums or put on static display, but twenty three were chopped up and buried.

Now that wasn't very polite!

(Since the publication of edition 1 I have since learned that the original purchase agreement specifically prohibited resale of the aircraft by Australia and consequently the sale of the aircraft to a major arms dealer was cancelled after the US

Government intervened. Apparently the aircraft could only be returned to the USA or rendered permanently unusable. Those they could not give away to museums and airbases as gate features were stripped and buried.)

Characters (In no particular order...)

I was asked whom the characters in Armageddon's Song were based upon, and to be honest there are a few who are amalgams of people I have met throughout my life.

'The President' is an easy one as I tend to picture a situation and hear dialogue form before I write. I found that the 'ideal' of a President was not a real person but rather one created by Aaron Sorkin. At least so far as speech and mannerisms, in my mind's eye anyway, President Josiah Bartlet, as portrayed by that brilliant American actor Martin Sheen, pretty closely fits the bill. Mine of course is a little more complex as will be discovered. A good person by nature who may have trouble sleeping some nights, owing to his being forced to work in dirty political waters.

'Regimental Sergeant Major Barry Stone, 1st Battalion Coldstream Guards' is a combination of three terrifying individuals (to be a young soldier in the British Army in the early 1970's)

RSM Torrance, Scots Guards, who reigned over the Infantry Junior Leaders Battalion at Park Hall, Oswestry in Shropshire.

Garrison Sergeant Major 'Black Alec' Dumon, The Guards Depot, Pirbright, Surrey and later Garrison Sergeant Major London District. And finally Regimental Sergeant Major Barry Smith, 2nd Battalion Coldstream Guards.

Sergeant Major Torrance was outwardly fierce but inwardly fair, and an ideal individual to be dealing with a couple of thousand 15 years old schoolboys who had to be turned into the next NCO Corps of the British infantry.

'Black Alec' is of course a legend. Those dark, sunken eyes and unblinking, cold stare. 'Captain Black & The Mysterons' except for that voice, the gruff Yorkshire accent that barked a command out on one side of a parade square and flowers in their beds outside Battalion Headquarters a quarter mile away would wilt and die.

RSM Smith was a pretty decent actor I think. The act was to make everyone, including young subalterns, believe he was perpetually angry and a heartbeat removed from downright furious.
I was on barrack guard one night when one of the old soldiers, an 'old sweat' with a few campaigns under his belt, and as it turned out at least one demon, went berserk. He had a rifle and bayonet attached to it in a barrack room he was trashing. The Picquet Officer voiced the possibility of arming the Picquet Sergeant, with obvious consequences, should the soldier in question make a fight of it, which he would have. The RSM intervened, whatever past trauma was troubling the soldier, he knew about it. He sent everyone away except for a couple of us and he waited out the storm. The RSM entered on his own an hour later, and spoke in a normal voice for long minutes before exiting and handing me the rifle before leading the soldier to the medical centre, speaking quietly to him all the time. Next day, RSM Smith was of course once more a heartbeat removed from outright furious.

General Henry Shaw USMC, another easy one, but also oddly out of time. It was back in 2004 when I added General Henry Shaw, and in my mind Henry is Tom Selleck as 'Frank Reagan' except that 'Blue Bloods' was not yet screened. Possibly Mr Selleck played another role around that time which was solid, professional and reliable-to-the-end in character. If I say so myself I do like General Henry Shaw, I could serve under a leader like that.

Sir James Tennant, the Commissioner of the Metropolitan Police is to me 'Foyle's War' Michael Kitchen an exceptionally talented British actor of the finest type.

WO2 Colin Probert, Coldstream Guards.

When we first encounter Colin he is out in the 'Oulu' shadowing a patrol on Sennybridge training area. He is a bit senior to be 'Dee

Essing' as a man of his rank should be running the office, keeping on top of the admin and as the company level disciplinarian; he should be ensuring no one is slacking off. Officers are not going to do that. However, Colin is a soldier, not an administrator and not a 'Drill Pig', so getting out with the students is something he would contrive somehow.

Colin is a Geordie from Newcastle who did not fancy shipbuilding, when there were still ships to be built of course, and made his way to the Army Recruiting Office armed with his O level certificates.

Brookwood station is where he arrived at 'The Depot' he may even have visited the gents before the 4 Tonner arrived, and seen 'Flush twice…it's a long way to the cookhouse!' graffiti on the wall of trap one.

'Cat Company' aka Caterham Company, is where Colin would have been introduced to the first mysteries of the British Army in general, and The Guards specifically.

A Platoon Sergeant and a buckshee Guardsman/Household Cavalry Trooper (the B.R.I, Barrack Room Instructor) would teach them how to iron, polish, bumper and buff, plus who and who not to salute.

I can see him sat on the end of his bed, sporting the haircut to end all haircuts as he polishes his boots for the first time, wondering what the hell he has let himself in for.

Colin is 6' 2"tall, so initially he would have been posted to 4 Company on arrival at Victoria Barracks, Windsor.

Selection takes place on height alone when you are a lowly and buckshee Guardsman. The tallest go into 1 Company; the next go to 4 Company. The short arses, 5'10" dwarves in comparison, find themselves in 3 Company. 2 (Support) was a mixed bag which could reduce a Drill Pig to drink as they were the specialists, the Mortarmen, Recce Platoon, Anti-Tanks and Assault Pioneers. They came in all shapes and sizes.

With promotion and courses such as Section Commanders, Platoon Commanders, and the All Arms Drill Wing, Guardsman Probert has become a Warrant Officer.

Sergeant Osgood.

Nobody knows his first name, and even Mrs Osgood calls him 'Oz', but he joined the army from the coal mines, tired of strike pay and bleak prospects.

Oz is already married when he joined the army, and Sarah had a baby on the way back then.

The Osgood's and Colin will have quickly to become friends. When Janet and Colin eventually marry, Sarah would take the newly wed under her wing and show her the ropes, guiding her away from pitfalls such as those purveyors' of innuendo, and assassins of character, the pad-hags.

With Colin and OZ away on exercise or deployed on operations the wives support each other.

Christina Carlisle/Svetlana Vorsoff.

I recall once seeing Anna Chapman, before she was notorious, and being struck by the way she stood out in a room, at complete odds with spooks such as Terry Jones in the book, but I fancy Svetlana would have that same effect.

At 5'10" tall, with curly chestnut hair to the backs of her legs and a dancers physique, Christina/Svetlana, is too strikingly beautiful to be a spy.

Having been robbed of a normal life and set to bedding whichever men and women the state required Caroline/Svetlana still had greater expectations. She does not object to the bedroom gymnastics it is just that it is not on her terms.

The Seventh Chief Directorate, into which she had been recruited, dealt with visiting foreign diplomats, politicians and businessmen. Her mind and high IQ are of little importance to her employer, it is her talent as a seductress and her talents between the sheets that are the only assets they value.

Somehow, Christina/Svetlana winds up in London with a flat in Knightsbridge and a legitimate six figure salary job at a leading merchant bank in the City.

She is living the life, or is she?

Major Constantine Bedonavich.

Constantine was an able and courageous pilot. He drove the SU27 Flanker until younger pilots were on the verge of making the old man of the regiment look precisely that.

His wife, Yulia, until recently the Prima Ballerina at the Moscow State Ballet, had friends in high places and instead of Constantine leaving the service he instead moved to London to take up the post of Deputy Military Attaché at the embassy of the Russian Federation. The good major did of course need to undertake a course in fieldcraft and trade craft for 'new agent and asset handlers' at the embassies.

Yulia's involvement with a billionaire entrepreneur and the divorce which followed, served to drive Constantine into his work rather than into a bottle, and the major developed into a highly capable spy handler.

Sir Richard Tennant.

Sir Richard wears two royal jubilee medals, his 'undetected crimes' medal aka Long Service and Good Conduct medal, along with the Queens Police Medal, but two other ribbons occupy the first two spaces. The General Service Medal with Northern Ireland clasp, and the South Atlantic medal. The Commissioner had not always been a copper; he had spent six years in the Blues and Royals, serving in the Falklands War as well as a couple of tours in Ulster.

Rather than sign on for another three years Corporal of Horse Tennant became Constable Tennant and attended the Metropolitan Police Training School at Hendon.

Theodore Kirkland (The President).

I have not given Mr Kirkland a political party affiliation. It does not really have any bearing on the story whether he is a Republican or a Democrat, he represents America in this story.

At the start of the tale the President has no affection, nor enmity either, for the military as he is just an academic who found himself in politics without actually encountering the military along the way.

I have left him as a good man but with a few flaws, because he is only human, and one who happens to be in the chair when a war starts.

Vadim Letacev (The Russian Premier).

My apology for coming up with a wholly unoriginal villain. He is Charles Dance (with his bad head on) and Vlad the Impalers more sadistic brother.

A man with no redeeming features, megalomania, a serious case of psychosis and probably halitosis too!

Lieutenant of Paratroops, Nikoli Bordenko.

"Ey, kak dela?" ("How are *you* doin'?")
I had a platoon commander once who was pretty much the suave and dashing Nikoli. The Joey Tribbiani of British Airborne Forces, until injury forced a change of pace, and he came to us. I was never quite sure whether the injury was caused by landing badly after jumping out of an aircraft, or a bedroom window?

Good officer and a good soldier.

Cast

The Americans

Theodore Kirkland	The President
Gen Henry Shaw USMC	Chairman of the Joint Chiefs
Terry Jones	Director CIA
Joseph Levi	CSA, Chief Science Advisor
Art Petrucci	CIA Chief of Station, London
Max Reynolds	CIA Langley
Scott Tafler	CIA Langley
Alicia O'Connor	Computer game programmer
Ben Dupre	Director FBI
Dr David Bowman	USS *Commanche*
Admiral C Dalton	USS *John F Kennedy*
Admiral Conrad Mann	USS *Gerald Ford*
Admiral Lucas Bagshaw	USS *Nimitz*
Captain Joe Hart	USS *Commanche*
Captain Rick Pitt	USS *Twin Towers*
Commander Kenny Willis	USS *Nimitz*
Lt Cmdr. Natalie Shaw	USS *Orange County*
Lt Col Matthew Shaw	USS *Bonhomme Richard*
Lt Nikki Pelham USN	USS *John F Kennedy* & USS *Nimitz*
Lt (jg) Candice LaRue	USS *Nimitz*
Col Omar Chandler	USAF
Major Caroline Nunro	USAF

Captain Patricia Dudley	USAF
Major Glenn Morton	USAF
Lt Col 'Jaz' Redruff	USAF, AC Air Force One
Major Sara Pebanet	USAF, Co-pilot Air Force One
Sgt Nancy Palo	USAF Air Force One
Major Jim Popham	82nd Airborne
Lt Col Arndeker	USAF
Captain Garfield Brooks	Green Berets
Senator Walt Rickham	US Senate
General 'Duke' Thackery	5th US Mechanised Bde
RSM Arnie Moore	82nd Airborne
Captain Daniel King	Black Horse Cavalry
Master Sergeant Bart Kopak	Black Horse Cavalry
Admiral Maurice Bernard	*Charles De Gaulle*
Admiral Albert Venesioux	*Jeanne d'Arc*, ASW Group
Lt Arnoud Bertille	21e Régiment d'Infanterie de Marine
Colonel Villiarin	Cebu guerrilla forces
Sergeant 'Bat' Ramos	Philippines National Police
Vadim Letacev	Premier
Admiral Pyotr Petorim	Red Fleet
Marshal Gorgy Ortan	Army Group West

General of Aviation Arkity Sudukov	Air Force
General Tomokovsky	Army Group West
Svetlana Vorsoff	KGB 'Sleeper'
Anatoly Peridenko	1st Chairmen of reformed KGB
Elena Torneski	2nd Chairman of KGB
Alexandra Berria	KGB stringer
Col Gen Serge Alontov	6th Guards Airborne
Lt Nikoli Bordenko	6th Guards Airborne
Major Constantine Bedonavich	Deputy Military Attaché, London
Vice Admiral Karl Putchev	*Mao*

The Australians	
Perry Letteridge	Prime Minister
Gen Norris Monroe	1st Brigade
Cmdr. Reg Hollis	HMAS *Hooper*
LS Craig Devonshire	HMAS *Hooper*
AB Philip Daly	HMAS *Hooper*
AB Stephanie Priestly	HMAS *Hooper*
Flt Lt Gerry Rich	15 Squadron RAAF

Flt Lt Ian 'Macca' McKerrow	15 Squadron RAAF
Sergeant Gary Burley	1st Armoured Regiment
Tpr Che Tan	1st Armoured Regiment
Tpr Chuck Waldek	1st Armoured Regiment
Tpr 'Bingo' McCoy	1st Armoured Regiment

The New Zealanders

| Barry Forsyth | Prime Minister |
| Sergeant Rangi Hoana | 1st Bn Royal New Zealand Infantry Regiment |

The Chinese

Guozhi Chan	Chairman
Tenh Pong	Defence Minister
Marshal Lo Chang	Peoples Liberation Army
Admiral Li	PLAN *Mao* Task Force
Captain Hong Li	PLAN *Mao*
Captain Jie Huaiqing	PLAN Special Forces
Captain Aiguo Li	PLAN *Dai*

The Brits (Second to None and therefore on the right of the line!)	
The Rt Hon Tony Loude MP	PM
The Rt Hon Peter Dawnosh MP	PM
The Rt Hon Victor Compton-Bent MP	PM
The Rt Hon Matthew St Reevers	Defence Minister
The Rt Hon Danyella Foxten-Billings	Defence Minister
Marjorie Willet-Haugh	'M' Head of SIS
Sir Richard Tennant Commissioner	Metropolitan Police Commissioner
Lt Col Hupperd-Lowe	1CG
Lt Col Pat Reed	1CG
Major Simon Manson	1CG& 2CG (pre Australia)
Captain Timothy Gilchrist	1CG
RSM Barry Stone	1CG
CSM Ray Tessler	1CG & 2CG (pre Australia)
WO2 Colin Probert	1CG
Sgt 'Oz' Osgood	1CG
Guardsman Paul Aldridge	1CG

Guardsman Larry Robertson	1CG
L/Cpl Steve Veneer	1CG AA Section
Guardsman Andy Troper	1CG AA Section
Guardsman Stephanski 'Big Stef'	1CG Sniper Section
L/Sgt 'Freddie' Laker	1CG Sniper Section
S/Sgt Bill Gaddom	RMP attached to 1CG Sniper Section
Major Stuart Darcy	Kings Royal Hussars
Major Mark Venables	Kings Royal Hussars
2Lt Julian Reed	Royal Artillery
Sergeant Rebecca Hemmings	REME LAD attached to 1RTR
Major Richard Dewar	Royal Marines, Mountain & Arctic Warfare Cadre (M&AWC)
Corporal Rory Alladay	Royal Marines M&AWC
Lance Corporal Micky Field	Royal Marines M&AWC
Sergeant Bob McCormack	Royal Marines M&AWC
Sergeant Chris Ramsey	Royal Marines, SBS
Major Guy Thompson	G Squadron 22 SAS
Guardsman Dick French	G Squadron 22 SAS
L/Sgt Pete 'Sav'	G Squadron 22 SAS

Savage

Lt Shippey-Romhead	Mountain Troop 22 SAS
Flt Lt Michelle Braithwaite	47 Squadron, RAF
Sqdn Ldr Stewart Dunn	47 Squadron, RAF
Rr Admiral Sidney Brewer	HMS *Ark Royal* ASW Group
Rr Admiral Hugo Wright	HMS *Illustrious* ASW Group
Captain Roger Morrisey	HMS *Hood*
Sub Lt Sandy Cummings	HMS *Prince of Wales*, Fleet Air Arm
Lt 'Donny' Osmond	HMS *Prince of Wales*, Fleet Air Arm
Lt Tony McMarn	3RGJ
Captain Hector Sinclair Obediah Wantage-Ferdoux	1RTR
Anthony Carmichael	KGB 'Stringer'
Janet Probert	Army wife
Annabelle Reed	Army wife
Sarah Osgood	Army wife
June Stone	Army wife
Jubi Asejoke	South London teenage criminal
Paul Fitzhugh	IRA 'Safe House' provider
PS Alan Harrison	Metropolitan Police
PC Dave Carter	Metropolitan Police

PC Sarah Hughes	Metropolitan Police
PC John Wainwright	Metropolitan Police
PC Phil McEllroy	Metropolitan Police
PC Tony Stammer	Metropolitan Police SFO SCO19
PC Annabel Perry	Metropolitan Police SFO SCO19
Cpl 'Baz' Cotter	Wessex Regiment 'Four One Bravo'
L/Cpl 'Dopey' Hemp	Wessex Regiment 'Four One Bravo'
Pte 'Spider' Webber	Wessex Regiment 'Four One Bravo'
Pte Adrian Mackenzie	Wessex Regiment 'Four One Bravo'
Pte 'Juanita' Thomas	Wessex Regiment 'Four One Bravo'
Pte George Noble	Wessex Regiment 'Four One Bravo'
Pte Mark Barnes	Wessex Regiment 'Four One Bravo'
Pte Shaun Silva	Wessex Regiment 'Four One Bravo'

Terminology & Acronyms

Terminology &	Acronyms

Numeric

1CG:	First Battalion Coldstream Guards
1RTR:	First Royal Tank Regiment
2CG:	Second Battalion Coldstream Guards
2LI:	Second Battalion the Light Infantry
3RGJ:	Third Battalion Royal Green Jackets
'5':	Slang term for MI5
'6':	USN carrier borne strike aircraft (Intruder)

'A'

A-6:	USN carrier borne strike aircraft (Intruder)
A-10:	US built single seat, close air support, tank killing aircraft (Warthog)
A-50:	Russian built AWAC version of the heavy Il-76 transport aircraft (Mainstay)
AA:	Air-to-Air
AAA:	Anti-Aircraft Artillery
AAC:	British Army's Army Air Corps
AEW:	Airborne Early Warning
AFB:	Air Force Base
AFV:	Armoured Fighting Vehicle
AGM:	Air-to-ground missile
AIM:	Aerial Intercept Missile
AK-47:	Updated derivative of the Kalashnikov assault rifle
AKM-74:	Romanian derivative of the AK-74
ALASAT:	Air Launched Anti Satellite missile
AMIP:	Area Major Inquiry Pool (Metropolitan Police)
AMRAAM:	Advanced Medium Range Air to Air Missile (Slammer)
AN-72:	Russian built transport
Apache:	US built helicopter gunship in service with US and Allied forces
APC:	Armoured Personnel Carrier
Army:	3 x Corps + combat and logistical support
Army Group:	3 x Armies
AP:	Anti-Personnel
ASW:	Anti-Submarine Warfare
AT:	Anti-Tank
ATC:	Air Traffic Control
ATF:	Bureau of Alcohol, Tobacco, Firearms
ATO:	Ammunition Technical Officer (Military bomb disposal officer)
AV-8B:	US developed version of the Harrier II.
AWACS:	Airborne Warning And Control System
AWE:	Atomic Weapons Agency (Aldermaston)

'B'

B1-B:	US built supersonic swing wing early stealth bomber (Lancer)
B-2:	US built stealth bomber (Spirit)
B-52:	Heavy USAF bomber (The Buff aka Big Ugly F***er)
Backfire:	Russian built supersonic swing wing bomber (TU-22M)

BAOR:	British Army Of the Rhine
Battalion:	3-4 Rifle Coy's + combat and logistical support (Bn)
BBC:	British Broadcasting Corporation
Bde:	Brigade (3 Bn's + combat and logistical support)
Binos:	Binoculars
Blackjack:	Russian built supersonic swing wing bomber (TU-160)
Blinder:	Russian built supersonic bomber (TU-22)
BMP:	Tracked AFV
Bn:	3-4 Rifle Coy's + combat and logistical support (Battalion)
Boomer:	Ballistic Missile Submarine (SSBN)
Box:	Slang term for MI5 (Post Office Box 500)
Bradley:	US AFV
BRDM:	Russian built four wheeled Reconnaissance vehicle
Brew:	Tea
BTR:	Russian built eight wheeled APC
Buckshee:	Free item
Buckshee:	New and inexperienced
Buff:	B-52 Heavy USAF bomber (Buff aka Big Ugly F***er)

'C'

CAD:	Computer Aided Dispatch
CAG:	Commander Air Group
CAP:	Combat Air Patrol
Carl Gustav:	84mm medium anti-tank weapon
CBU:	Cluster Bomb Unit
CCCIR:	Police Information Room Senior Controller
CCCP:	Cyrillic alphabet for 'Union of Soviet Socialist Republics'
CG:	Coldstream Guards
Challenger:	Current series of British MBTs
Charlie Gee:	84mm medium anti-tank weapon
CHARM:	120mm self stabilising main tank gun with rifled barrel
Chieftain:	Former series of British MBTs
CIA:	Central Intelligence Agency
CIC:	Combat Information Centre
CIC:	Commander In Chief
Civvy:	Civilian
CNN:	Cable News Network
CO:	Commanding Officer
CO:	The Commissioner's Office (NSY: New Scotland Yard)
Colly:	Her Majesty's Military Correction and Training Centre (HMCC)
Company:	3 x Pl's + logistical support (Coy)
COMSUBPAC:	Commander Submarines Pacific
Corps:	3 x Div's + combat and logistical support
Coy:	3 x Pl's + logistical support (Company)
CP:	Command Post
Cpl:	Corporal
CQMS:	Company Quarter Master Sergeant (Colour Sergeant rank)
CSA:	Chief Scientific Advisor

CSM:	Company Sergeant Major (WO2 rank)
CTR:	Close Target Reconnaissance
CVR(T):	Combat Vehicle Reconnaissance (Tracked)
CVR(W):	Combat Vehicle Reconnaissance (Wheeled)

'D'

DEEP STRIKE:	Air and SF attacks on logistical targets 100k + behind the lines
DefCon5:	Peacetime
DefCon4:	Peacetime; Increased intelligence; Strengthened security
DefCon3:	Increased force readiness
DefCon2:	Increased force readiness – Less than maximum
DefCon1:	Maximum force readiness
DF:	Defensive Fire
DF:	Direction Find
Div:	3 x Bde's + combat and logistical support (Division)
DPM:	Disruptive Pattern Material (Camouflage)
DZ:	Drop Zone

'E'

E-2C:	US built Carrier borne early warning aircraft (Hawkeye)
E-3:	US built AWACS based on Boeing 707 (Sentry)
Eagle:	USAF swing wing, twin engine, single seat, all weather, fighter (F-15)
ECM:	Electronic Counter Measure
ELINT:	Electronically gathered Intelligence
EMCON:	Electronic Emission Control (Radio and Radar silence)
EMP:	Electro Magnet Pulse
ESM:	Electronic Surveillance Measures
Expo:	Explosives Officer (Police bomb disposal officer)
Extender:	Aerial Tanker derived from Boeing 707 (KC-135)

'F'

F-14:	USN swing wing, twin engine, two seat, strike fighter (Tomcat)
F-15:	USAF swing wing, twin engine, single seat, tactical fighter (Eagle)
F-15E:	USAF swing wing, twin engine, single seat, all weather, strike fighter (Strike Eagle)
F-16:	US built multi-role fighter (Falcon)
F-117A:	USAF stealth fighter bomber (Nighthawk)
F-117X:	Northrop experimental stealth fighter bomber testbed in service with USAF
FAC:	Forward Air Controller
Falcon:	US built multi-role fighter (F-16)
FAO:	Forward Artillery Observer
FBI:	Federal Bureau of Investigation
FEBA:	Forward Edge of the Battle Area
Fencer:	Russian built two seat interdiction and attack aircraft (SU-24)
Flanker:	Russian built single seat, twin engined fighter (SU-27)
FLIR:	Forward Looking Infra-Red
Flogger:	Russian built single seat, single engine fighter (MIG-23)
FLOT:	Forward Line Of Troops

Fox One:	Radio call from a pilot announcing his firing an AIM-9M Sidewinder missile
Foxbat:	Russian built high speed interceptor (MIG-25)
Foxhound:	Russian built high speed interceptor (MIG-31)
Foxhound:	Infantryman
FPF:	Final Protective Fire
Frogfoot:	Russian built close air support, ground attack aircraft (SU-25)
FRV:	Final Rendezvous Point
Fulcrum:	Russian built single seat, twin engined fighter (MIG-29)
Fullback:	Russian built advanced two seat fighter bomber (SU-32)
FUP:	Forming Up Point

'G'

Gdsm:	Guardsman
Gimpy:	General Purpose Machine Gun
GPMG:	General Purpose Machine Gun
GPS:	Global Positioning System
Green Beret:	US Army special forces unit
Green Maggot:	Sleeping bag
GRI:	General Research Institute (Chinese espionage service)
Grumble:	Russian built anti-aircraft missile system

'H'

HARM:	High speed anti-radiation missile
Harpoon:	Anti-shipping missile
Harrier:	British designed VTOL Strike fighter
Hawkeye:	US built Carrier borne early warning aircraft (E-2C)
HE:	High Explosive
HESH:	High Explosive Squash Head (shaped charge warhead)
Hind-D:	Heavily armoured helicopter gunship
Hornet:	US built all weather strike fighter (F/A-18)
HUD:	Heads Up Display
HUMINT:	Intelligence gathered by humans

'I'

ICBM:	Inter-Continental Ballistic Missile
IFF:	Identification Friend or Foe
IL-76:	Russian built heavy transport aircraft
Intruder:	USN carrier borne strike aircraft (A-6)
IR:	Information Room (Metropolitan Police)
IR:	Infra-Red
IRST:	Infra-Red Search and Tracking

'J'

Jaguar:	British/French ground attack aircraft
JNAIRT	Joint Nuclear Accident and Incident Response Team
JSTARS:	Joint Surveillance and Target Attack Radar System (air to ground surveillance)

'K'

KC-135:	Aerial Tanker derived from Boeing 707 (Extender)
Kevlar:	Carbon fibre armour
Klick:	Kilometre / a thousand metres

'L'

L/Cpl:	Lance Corporal

L/Sgt:	Lance Sergeant
Lancer:	US built supersonic swing wing early stealth bomber (B1-B)
LAW:	Light Anti-Tank Weapon
LSW:	Light Support Weapon
Lynx:	British, fast, tank hunting helicopter
LZ:	Landing Zone

'M'

M&AWC:	Mountain & Arctic Warfare Cadre (RM Specialists)
MAC:	Military Airlift Command
Mach:	Speed of sound (at sea level = 1,225 KPH / 761.2 MPH)
Maggot:	Sleeping bag
Mainstay:	Russian built AWAC version of the heavy Il-76 transport aircraft (A-50)
MAW:	Medium Anti-Tank Weapon
MBT:	Main Battle Tank
Mess:	Sleeping quarters/Dining area/Bar/social organisation
Met:	Metropolitan Police
MFC:	Mortar Fire Controller
MIG-23:	Russian built single seat, single engine fighter (Flogger)
MIG-25:	Russian built high speed interceptor (Foxbat)
MIG-29:	Russian built single seat, twin engined fighter (Fulcrum)
MIG-31:	Russian built high speed interceptor (Foxhound)
Mirage:	French air superiority fighter
MLRS:	Multi Launch Rocket System
MP:	Member of Parliament
MP:	Military Police
MP5:	Heckler & Koch MP5 9mm SMG and carbine
MRCA:	Multi Role Combat Vehicle
MRR:	Motor Rifle Regiment
MSTAR:	Battlefield radar system

'N'

NAAFI:	Navy Army Air Force Institute (shop and bar facilities for British forces)
NAS:	Naval Air Station
NATO:	North Atlantic Treaty Organisation
NAVSAT:	Navigation Satellite
NBC:	Nuclear Biological Chemical
NBC:	National Broadcasting Company
NCIS:	National Crime Intelligence Service
NCO:	Non Commissioned Officer
Nighthawk:	USAF stealth fighter bomber (F-117A)
NSA:	National Security Agency
NSY:	New Scotland Yard
NVG	Night Vision Goggles

'O'

O Group:	Orders Group (Briefing)
OP:	Observation Post
Oppo:	Buddy
Oulou	In the countryside. In the middle of nowhere.

'P'

PC:	Police Constable
Peewits:	Possession With Intent to Supply (The Misuse of

	Drugs Act 1971. S 5 (3)
Pickle:	Release bombs
Pl:	Platoon: (3 x Sections)
PLA:	Peoples Liberation Army
PLAAF:	Peoples Liberation Army Air Force
PLAN:	Peoples Liberation Army Navy
Platoon:	3 x Sections (Pl)
PLCE:	Personal Load Carrying Equipment (Webbing)
PM:	Prime Minister
PNG:	Passive Night Goggle
PRC:	Peoples Republic of China
PS:	Police Sergeant
Ptarmigan:	British, secure battlefield communications system
Pte:	Private

'Q'

Q Bloke:	Quartermaster
QM (T):	Quartermaster (Technical) - (W01 rank)
QRF:	Quick Reaction Force
QRH:	Queens Royal Hussars

'R'

RA:	Royal Artillery
RAC:	Royal Armoured Corps
RAF:	Royal Air Force
Rapier:	British AAA missile system
RE:	Royal Engineers
REME:	Royal Electrical and Mechanical Engineers
Replen:	Replenish
Rfn:	Rifleman
RIO:	Radar Intercept Officer
RM:	Royal Marines
RMP:	Royal Military Police
RN:	Royal Navy
ROC:	Republic Of China (Taiwan)
ROC:	Generic term for the Taiwanese military
ROE:	Rules Of Engagement
RORSAT:	Radar Ocean Reconnaissance Satellite
RQMS:	Regimental Quarter Master Sergeant (W01 rank)
RSM:	Regimental Sergeant Major (W01 rank)
RV:	Rendezvous Point
RVP:	Rendezvous Point

'S'

SA:	Surface-to-Air
SA80:	British 5.56mm calibre individual weapon
Sabre:	British tracked reconnaissance vehicle
SACEUR:	Supreme Allied Commander Europe
SAM:	Surface to Air Missile
Samaritan:	British tracked armoured ambulance
Samson:	British tracked armoured recovery vehicle
SAR:	Search-And-Rescue
SAR:	Synthetic Aperture Radar
SARH:	Surface to Air Radar Homing
SAS:	Special Air Service (recruits from British Army)
SASR:	Special Air Service Regiment (recruits from Australian Army)
Saxon:	British, wheeled APC
SBS:	Special Boat Service (recruits from Royal Marines)
Scimitar:	British tracked reconnaissance vehicle

Sea Harrier:	RN V/STOL Fleet defense aircraft
Sentry:	US built AWACS based on Boeing 707 (E-3)
SFO:	Specialist Firearms Officer (Police)
SIS:	Secret Intelligence Service
Sitrep:	Situation report
Six:	Directly behind (Six o'clock position)
SLBM:	Nuclear powered ballistic missile submarine
SLR:	Self-Loading Rifle
SMG:	Sub Machine Gun
SO12:	Special Branch (Metropolitan Police)
SO13:	Anti-Terrorist Squad (Metropolitan Police)
SO14:	Royalty Protection (Metropolitan Police)
SO16:	Diplomatic Protection Group (Metropolitan Police)
SCO19:	Specialist Firearms Unit (Metropolitan Police)
Spartan:	British tracked vehicle for AAA, MFC, Engineer or Recce
SP HVM:	Self-Propelled High Velocity Missile
Spearfish:	British advanced, high speed, wire guided torpedo
Spirit:	US built stealth bomber (B-2)
SRAM:	Short Range Attack Missile
SS:	Surface to Surface
SSBN:	Ballistic Missile Submarine (Boomer)
SSG:	Diesel powered guided missile submarine
SSGN:	Nuclear powered guided missile submarine
SSK:	Diesel powered attack submarine
SSN:	Nuclear powered attack submarine
Starstreak:	British advanced, high speed anti-aircraft missile
Striker:	British tracked AT vehicle
STOL:	Short Take Off and Landing
SU-24:	Russian built two seat interdiction and attack aircraft (Fencer)
SU-25:	Russian built close air support, ground attack aircraft (Frogfoot)
SU-27:	Russian built single seat, twin engined fighter (Flanker)
SU-32:	Russian built advanced two seat fighter bomber (Fullback)
Sultan:	British tracked, armoured command vehicle
SWAT:	Special Weapons and Tactics

'T'

T-64:	Russian designed MBT
T-72:	Russian designed MBT
T-80:	Russian designed MBT
T-90:	Russian designed MBT
TAO:	Tactical Action Officer
TAVR:	Territorial Army Volunteer Reserve
TEL:	Transporter Erector Launcher
Thunderbolt:	US built single seat, close air support, tank killing aircraft (A10 / Warthog)
Tomcat:	USN swing wing, twin engine, two seat, strike fighter (F-14)
Tornado F3:	British/German twin seat, swing wing fighter
Tornado GR:	British/German ground attack aircraft
Tpr:	Trooper
Triple A:	AAA (Anti-Aircraft Artillery)
TU-22:	Russian built supersonic swing wing bomber

	(Blinder)
TU-22M:	Russian built supersonic swing wing bomber (Backfire)
TU-160:	Russian built supersonic swing wing bomber (Blackjack)

'U'-'V'-'W'-'Z'

UGM:	Un-Guided Missile
USAF:	United States Air Force
USMC:	United States Marine Corps
USN:	United States Navy
USSR:	Union of Soviet Socialist Republics
VTOL:	Vertical Take Off and Landing
Warrior:	British AFV
Warthog:	A-10: US built single seat, close air support, tank killing aircraft
Wild Weasel:	Dedicated, specialized, AAA suppression mission
Willy Pete:	WP: White Phosphorus
WO:	Warrant Officer
WP:	White Phosphorus
ZSU:	Russian designed series of Self –Propelled AAA vehicles

ABOUT THE AUTHOR

Andy Farman was born in Cheshire, England in 1956 into a close family of servicemen and servicewomen who at that time were serving or who had served in the Royal Air Force, Royal Navy and British Army.

As a 'Pad brat' he was brought up on whichever RAF base to which his Father had been posted until he joined the British Army as an Infantry Junior Leader in 1972, at the tender age of 15.

Andy served in the Coldstream Guards on ceremonial duties at the Royal Palaces, flying the flag in Africa and on operational tours in Ulster, and on the UK mainland during Op Trustee.

In 1981, Andy swapped his green suit for a blue one with the Metropolitan Police but continued an active volunteer reserve role in both the Wessex Regiment and 253 Provost Company, Royal Military Police (V).

After twenty four years in front line policing, both in uniform and plain clothes he finally moved to a desk job for six years at an inner city borough, wearing two hats, those of an operation planner, and liaison officer with the television and film industry.

His first literary work to be published was that of a poem about life as a soldier in Ulster, which was sold with all rights to a now defunct writers monthly in Dublin for the princely sum of £ 11 (less the price of the stamp on the envelope that the cheque arrived in.) The 'Armageddon's Song' series began as a mental exercise to pass the mornings whilst engaged on a surveillance operation on a drug dealer who never got out of bed until the mid-afternoon. On retirement he emigrated to the Philippines with his wife Jessica where he took up scuba diving and is a member of the famous IGAT running club.